BEHIND THE BOATER'S COVER-UP

ETTA FAIRE

CHAPTER 1

DATE KILLERS

I realized I was making my ice-skating face again. My cheeks naturally scrunched into an odd, fake smile whenever I had to pretend to adore something I really hated. It wasn't something I had control over, and it happened whether I was on the ice or not.

Snow fell along my path. My toes were numb in the skates I'd had since I was 14 and swore to my mother that my feet were done growing so she could go ahead and buy those expensive skates that everyone else had at school because *I just loved ice skating*. That day marked the beginning of my ice-skating face. I make that face a lot around my dead ex-husband now, whenever he wants to buddy up and solve another murder together.

The five-year-old little pink puff in front of me skated backwards, sticking out her tongue. "Come on, slow poke," Lil Mil said, wiggling her hips in a mocking fashion. I tried to catch up but I lost my balance and fell into the six-foot, dark-haired man skating by my side.

"Don't worry," Justin said. "She'll come 'round again in a second. You can catch her next time."

His already large arm was made even thicker by the puffer

jacket he was wearing. We'd been dating for three months now, and it was nice, but not serious. I wasn't sure if I was ready for serious yet, but I was sure enjoying the nice part.

Partiers' Loop was the one part of the lake everyone came to ice skate on whenever the weather permitted, and it was packed with people today, enjoying a winter Sunday on Landover Lake. Soft rock music played out from the speakers that someone had set up along the side. I tugged Justin in tighter, trying to warm myself on his chest as we passed under a tree limb.

I watched every branch intently as we went under, not quite trusting nature just yet, not after Delilah Scott said she heard "those birds" again last week.

Mrs. Carmichael came up behind me and grabbed my arm, making me lose my footing and fall onto the ice, mostly because I'd been thinking about the birds. Pain shot up my back, but I tried to laugh it off.

She put out a gloved hand to help me up. "Sorry about that, Carly Mae. You would think that's why they call this Accident Loop, wouldn't ya?" She looked different without her pink Spoony River uniform on. Her blonde hair was dotted with gray and flew crazily out of her knit cap as she talked. In or out of the diner, Mrs. Carmichael was still hands down the town's biggest gossip. And I could tell, she couldn't wait to tell me something here.

"I thought it was called Partier's Loop," I said.

"Same thing." Old George grunted by her side. He pointed down to the ice we were skating on. "Terrible boating accident happened on this side of the lake." His voice sounded straight out of a horror movie.

"Let me tell it," Mrs. Carmichael teased, hitting his arm in a way that made me wonder if old George and Mrs. Carmichael were becoming the town's latest bit of gossip. "Sometime in the 1950s. Oh no, it was the 1960s... Oh I don't know. A while back, some kids went partying on a boat after dark. Four people didn't come back. Drowned."

"No, they got run over by their boat, mangled in the propeller," George said.

"They drowned. They were high and drunk and they swam too far from the boat. Their bloated remains washed up right here." She pointed.

He shook his head and she shot him a look.

"Well, it's a lovely story either way," I said, making Justin smile at me as the older couple skated on still arguing over the gruesome details.

Justin was a man of few words, but I was really enjoying the quiet way he communicated, especially since I lived with a loud-mouthed ghost of an ex-husband.

We skated by Parker Blueberg, who was off to the side holding onto his three-year-old son's back as they shuffled slowly along the ice. The kid could barely move he was so bundled up, but he sported a wild grin and rosy chubby cheeks.

"Thanks for inviting us," Parker said when he saw me watching him. He had his hood down, and his thick sandy brown hair was flaked with snow. He smiled just enough to show he probably wore his retainer a lot more than I did; perfectly straight, white teeth.

Justin pulled me in tighter.

"Of course," I said as we skated over to him. "You're the newbies in town. And this is the best entertainment we have here in January. Cheapest too. Okay, it's the only entertainment. Sorry."

"I'm always looking for cheap entertainment for the kids," he said. "Mostly because I'm also still looking for a job."

I turned to Justin. "Parker was a personal trainer back in Chicago."

"No kidding." Justin puffed out his chest. "What do you bench?"

"I mostly taught spin class and yoga."

"That's bike riding, right? You taught bike riding to grown-ups."

"It's a little more complicated than that," Parker said.

"Two-fifty," Justin replied, still puffing out his chest, which made me wonder if he'd exhaled yet. "I bench two-fifty."

"If I hear of anything, I'll let you know," I said and skated ahead, leaving the testosterone competition behind.

Jackson appeared by my side. "Well, they certainly are impressive, aren't they." He motioned toward the men behind us. "You don't often see two jocks using almost complete sentences at the same time."

I hit a slippery patch and struggled to catch my footing again. "Go away," I muttered under my breath to the annoying ghost hovering by me. My ex-husband's coloring seemed particularly pale against the snow surrounding us, his full beard and thin frame fading into the background. I looked around before saying anything else, just to make sure no one was watching me. I tried to avoid looking crazy in public, whenever possible. And no one else could see the ghosts I talked to. "You promised you wouldn't go with me on dates. You're being a date killer again."

"I'm actually here on official business, not as a date killer. Although you seem to be your own biggest date killer right now."

I turned to him, hands on my hips.

"Come on, Carly doll," he said, raising an almost transparent eyebrow at me. "Why did you invite Parker and the kids along on a date with Justin?"

"I thought the kids would like this, and… I don't need to answer that. Justin and I are happy. What's your official business?"

"That boating accident they were talking about. One of the partiers is coming home with us."

"Of course he is. Let me guess. It wasn't an accident."

"It's a she. And no. She's absolutely certain it wasn't, but she doesn't remember what happened. She's been waiting a long time for a strong medium to come to this part of Landover Lake so she could finally figure things out. It's why she haunts here. Since 1957."

I nodded, but my face felt oddly frozen when I moved it. I was ready to head inside, defrost, and get some hot chocolate.

Jackson continued. "She's also got strong memories from 1954." His voice took a sing-songy lilt to it. He knew that was going to be the kicker. A ghost with memories from 1954 was too enticing for me to pass up. I'd recently started a keepsake box full of articles and information from 1954 and a little bit of 1955, the years when the strange growling crows with large yellowed beaks had taken over Potter Grove, apparently dive-bombing victims' skulls seemingly at random. They killed five people and seriously wounded several more before leaving the area as mysteriously as they came.

A few people believed they were back. I was one of them.

"You don't need to convince me," I said to my ex. "I was already going to do it."

Justin skated up and took my hand again. "You were already going to do what?" he asked, turning his head to the side. Justin knew I was a medium. He knew I talked to ghosts at my haunted house, and I could tell he was slowly starting to believe that maybe they weren't just pretend friends. But I never told him they sometimes followed me around or that I more than occasionally helped them solve a murder case or two. I needed to ease people into my crazy.

"Nothing," I said, pulling my hat off so I could adjust it over my blondish-brown curls in a way that would hopefully frame my face in something that looked cute and not clownish. "You ready to go?"

The wind picked up, blowing my hat off my fingers and sending it sliding along the ice. Of course this also made my hair fly out in all directions, and I struggled to press it back down to normal-poof as I skated after my hat. My nose dripped and my ears stung, and I realized after a while that I was skating with my tongue out, but I'd paid way too much for that cute hat to let it go that easily. It landed under the tree limb, and I bent down to grab it. Parker did too, and our hands touched. Technically, our gloves.

"Sorry," I said, pulling my hand back like he'd assaulted me.

Parker smiled and handed me my hat. "Thanks again. We had a great time."

"You too." I said. "I mean, me too. I had a great time too."

"Oh my. Awkward," my ex-husband said, popping in to commentate. I ignored the annoying ghost. "Don't mind me," Jackson continued. "I only wonder if your boyfriend is watching this completely natural exchange with the man you invited on your date."

As soon as Parker left, I glared at Jackson. "There is nothing wrong here. I only invited this man to this lake because I told Mildred I would help her grandson acclimate to the area." I tried to remember if I actually said that to Mildred or not.

"Tell yourself whatever you want," Jackson replied.

The wind pummeled my face again but this time I heard a low, humming kind of a noise along with it. It lifted along the breeze, an almost growling sound. Like nothing I'd ever heard before, different than the growls at the bed and breakfast months ago. It was almost human sounding.

I looked all around, searching the branches overhead for the birds I knew must be there, a chill running up my spine. When the wind died down, I covered my skull and shushed my ex-husband even though he wasn't talking and listened intently to the wind again. But I didn't hear anything else.

It had to have been my imagination. I was just being paranoid. Still, I quickly caught up to Justin who was sitting on the bench, putting his boots on, oblivious to the hat hunt and the birds growling. I scooted in close and grabbed his hand faster than I'd intended.

"Let's go," I said.

"That's what we're doing, right?" He shrugged. "You gonna change out of your skates?"

"Nope," I replied, not even listening to my mother's nagging voice echoing through my head about how she knew I wasn't going to take care of those expensive skates. I stood up and wobbled across the snow and dirt in them.

Justin didn't say much as we trudged over to his truck while we held hands, me trying to make the pace as fast as possible in a clunky pair of ice skates as I checked all the branches along the way. When we reached the parking lot, he looked back at the makeshift skating rink set up along the ice behind us, his eyes wet from the wind. "Spin class and yoga," he said, shaking his head.

I looked back too just in time to see a very large crow flying across the rink toward the bench where Justin and I had just been sitting. I couldn't move. I just stood, holding onto the truck door, staring at the tree. The bird looked completely normal, yet something seemed off.

"You okay?" Justin asked, starting the truck, motioning for me to get in.

Squinting into the wind, I caught the eye of another black bird. This one was in a higher branch when our eyes met. A bigger one. It seemed to be looking for me too, with a surprisingly human glare, and a thick yellowed beak.

CHAPTER 2

ACCIDENTS HAPPEN, SOMETIMES ON PURPOSE

I snuggled into the crook of Justin's arm and tried to focus on the superhero movie streaming on my flatscreen. Justin smelled like soap mixed with sex appeal, and he was wearing the dark gray sweater I told him I couldn't resist. But still, the only thing I could think about was my ex-husband and the partier we'd just taken home with us.

They were here somewhere, watching and waiting, probably tapping on their ghost watches.

Rex sat quietly at our feet. My dog was finally getting used to my boyfriend. He used to bark at Justin a lot, but it only happened every once in a while now.

"Did I tell you," Justin said, leaning over toward me. "You look beautiful tonight?"

"It's completely okay if you repeat yourself. I hear that's a sign of extreme intelligence."

He brushed a strand of my curls away from my face and moved in for a kiss. His face was wonderfully scratchy and soft all at the same time. He ran a hand along the back of my neck as he pressed his lips over mine and a tingle ran all the way to my toes. I was just starting to get into it when I opened my eyes for a split second. Jackson was hovering directly above us.

I closed my eyes again and tried to ignore him. *He's just looking for attention, and if you give it to him, things will only continue down this path,* I told myself like I was dealing with a toddler and not a 50-something-year-old ghost.

I peeked again. He was still there. The man was bound and determined to break Justin and me up, again. Twelve years ago, I broke up with Justin to date and marry Jackson, and it wasn't about to happen again, not that you could date and marry a dead guy. Or that I would want to.

Justin stopped kissing me and pulled away. "Is something wrong?' he asked.

"No. It's nothing," I replied, mostly for the benefit of the hovering ghost.

"It's your ex again, huh?" he said. He looked around my living room. "I think I like hanging out at my place better. No offense."

"None taken. I'm sorry."

"It's okay," he said in a way that made me think it really wasn't. "I have to get up early anyway."

It was a sore spot all the way around. Even though Justin would never admit it, I knew he resented Jackson again, and probably wondered if I was even making him up.

I followed my boyfriend to the kitchen where he paused at the back door that led to the veranda. "Next time, my place," he said, gently lifting my chin up with the tip of his finger so he could kiss me again. Then he left. And my heart sunk into my gut.

These ghosts were ruining my love life.

Plus, I didn't really want to hang out at Justin's apartment all the time. That place gave me the creeps, and this was from a woman who lived in a haunted house. His apartment complex sat right at the edge of the Dead Forest, a wildlife preserve that spanned a whole side of Landover County, reaching for miles, like a divider that kept us apart from the rest of civilization.

Every place in Landover had its myths. You couldn't live here and not know about them. But the Dead Forest had the creepiest one. People who went into the Dead Forest didn't come out, hence the name. And it was this fact that made the myth so creepy. Nobody knew why people didn't return because nobody returned.

Logically, I knew it was just a rumor. And, I'd never actually heard of anyone going into the forest. But when you live in a town where rumors seem to be proving themselves true right and left, you don't test things. You don't decide to be that person who goes in.

So now, because my jerk of an ex-husband was ruining my love life, my only choices were be the pervy ghost's sex show or hang out by death's forest.

Of course Jackson appeared as soon as the door closed. "I thought he'd never leave," he said.

"He shouldn't have to. He's my boyfriend."

"Just until someone better wins you back." He winked.

"So your plan is to annoy your way back into my heart?"

"Worked the first time."

I grabbed one of the dishes drying along the side of the sink and somehow resisted the urge to chuck it out the window. I needed privacy around here. I needed to be free from this house agreement and these ghosts. Clutching the dish so hard I almost broke it with my bare hands, I gently placed it into the cabinet where it belonged. One after another. Then, I grabbed Rex's dog food and plopped it into the microwave. The thermometer to check the food's temperature was right where it always was. Everything was always right where it should be. Things were too routine. Too strict.

"No wonder I'm 31 and still dating. Justin's not going to stick around if he has to put up with weird house rules and ex-husband ghosts."

"Now, Carly. If a boy really likes you for you," Jackson began. "He won't care."

"Oh shut up," I replied as the microwave beeped. I whistled for Rex then checked another box off the house agreement checklist I kept on the fridge. "I'm going to burn the sage again, a whole truckload this time."

As the familiar sound of dog claws along the hardwood sounded, I felt another presence, and I remembered we had a guest. I felt guilty for yelling at my ex in front of her. But then, it wasn't the first time my ex-husband and I had done that. In fact arguing in front of company and almost demanding they take sides was pretty much our MO back in the day.

"I'm sorry to intrude," the timid voice said, making me instantly feel sorry for her.

"Allow me to introduce our guest," Jackson said. A woman appeared with dark bobbed hair, full eyebrows, and a cute button nose. She was dressed in a sleek navy blue skirt and a polkadot sleeveless shirt. She was absolutely stunning.

"Carly, this is Gloria Elenore Thomas, our newest client," he said.

The girl smiled softly at me, hands behind her back as she nervously hover-rocked back and forth. She couldn't have been older than 18, max.

I searched my brain for something appropriate to say. "Sorry about your accident," I managed. "I mean, if it was an accident."

She nodded. "It wasn't."

"Let's go into the dining room and you can tell me everything you remember."

I knew it wasn't going to matter much, as far as the story's accuracy went. Ghosts didn't always remember things correctly after they died. It was only when we joined forces during a chan-neling that we relived the memory, exactly as it happened at the time it happened, second by second.

I pulled open the top drawer of the credenza in the back of the dining room, grabbed my notebook and pencil, then sat down.

"I don't know where to begin," she said.

"Gloria wasn't a regular on Landover Lake," Jackson said. "She's from California."

"Los Angeles," she chimed in, looking up at the ceiling like she was trying to remember. "We always rented a house on the lake, every summer since I was six, for two weeks with my aunt's family. My mother and my aunt grew up in Wisconsin, so even though we all lived in California, we always went to the lake to vacation." She sat on the chair next to me, such a small spirit, one I suspected was pretty easily taken advantage of in her day.

She continued. "I looked forward to it every year, eating fresh-picked corn while we caught fireflies and fished. I have to say, we were much more successful at catching fireflies than fish."

I nodded along, not much to take notes on yet. "So, the night you passed away. You were renting on the lake? What happened?"

"My cousin Nettie is what happened. Annette, but everyone called her Nettie. We'd both just graduated. Most years we kept to ourselves, just our families on the lake. But that year, Nettie got it in her head she wanted a boyfriend. A summer fling, she'd said. And the boys on the lake were so cute I found myself wanting that too. The boys only liked Nettie, of course. She'd just dyed her hair, like Marilyn Monroe's."

I wrote Nettie's name into my notebook along with a short description.

Gloria squinted her eyes up. "Honestly, I don't remember too much from the night itself. We went to the sock hop at the dance hall. Nettie found a boy and ditched me like always. I'd just turned 18 and this was my first country club dance. But I didn't really know anyone, so I was happy when the party broke up early. I wanted to go home."

"So the party ended early, huh?" I asked, scribbling as I talked. "Why?"

She looked at the ceiling. "Somebody spiked the punch and some kids were getting out of control, I think. I don't really remember. Nettie wasn't ready to go home, though. I do remember that. She convinced me to sneak on a boat with her. Man, it was the largest, most luxurious boat I'd ever been on, with a downstairs and everything. We thought the people on the boat would be cranked to have us along for their after-party. But I only remember their faces when they found us. They went ape, and not in a good way. I woke up in the water with Nettie."

"You're sure you didn't fall overboard?"

"Oh no. I don't remember how we got in the water, but it wasn't a fall. And when we were there, treading water, another boat showed up and yelled to us over a megaphone or something. I tried to wave my arms to get their attention, but when I looked up, the boat was coming right for us…"

I wrote as fast as I could at this point. These girls hadn't been partiers who met with an unfortunate accident. Something else had gone on entirely, and I was going to figure it out.

"So, will you help me?" she asked. Her voice seemed weaker now, her body almost completely transparent.

"Absolutely," I said. "Tomorrow morning, I'm going to find out everything I can about this so-called accident. We'll start gathering evidence, schedule a channeling of that night as soon as you're up for it. And if there's anyone left from that boat still alive today, they're going to wish they were dead. Mark my words."

I was feeling especially confident for someone who had no idea where she was going with this.

Gloria vanished, and I continued writing out our schedule and my plan to help her.

Jackson hovered by my side, reading over my shoulder in that annoying way he always did, even when we were married. "That's a lot of channeling you've got planned. Are you sure you're up for that?"

"Of course," I said in my most confident voice.

I knew he was concerned about the effects the channelings

were starting to have on me. Truth was, I was concerned too. But I was also starting to feel drawn to them. I needed those channelings, and the ill effects that went with them. Possible hallucinations. White specks impeding my vision. Dizziness. The whole thing was like an intoxicating package that needed me to unwrap it, again and again.

I pulled the shoe box off the bookshelf in the living room and sat down at the coffee table. It was where I kept all the research I'd done on the crows and the history of Gate House. All the articles from 1954 about skull-crushing birds with thick yellowed beaks. And my notes. If anyone told me anything about Gate House, shapeshifters, curses, the Dead Forest, or birds, I put it in there, along with the things I remembered from every channeling and seance. I didn't have much so far.

There seemed to be a curse, all right, and I felt like I was supposed to end it somehow. But that was about as much as I knew, except for the fact I looked exactly like the woman who put the curse on the house in the first place. No idea why, but a coincidence didn't really seem possible.

My mother wouldn't tell me anything about my biological parents or my adoption, except to say the lawyer in the case resembled the lawyer I had now, a man who didn't seem to age, and kind of looked like he'd just stepped off the field of a Civil War reenactment.

Every week I'd think of some other thing to research, some other key word that might unlock the mystery behind this curse and my life, so I'd head optimistically over to the library.

But Parker's grandmother Mildred had been right. There wasn't nearly enough coverage in Potter Grove about the things that mattered, the supernatural things that terrorized this town. And might be back.

But with Gloria's help, I was about to do my own firsthand research and see things for myself in real time.

CHAPTER 3

I bumped the library door open with my butt because my hands were full of to-go cups of coffee. Stopping just inside the doorway, I closed my eyes a second, enjoying the warmth from the vent blaring out heat right above me. Giggles, screams, and squeals interrupted my thoughts, so loud they echoed off the walls.

There were kids in the kids section?

We had a kids section?

"You didn't get me," a little voice taunted. "Come on, at least try."

A toddler screeched.

"Lil Mil, sit down. Mrs. Nebitt is still reading the story."

I recognized the voices immediately. Landover Lake's newest single dad, Parker Blueberg, and his family. I walked toward the sounds and leaned against one of the book racks to watch the very first story time this library probably ever had. Mrs. Nebitt's frail, veiny hand shook as she struggled to hold the book out so the pictures would show to her audience as she sat on one of the metal chairs in the children's section, a section about the size of a small bathroom.

Parker grabbed Benjamin, his toddler, and secured him on his lap even though he was squirming to break free, while Lil Mil, his five-year-old daughter with wild curls, was spinning around on the floor in front of them. He smiled and waved to me when he noticed me standing there.

Mrs. Nebitt ignored the interruptions. "Where was I? Oh yes. *'This must be a home,' he said. 'I know I've always wanted a home.'"* The 80-year-old closed the book with a soft sigh. "Corduroy. One of my favorites. I remember your great grandmother reading it to your dad when he was a baby. You might not know I am very good friends with your great grandmother."

Benjamin got up and started spinning with his sister. Mrs. Nebitt was quickly losing her audience, but oddly, not her patience. She picked up another book, seemingly oblivious to the children who were now chasing each other through the stacks in the nonfiction section. That woman used to shush me whenever I'd move a chair too loudly and now she had children screaming through the library and she hardly noticed?

I handed her the coffee while she carefully put the children's books back, in their exact right spots along the shelves. She hesitated to take it, glancing over at the "No food or drinks" sign posted along the side wall next to the sign that read, "Quiet Please." Lil Mil screamed louder from the back, and Mrs. Nebitt snatched the coffee from my grasp, thanking me.

"I need research on another ghost," I said. "For my book." I added that last part so Parker would know I wasn't crazy. "Someone named Gloria Thomas. She was one of the partiers from 1957 who died in that unfortunate boating accident."

Mrs. Nebitt's smile dropped and she stammered her words a little. "Microfilm section again," she finally said after a couple seconds.

Parker leaned against a table, like he didn't have kids running crazy in a library right now. "I heard you were writing a book," he said. "I'm very impressed."

"Don't be. So far it's just a lot of research."

Even though I had the first chapter written about the suffragette's suicide sitting at home on my laptop, I would rather jump into a vat of hepatitis needles with it than have anyone read it yet.

I caught Parker's profile as he craned his neck to look for his kids. Beige sweater and jeans, his hair tousled like he hadn't had time to brush it. He rocked the frazzled, single-dad look; that was for sure. I looked at my phone, pretending not to be looking at Parker. Jackson's voice echoed in my head, something about wondering if Justin would approve.

A loud crash came from the back, followed by even louder laughter, and Mrs. Nebitt shot Parker a look.

"Sorry, Mrs. Nebitt," he said. "I'll take care of it." He ran after the noise as Mrs. Nebitt and I walked to the periodicals section together. It was a short walk.

She mumbled to herself, tugging on an ear. "So, let's see. 1957…" She set her coffee down on top of the cabinet and opened a drawer.

"You were here in 1957," I said, thinking about the large black-and-white photo that hung on the wall over the copiers. The library's ribbon-cutting ceremony had to have been from around that time. "Do you remember the boating accident?"

She hummed loudly to herself as she sifted through the boxes in the drawer, like she was ignoring me.

"Did you know the people involved? Were you at the dance?"

Still nothing.

Parker came back over, carrying a grinning toddler on his shoulders while holding Lil Mil's hand. "Tell Mrs. Nebitt thanks for the story time, kids," he said, heading for the door.

"Thanks for the story time, kids," Lil Mil echoed back in a gravelly deep voice that sounded a lot like her great grandmother's. Benjamin just waved and blew kisses. And I bit my lip, mentally yelling at my uterus to stop being so needy. We would have kids when we were meant to, if we were meant to.

Mrs. Nebitt pulled on her ear. "What was that?" she asked Parker in a soft, faraway tone. "My hearing aid was down."

I knew from helping my mother take care of my grandmother just before she passed away that hearing aids didn't just turn down on their own. Older people turned them down when they didn't want to hear you anymore.

I walked Parker and the kids to the door so I could get a look at the photo of the ribbon-cutting ceremony again. He put his hand on my shoulder before he left. "That accident you're looking up. That was very hard for Mrs. Nebitt and my grandmother."

I looked at him sideways.

"They were chaperones at the dance and were pretty much blamed for the accident. Someone spiked the punch and kids got out of control. And when some kids drowned because they were drunk… It was a rough time for the family."

I gasped. "I had no idea."

"Just tread lightly," he said then left with his kids.

Mrs. Nebitt waddled over to me as soon as the door closed behind them. "They are driving me nuts, running around like that. Parker asked if we did story time. What was I going to say? Poor guy's looking for cheap entertainment for those kids. But honestly, I don't know how to do a story time for toddlers. Run a book club for 90-year-olds, sure. But toddlers…"

"I can do it next time," someone said, and I realized it had been me. I immediately tried to back peddle. "I know you would hate that, though, because you would hate for someone else to take over. And there probably won't even be a next time."

Mrs. Nebitt's face relaxed, so it was only halfway scowling now. "I will take you up on your very kind offer," she said.

Why had I made such a very kind offer, anyway?

"We'll talk about the details later. I set up the microfilm

machine for you," she said, sashaying off to her humungous desktop computer at the front, leaving me to do my own research for once. Every other time, she'd kept me company.

I looked up at the photo above the copiers before making my way to the periodicals section again. In it, Mrs. Nebitt stood with a pair of humungous scissors next to four smiling men in dark suits and one young woman in a beauty queen sash, *Miss Potter Grove 1950-something*. The woman was standing behind one of the men, so I couldn't really tell the date on her sash. Mrs. Nebitt looked remarkably similar to the way she looked today, except in the picture her hair was dark and her glasses were thick and cat-eye looking as she glared down at the ribbon she was about to cut, like she might want to stab it instead.

I went back over to the periodicals section and sat in front of the machine. Mrs. Nebitt was humming to herself, causing a very loud distraction. The woman didn't hum. She hated noise. I could already tell this case was going to be different.

Young Party Goers Meet Tragic End; Alcohol Suspected

   Gloria Thomas and Annette Jerome, recent high-school graduates and cousins from Los Angeles, CA, were two of the four victims in the boating accident late Saturday night. Witnesses say alcohol was most certainly involved. After attending what was supposed to be a "sock hop" at the country club's recreational center, the girls surreptitiously boarded a yacht owned by the Donovan family with Frederick Linder, 18, of Landover and his friends Clyde Bowman, Myles Donovan, and Darren Wittle. Also in attendance were Bill Donovan and Dwight Linder.

My jaw dropped. There, on the screen, were some of the biggest names in Landover County. Clyde Bowman was the mayor of Potter Grove (and was also Jackson's uncle) while Darren Wittle was the mayor of Landover. And Myles Donovan was *the* Myles Donovan, the man in the largest house on the lake, the richest man in Landover. He was also Delilah Scott's distant cousin. I didn't recognize the Linders, though, even though there was a photo of them. I read on.

> *"I am actually surprised this didn't happen sooner," one of the mothers of a young party attender said. "We've been warning the country club for years. They need to do a better job chaperoning those dances. The punch was spiked again, and I suspect funny cigarettes were a part of it, too."*
>
> *Witnesses on the boat say the teenagers jumped overboard for a late-night swim, but were too inebriated to make it back and quickly became lost in the water.*
>
> *Frederick Linder's father, Dwight, apparently jumped in to save the kids, but was quickly lost too. A police vessel was summoned to the scene, but in the chaos, accidentally ran over the women who were still struggling to stay afloat. The search for the Linders continues. Ms. Thomas is survived by her parents, Tony and Velma Thomas and her sister, June, of Los Angeles...*

Below the article were all three of the kids' senior high-school photos. Gloria and Nettie smiled at me in velvet wraps and pearls. And Freddie Linder was a lanky kid in a bow tie and suit, his thinning hair parted neatly to the side.

"Who's Frederick Linder?" I called out across the library.

Mrs. Nebitt shushed me and took another sip of her coffee. "This is a library, Carly Mae," she said, like it hadn't just been a daycare about 20 minutes ago.

In the middle of the article, there was a small grainy photo of the lake, with a couple large boats sitting along the bank and what looked like stretchers loaded with lumpy white sheets being wheeled along the dirt. The caption underneath said: *"We didn't know they were swimming when we pulled anchor and drove off. By the time we realized they were in the lake, we turned around but it was too late to find them. Freddie's dad jumped in and we called the police."* — Clyde Bowman

I noticed the inconsistencies right away. Did the "witnesses" know their friends had jumped overboard or were they surprised not to see them onboard? And almost none of this went along with Gloria's account.

I printed out the article and wrote down every person's name I could find in the margins, circling June Thomas, Gloria's sister. There was very little chance Gloria's parents were still alive, but maybe her sister was. Finding her might be a challenge, though.

I could only find a couple other articles about the accident. Apparently, the other two victims had drowned. Mrs. Carmichael and old George had both been right. While I was printing out every article I could find, I looked up at the 50's photo just above the copiers again.

I didn't care that this happened 60 years ago. Someone from that boating accident was going to talk to me. And I was going to start with the person I didn't have to look too hard to find. The mayor.

$\mathcal{M}$ayor Clyde Bowman was a predictable man who loved three things: money, himself, and food. And Mondays were the day he could celebrate all three. The investment club always met at the Spoony River Cafe because chicken fried steak was on special, and that was an investment most people could agree on, even without an investment club.

After work I went over there. It was warm and loud, and smelled like grease mixed with blood pressure medication.

Mrs. Carmichael rushed over to me, strutting to *Runaround Sue* playing softly in the background. "There's a spot open along the counter, hon. Coffee and chicken fried steak?"

"Just coffee," I said, sitting down at one of the stools close to the investment club. The mayor was right behind me at his usual spot in the large corner booth next to five other men, leaning back into the sticky white vinyl of their seats, laughing, probably at some joke about poor people or taxes, or how they avoided both.

I knew this was a bad idea. There were too many people and it was weird to ask an almost 80-year-old man about a horrific boating accident that happened when he was 18. I gulped, but scooted my barstool over a little so I'd be close enough to over-hear them.

Landover's mayor, Darren Wittle, was among the group, a man who looked more like Pee Wee Herman's creepy uncle than an authority figure worth voting for. He and Mayor Bowman were talking about how they might be able to take a trip to Florida together soon, on the taxpayer's dime for business reasons.

Nobody glanced in my direction or smiled, even though they all knew me and saw me there. But then, I was the awful woman who had somehow swindled Gate House out of the Bowmans' grasps, so I was getting used to being ignored.

Mrs. Carmichael carried a pot of coffee when she came back over. She fixed her pink waitress hat and set a white coffee cup by my place mat.

"When you told me about Accident Loop yesterday…" I began, loudly. I paused to see if the investment club at the large booth was looking over at me like I wanted them to. They weren't, so I made my voice even louder. "I did a quick library search to see what you were talking about."

Mrs. Carmichael stopped pouring mid-cup, suddenly inter-ested. "So, tell me. Who was right? Was it a drowning or were those kids mangled by a boat?"

I studied the woman's face. I had no idea how old anyone was, really. But I guessed Mrs. Carmichael must have been in her late 50s so she probably hadn't been around when the accident happened. And since not too many people talked about it anymore, she might not have known that two of the people involved were sitting at the booth next to us right now. I was about to fill her in, though.

"You were both right. Two of the victims were hit by a boat, the other two drowned." She almost looked disappointed not to be fully right.

I pointed over to the booth with the investment club while

she filled my cup the rest of the way. "I also found out the mayors of both Landover and Potter Grove were on one of the boats when it happened."

Mrs. Carmichael turned so fast she almost spilled coffee on them. "These two?" She motioned with her coffee pot at the mayors. "Well, I'll be," she said, mouth open. Mrs. Carmichael prided herself on being the town's biggest gossip, and now I'd scooped her on a story that George had already partially scooped her on.

Mayor Bowman cut her off. "Just a splash more coffee, Patsy," he said, raising his cup. "And before you even ask, I don't talk about that night. It was a horrible, tragic accident. One we all want to forget about."

Mayor Wittle nodded his thin, turkey neck so hard in agreement, I worried for a second I'd hear a twig-snapping sound. "Horrible," he repeated, voice nasally and shaky.

Mayor Bowman went on. "And it happened a long time ago. There is no reason on God's green earth to relive it."

"What if I gave you a reason? I don't believe the accident happened like it was reported."

He went back to his food and his friends. "Some people don't know when to quit. Nobody cares about something that happened that long ago."

"The dead do," I said, then after realizing that sounded crazy, added. "I mean their families do, and I care too."

Dr. Vernon Gleason, the town's only veterinarian and the youngest one in the investment group at age 60, leaned in my direction. Rosalie called him *Dr. Dog*, mostly because he hit on every woman at his vet clinic. "She's just trying to drum up some business over there at the Purple Pony. Charge good people millions of dollars to watch another silly seance. I heard they're not doing very well over there." He ran a thick freckled hand through his greasy dyed bangs and winked at me. "You should come on over and work for me, Carly Mae. I'll keep you busy."

I was happy my stomach didn't have anything to possibly throw up.

I grabbed my coffee and took a larger sip than I'd intended, burning my tongue. I hadn't heard the Purple Pony wasn't doing well. I mean, I should have guessed. My hours had been cut again, but Rosalie just said that was because it was winter and we didn't have rich tourists here for the summer yet.

The diner seemed silent, except for the occasional sounds of forks scraping along plates, and a mumble about me and the Purple Pony. I shook myself out of my stupor.

"Stop trying to change the subject. Gloria Thomas did not die by accident. And I'm going to prove it," I said, loudly, so the whole restaurant could hear me. That got the murmurs really going.

The mayor pointed a shaky finger at me. "We know how you operate, and we're all tired of it. Aren't we?" he asked the members of his table. They all nodded like the old man was making sense.

He went on. "You sure like to stir up trouble where there isn't any. Well, that might have flown with the country club ladies who like to take on ridiculous causes like helping mediums change death certificates on old suffragettes. But this is different. You could hurt people's reputations. And I, for one, will fight for mine."

We were both talking for the benefit of the entire restaurant now. Mrs. Carmichael and Shelby were the only ones shuffling about, grabbing empty plates and filling coffee cups, but even they were really looking over, listening.

And the ball was back in my court. "I thought just a couple months ago, you said every life mattered in this city and so did every death. Gloria Thomas was a life. So was her cousin Annette and your friend Frederick. Apparently, life and death only matter when precious reputations aren't also on the line."

"The good people of this town have suffered enough with this case," he said. "You're right. Freddie was my friend. And he was lost in a tragic accident. I think everyone here will agree with me when I say we're done reliving it. Certain things should stay in the past."

He was good, better than I thought. Just like the politician he was trained to be, he knew exactly when to bring the crowd to his side, and how to do it. I could tell he'd just won this round. Everyone went back to their chicken fried steaks and their conversations about what a bad winter this was going to be.

I took another couple sips of coffee, threw down five dollars onto the counter, and hopped off my bar stool. Someone who probably wasn't on the verge of losing her job should have my spot. Someone who could afford chicken fried steak and not just coffee.

CHAPTER 5

TREAD CAUTIOUSLY

"Jackson is seriously getting on my nerves," I told my boss the next day when we were standing by the main storefront window, pulling the stiff arms of a headless mannequin into a cable knit, vintage, 70s sweater for the Purple Pony's window display. "I have no privacy."

"And that's surprising to you how? I'm pretty sure Jackson didn't have boundaries when he was living either."

"And the other day, when Justin and I were on the couch…" I stopped myself. It was strange talking about my love life in front of someone I thought of as a mom.

"I get it. You don't want Jackson popping in. Maybe I can find a recipe to help."

I nodded like I knew what that meant. One of my curls caught on a random Christmas bulb hanging from the side of the window and I yanked it free, leaving a chunk of blondish brown strands dangling off of it like tinsel.

Even though we were well into January, the Purple Pony still had Christmas lights hanging everywhere because Rosalie "loved that time of year." What she probably loved best was that it was the last time we had any customers. I didn't mention the part where Dr. Dog said the Purple Pony was in trouble.

Instead, I told her all about my new client and the run-in I had with the mayor.

Rosalie pulled her dreadlocks into a bun and steadied herself on the stool by her side, resting her bad hip as she straightened out the neckline of the mannequin's sweater. "If the mayor had that kind of a reaction when you just brought up the boating accident, he's hiding something."

"Yep," I said.

"You could uncover a whole mess of trouble," she mumbled with a pin in her mouth. She bunched the mannequin's skirt a little in the back and pinned it so it would fit its curves better. "Tread cautiously."

That was the second "tread cautiously" I'd heard in the last couple days.

"Were Woodward and Bernstein told to tread cautiously by the Washington Post?" I asked.

"How should I know? They didn't have to deal with the good-ole-boys club of Landover County. I do know that. Now, go on outside and tell me how this dummy looks from the window."

"It's below freezing outside," I said. "I can already tell you. It looks fine."

She gave me a look, so I went in the back and grabbed my coat, gloves, and hat. She waited to roll her eyes until I got back to the front. "I asked you to make a two-second assessment. You're dressed like you're going camping in the Arctic."

I smiled behind my scarf and opened the door, blinking into the sunlight that always seemed brighter when it reflected off snowbanks. A cold wind shot through my body, and the many layers of clothes I was wearing weren't doing much to help.

The sidewalk under my feet hadn't been salted properly and I slipped a little as I cautiously trudged out to the window in the front. Just like I thought, the mannequin looked fine, although very Christmasy for nowhere near Christmas with all the red and green lights surrounding it.

"Thanks again for the rush delivery," a familiar voice said as the door to the Bait 'N Breath opened, and Paula Henkel stepped out, carrying a large box. The hippie store couldn't even get one customer during the off season but the tackle shop next to us in the strip mall had customers galore.

Last time I saw the spiky-haired, bleach-blonde woman, her face was stuck in a bucket of fish as a polar bear. Apparently, there were many shapeshifters here in Potter Grove. So far, I'd only discovered two bears for sure: her and Bobby Foreman, Shelby's fiancé. I avoided both.

"Going ice fishing?" I asked, pointing toward her box. "Or buying a few snacks?"

Paula glared at me. "How's business?" she said in such a way I knew she was dying for me to ask her the same question. The winter business season in Potter Grove was even deadlier than winter itself.

"Oh, it's always slow in January," I said. "But we're making do." I added that last part to try to quell the rumors already circulating.

She waited a second for me to ask her about the bed and breakfast. I didn't. "Still going strong at the bed and breakfast," she replied, trudging out to her large white truck. "But then, I know how to cater to the locals. That's the secret. I'm running a local lovebird special right now if you and Justin are interested."

"Thanks, but I live in a beautiful Victorian. Every day's like waking up in a bed and breakfast." If cursed haunted houses were charming and had privacy. I looked down at my scuffed-up puffer coat, which was the same coat I'd been wearing for five years. Who was I kidding? She knew the truth.

She smiled a little too enthusiastically. "Well then, have a good day."

I needed to figure out a way for the Purple Pony to cater to the locals, too. I was just about to go back inside when I thought of something. *Why not take the investment club's advice?*

I sucked in my pride and yelled to Paula. "I think I have a ghost story the locals will be very interested in if you feel like partnering to do a seance again. I'd do it myself, but you were great with marketing last time."

She stopped and looked over. "I'm listening."

"Sixty years ago, four people died on the lake. It was deemed an accident, but I've talked to one of the ghosts, and it was no accident."

"You talked to one of the ghosts?" She chuckled to herself, her cheeks bright red from the cold.

"You're right. That's crazy. Enjoy your fish, from your bucket."

She paused at her opened driver's side door. "I'm always up for a business proposition," she said, sliding her box of polar bear food across to the passenger's seat. "But just so you know, if we work together, I won't be paying for damages this time around. And windows probably cost double to replace in winter."

She was referring to the last seance we'd done when my suffragist client was so angry with her lying fiancé that she blew out some windows at the bed and breakfast. It made negotiating the terms of our agreement with Paula pretty sticky.

I tried to make my voice as confident as I could. "We'll have sage on stand-by this time. Burning sage will keep the ghosts in check."

She looked at me like I just told her I still believed in Santa. "C'mon, Carly. That's an old wive's tale, and ghosts aren't real."

"They're real, and it works. But even if it doesn't, we'll pay for any damage caused by ghosts. You paid for it last time."

Her smile grew to an evil length. "We'll talk," she said, getting into her truck.

Snow fell heavily as I walked back toward the Purple Pony, a new-found confidence in my step. All I had to do was convince Rosalie to work with Paula again, and get a ghost or two from the boating accident to show up. I pictured the whole county getting behind me on this one. The truth would prevail.

I looked up at the sad headless mannequin celebrating Christmas from 1976, a hairy bulb behind her neck. Truth was, we couldn't afford for the truth not to prevail.

Rosalie was just as curious as I thought she'd be when I got back inside. "What were you talking to Satan about?"

"Business."

"My soul's not for sale."

"He said he needs 'em pure, anyway," I joked. I wanted to say a lot of other things, like how I knew the Purple Pony wasn't doing well, maybe remind her that we needed to figure out ways to cater to the locals. But I didn't say any of that. Instead, I just nodded like we weren't about to do business with the dark lord.

AT THE END of the day, when the window mannequin was sporting her third 70's Christmas look in January because we were bored, I stood at the mirror by the dressing room, touching up my mascara. Justin and I were hanging out at his place tonight and I was counting down the seconds until I could leave.

The wind chimes on the front door clanged, and Rosalie darted in from the back like she was prepared to pounce on our one-and-only customer. She stopped when she saw it was Justin, and limp-walked back.

"You're early," I said to him. "I can officially go in…" I looked at my cellphone clock.

"Just go," Rosalie said.

Justin didn't say a word as we walked out to his truck. And, it dawned on me that he hadn't kissed me hello either. Snow fell all around us, but it wasn't why I was feeling cold.

"Everything okay?" I finally asked when we reached his truck.

"Fine."

I nodded and got into his spotless passenger's seat, turning the vent over toward me and adjusting my temperature to max heat. "I wish everything was fine with me. I think I'm about to get my hours cut again."

He took a deep breath like he was going to say something then exhaled without saying a word. I hated it when people did that. My mother made that same sound every time she asked how my career was going.

It was the sigh of disappointment. I never thought I'd hear it from my boyfriend, though. I turned the radio up so we wouldn't have to make conversation then looked out the window because staring at darkness was much more interesting right now.

"Do you know what I did all day?" he finally asked.

"I have no idea," I replied to the window, never looking over at him.

"I filled out paperwork and filed it. I cleaned trashcans and wiped toilets. That's what I did."

"That sucks."

"Yes. It did suck." His voice was cold, distant.

I didn't say anything and he didn't either, but after his third sigh-of-disappointment, I'd had enough. "Look, okay it sucked. But I have been in enough years of therapy to know that what you're doing right now is inappropriately displacing your anger. You're mad at Caleb and taking it out on me."

He stared at the road.

I went on. "Now, *my* anger about your anger, on the other hand, is very understandable. I'm pretty sure even a therapist would say, 'Good job on this anger, Carly. Totally appropriate use of it there.'"

Justin clenched his teeth and furrowed his thick eyebrows. "When I asked Caleb what was going on, why I was cleaning and filing stuff. You know what he told me?"

"I don't care."

"He said, 'Ask your girlfriend.' So now I'm asking. What does that mean?"

I took a deep breath like I was about to say something, but only exhaled. The sound of Justin's wipers swishing away the fast-falling snow was the only sound.

My mouth fell open. "He said to ask me?"

"Yes."

I sat listening to the wipers. That comment must've been the mayor's attempt at trying to silence me. I tried to hold in my smile. "I think it means I'm on the right track. I met a new ghost…"

"Ghost," he said with an almost laugh in his tone. "I have to clean trashcans and file because of a ghost. Listen to yourself."

"I am listening to myself," I said. "You're the one not listening. Just take me back to my car. I'm not in the mood to hang out with your illegitimate anger issues."

"You always do this," he said. "You did it twelve years ago, and you're still doing it."

"Do what?"

"Make me out to be the villain."

We didn't talk the whole way back to the Purple Pony. And I didn't even give him the chance to kiss me good-bye. I slammed the door shut and stumbled through the piling snow over to my car, never looking back.

I could tell the man of few words was holding in a lot of them at that moment. Good. That made two of us.

CHAPTER 6

SLIPPERY SLOPES

*I*t was just one simple question. For my investigation. It had nothing to do with the argument I'd just had with my boyfriend. I hit the little phone icon and waited on the side of the road for him to pick up. The snow had really piled up while I was at work and it was still coming down. It was going to be slow-going, getting up Gate Hill tonight, and this was my last chance to use my cell phone.

"Hey Carly. I've been meaning to call you," Parker said when he answered.

I lost any semblance of thought. "Whymever for?" I managed. *Whymever for?* I cursed my ex-husband for making me feel nervous around this man. Maybe Parker hadn't heard me.

He went on. "Mrs. Nebitt said you were going to take over story time at the library for her. She wants us to coordinate a day to do it so she can put it on the library's online calendar. She's hoping more kids'll show up next time so Lil Mil and Benjamin can maybe make some friends."

"Oh," I said, cluing in that this was a business call. I tried not to show my disappointment. "Pretty much any morning works for me. I work at the Purple Pony in the afternoons," I said. "But I'll be honest. I have no idea how to run a story time."

"It's simple." He laughed. "You just read stories."

I breathed a sigh of relief. I had two English degrees. I could read.

"And maybe do a puppet show or a sing-a-long."

I coughed on air. "A puppet show? Where do you even buy puppets? Is there a puppet store somewhere? And do kids really like those creepy things?"

He laughed even harder, probably thinking I was joking. "You're creeped out by puppets, huh?" His voice had a teasing quality to it that made me want to get teased more. "They're Lil Mil's favorite."

"Well, then," I said. "I don't want to piss off Lil Mil. She seems like a tough cookie."

"Takes after her great grandma."

"Speaking of her great grandma," I said. "I'm calling because I lost her phone number and I need it."

There was a long pause. "Whymever for?" he asked, making me kick myself even harder for saying that before. So much for thinking he hadn't heard.

"I just want to ask her a few things."

"You're not going to…" he hesitated. "Ask her about the night of the dance, are you? Honestly, I don't think that's a good idea."

"Your grandmother's a grown woman, Parker. And a tough cookie. You just told me that. She can handle my questions."

"Okay, but you saw how Mrs. Nebitt reacted when you asked her about that night? My grandmother is ten times worse."

"Don't worry. I'll tread cautiously," I said, before he had a chance to say it.

Parker agreed to text me the number and I agreed on a week from Monday for the story time. Then I slowly maneuvered my way up Gate Hill, along the barely-visible path that had supposedly been snowplowed for me that afternoon.

My car skidded on what felt like a block of ice and I turned my steering wheel in the direction of the skid, just like my mother taught me to do, taking my foot off the gas. My heart pounded through my sweater as I mechanically went through the steps of coming out of a skid, but ended up sliding out of control for a full 10 seconds. The only light around was coming from my headlights as they bounced crazily over rocks and trees. I finally stopped in a snowbank and took a deep breath.

Quickly, I put my foot on the gas again to make sure I wasn't stranded. Commuting to work was not as safe as it used to be. It was definitely not worth the short hours and minimum-wage pay.

After lurching my car forward enough to know I was okay, I threw it into park and took a second to calm down, let my hands stop shaking before I moved on. And I remembered now how Justin and I had broken up originally more than twelve years ago. It had been a similar night to tonight.

I had a different car, though, a God-awful orange Volvo that I nicknamed the politician because I couldn't count on it for much more than money-sucking and broken promises. This was around the time when Jackson started noticing me too, and unfortunately for me, I was a dumb 19-year-old who apparently liked to be noticed, and couldn't tell the difference between a nice guy and a pile of... cash.

And I'll just admit it; it felt good to have somebody rich treat me special, flaunting money, saying all the things I liked to hear like, "Here's some more money."

I didn't choose Jackson over Justin for the money, but it sure made things confusing. I mistook generosity for kindness and love. It didn't help that Justin looked the part of the bad boy. He had a motorcycle and tattoos, pretty much everything my mother hated in my boyfriends from high school because they'd all been selfish pricks. And before I knew it, I'd put Jackson in the nice category and Justin in the jerk one. I was a shallow, confused teenager.

The night we broke up, I knew I had to tell him it was over, but I didn't know how. We were just about to snuggle on the couch like usual when I blurted out, "I can't do this anymore. I'm not a kid. This was fun, but I need somebody stable and secure who cares about me for me."

The politician wouldn't start in the snow when I got back out to it. And after about 10 minutes of me sitting in my car outside his home, cursing into my steering wheel, trying to get the damn thing started, I got a text on my flip phone.

"You okay?"

I ended up staying over. He even insisted I take the bed.

I kicked myself a little just now in my Civic for not seeing true kindness back then, especially when it let me stay the night, after I'd been the villain.

Did justice for the dead really matter that much? Finding out what happened the night of the boating accident wasn't going to change what happened the night of the boating accident. But it might change a lot of things for the people I cared about right here, right now.

I turned the heat higher and warmed my fingers on one of the vents, suddenly feeling like something was watching me. I looked around but didn't see anything. That's when I heard high-pitched screaming from up above. The sound grew louder and louder like it was plunging straight for my car. I screamed too, ducking, covering my face, certain whatever it was was coming straight through the windshield. I looked up just in time to see it stop. A crow zoomed past my windshield and down the road.

That was crazy.

I wasn't sure if it was one of the thick-beaked bomber birds, or a shapeshifter, or just a regular bird who forgot to fly south and had apparently frozen in midair, plummeting to the ground like a screaming piece of hail. I maneuvered my way back over to the path again, the bird just in front of me now, soaring ahead like it was guiding my way. I got a look at its beak. It wasn't crusty yellow, but still, that was not as comforting as you would think it'd be.

It took me more than an hour to inch up Gate Hill and I must've looked like hell frozen over when I finally stomped through the veranda door, kicking my boots off on the porch, as was required by my agreement. I leaned against the wall of the kitchen and closed my eyes, trying to feel safe.

Jackson appeared as soon as I opened my eyes again.

"Don't start," I said, my eyes stinging with rage. "I cannot get stranded on that hill without cell phone coverage. We will be making some upgrades to this place or I am leaving it. We need lights on Gate Hill. And paved roads."

He didn't say anything. He just calmly listened to me ranting about safety issues and improperly plowed roads. And then when I was finished, he looked at me with the kind of sad concern I saw way too much of nowadays, and I wanted to strangle him for it.

That's when I noticed Ronald was there too, standing in the kitchen. Jackson's lawyer, and probably the lawyer in my adoption 31 years ago.

He was a rail thin man in a perfectly-pressed, buttoned-down white shirt and a waxed mustache that bordered on handlebar, his hair neatly side-parted with a little swoop.

"The trust pays handsomely for that road to be maintained," he said. "I made a full inspection on my way in, and I can conclusively say it hasn't been touched. I'm very sorry. I will immediately stop further payment to the city…"

"To the city," I said, suddenly suspicious.

"We have never had problems contracting with the snowplow service they use."

And now, I understood. I hadn't even had a channeling with Gloria Thomas and the mayor was so scared he was trying to convince me to go no further with this. At least I knew what tread cautiously meant. "Yes, thank you, Ronald. Please do whatever you can to make sure that road is safe." I thought about the bird I saw on Gate Hill. "And thanks for directing my way in. Bird's eye view of the road helps, huh?"

I'd long suspected that man was a ghost. Now, I also suspected a shapeshifter too.

His face never changed expression. "We'll go directly with a private contractor from now on," he said, ignoring my comment. "I'll call to see if they can come out tomorrow morning. And you're right. It's time for some upgrades this spring. I'll put in an order."

I had no idea what "putting in an order" meant, but I knew it was futile to ask. I was the owner of this place, but I had very little control over it. I had to follow a house agreement and, apparently, I also had to wait for approval before doing any upkeep.

I sat down on the couch and sunk into the cushions, yanking my super-soft throw blanket over myself. This case was already getting dangerous. Rex bounded over to me and I scratched him behind his ear. "I'll feed you in a minute," I said, knowing that was about all the time I had before I'd get docked for not feeding him on time.

My laptop was on the coffee table in front of me and I pulled it over so I could look up as much about this boating accident as I could before my channeling tomorrow. The Donovans. The Linders. The Bowmans and Wittles. The mayor was not going to stop me that easily. This investigation was moving forward. Like it or not.

"Sorry, Justin," I said in my head. "Looks like you'll have trash duty for a while longer because I'm choosing to be the villain again."

CHAPTER 7

*M*y mother didn't answer when I tried calling her the next day just before the channeling. I expected to get her voicemail. I didn't expect to get her friend's voicemail as well.

"Hi, this is Marlene," my mother said.

"And Brenda," said her friend.

"We're not here right now," they said together, giggling. "But leave a message."

I left one. But not the one I wanted to leave, which was, "What the Golden-Girls is going on here? Are you and Brenda room-mates now? And why are you so happy?"

It wasn't any of my business, but I thought it was odd that I hadn't heard a thing about anyone moving in.

"Call me when you get this," I said, instead.

My choppy internet had been extra choppy last night, and I hadn't been able to look anything up, so I was happy to have the printed library articles.

I spread them out along the dining table and glanced over them one by one. There were so many inconsistencies, it was crazy. From the misspelling of names (Linder vs. Lender) to the "blame the victims" defense, the Landover Gazette had dropped the ball on its reporting all over the place. And it seemed to be on purpose.

> *According to police reports, Miss Thomas and Miss Jerome secretly boarded the Donovan's yacht after the Landover Country Club dance ended, apparently hoping to continue a night of carousing and debauchery.*
>
> *"Myles's dad had no idea the girls were even on there. He and Mr. Linder were asleep downstairs," Clyde Bowman, 18, said. "Freddie and the girls were drinking. Beer bottles were everywhere, onboard and in the water, all over the place. Freddie didn't do stuff like that. These girls were party girls from California. I think they were pretty 'loose.' They must've talked him into it. I bet that's how he got drunk at the dance too."*

It went on to lecture about the perils of being "talked into stuff," with advice backed by "experts," of course. *"It's one of the dangers our young people face on the lake every summer, and when the university's in session," said Mayor Lawrence Peterton. "Outsiders who come here with questionable values and nothing but partying on their minds."*

The byline said the article was written by Ethel Peterton, same woman who wrote the other articles, and the same last name as the mayor.

Jackson appeared beside me. "I see you've found the work of my great aunt Ethel," he said. "Henry Bowman had four children. Ethel was one of them. Such a dear, dear woman. Loved by all."

"Sounds like she and the mayor pitted the whole town against the *outsiders*," I said. I'd been an "outsider" once too. And I'd felt every bit the pitted part. "I take it the mayor's her husband?"

He nodded. "They made a great team, like a deadly version of Bonnie and Clyde."

I snatched my laptop from the middle of the table, happy to see the internet was working again.

I looked up the Landover Gazette itself, clicking on the "about us" tab on its website. *A rich history of serving Landover County with accurate and timely reporting for more than a century.* I also saw that it had been established in 1888 when Landover was just becoming a rancher town, but was sold to the Peterton family in the 1930s and then to the new owners in 1993.

"If you think my uncle is a crooked mayor," Jackson said. "Ethel's husband, Lawrence, made Uncle Clyde look like the Dalai Lama. Lawrence was supposedly an ex-mafia lawyer."

"Interesting," I said, taking mental notes to keep the couple in mind as potential suspects. I couldn't decide which was more crooked. The mafia or the Bowmans.

At that moment, Gloria appeared. She was brighter now. I could see the blonde highlights in her brown hair where it had lightened over the summer. A good sign she was strong enough for a channeling.

Jackson whispered in my ear. "Be careful. This is harder on your body than you think."

"I'll be fine," I said, even though I had no idea if I would be fine or how to be careful, anyway. I hadn't done a channeling in a couple months. But I was still having weird side effects that included a hallucination or two. I kept hearing birds when there weren't any. But then, maybe I was fine and there were just ghost birds flying around my house. Anything was possible nowadays.

I asked Gloria about her sister.

"I do have a sister," she said like she was just now remembering that fact. She closed her eyes. "June. June Bug, that's what I called her. I don't know what happened to her, or anyone for that matter. I couldn't get myself to leave the lake. I got so caught up in knowing the truth." She hovered back and forth. "Bug was thirteen when everything happened."

I quickly did the math in my head. "So she'd be in her 70s

now. What's her full name?"

It took Gloria a good ten seconds before she answered. Ghosts seemed to have a very hard time recalling specifics outside of a channeling. "June Marie Thomas," she finally replied. "Dark-haired girl with freckles. Please, let me know if you find anything about her." Her voice trailed off. "I should've sought her out. I should've been a better sister."

"I've found it's never too late for that one," I said, mostly thinking about the case I had with the suffragette not too long ago.

Jackson left "to give us our privacy," and I stacked my articles up into a short pile on the table, the afternoon light shining in on them from the opened curtains. "I'd like to go back to the beginning of the dance, if you're able to," I said, pulling the curtains closed so the room would be darker, the mood more appropriate. "We'll channel until one of us gets tired."

I said that like I knew how to get myself out of a channeling. They'd ended before with either a death, a pass-out, or someone shaking me from the present.

For some reason, my heart raced thinking about this one. Seeing the town back then and the people in it might change the way I felt about them now. And truth was, we were all different people. I sure wasn't that same dumb 19-year-old who'd picked Jackson over Justin.

I took a deep breath to calm down, reminding myself I could be a fair and nonjudgmental bystander no matter what I saw or went through. And I could go through death again. I could do this. "I'm ready whenever you are." I lied.

She nodded. And I stared at one of the golden fleur de lis in the wallpaper, concentrating on its curves and shimmers, trying to think of nothing.

I barely felt her entering. It was a lighter touch this time, much different than when I channeled with Jackson, Martha, or Bessilyn. They had all been heavier, more confident ghosts.

Gloria was a bit reluctant, almost like she was as afraid as I was. Maybe she didn't really want to relive this. It's one thing to want to know what happened and a whole other thing to want to go through it again, second by second.

A mild tingling began in my fingertips, travelled up my spine, and spread across my face.

Music played all around me, along with lots of talking and laughing. The smell of adolescent sweat mixed with chips and punch.

"He was absolutely the cutest. The cutest," a girl's voice said while *See You Later, Alligator* played in the background. "He says he's one of the richest boys on the lake." She squealed. "His name's Freddie. So cute."

"You can open your eyes now," Gloria said to me in our now-meshed mind. I looked around. A large dance floor was surrounded by a pool table and some couches. A couple of girls with short curled hair and high-waisted shorts with no shoes or socks sat on a couch in front of us. One of the girls bounced up, folding her legs underneath her. "My parents told me we can't afford Purdue anymore. Can you believe it? They actually suggested secretarial school," she said. "Who are they kidding?"

I didn't recognize them. The dance floor was also filled with kids I didn't know. Some were twirling around in a jitterbug fashion, others bobbed up and down, squatting and twisting to the beat. Most the girls were in tight long skirts but some had casual shorts or capris on and sandals like they'd thought to come straight off the lake.

Gloria was an out-of-towner, so I knew she was not going to be able to show me around. I scanned the room for people I recognized myself. Their faces were all so round, rosy, and wrinkle-free. How would I be able to tell anyone?

A chubby dark-haired college girl stood at the entrance to the dance hall. She was wearing a puffy pink dress and an awkwardly large corsage. Every once in a while, she looked over at the tall, thin man beside her who was wearing a suit slightly too short for him. And I knew instantly who they were. Mildred and her now-husband, Horace.

"Please don't leave me here alone. Promise me you won't go off with anyone," Gloria begged the girl standing by her side who was wearing a tight-fitting black dress with her bleach blonde hair done in a high ponytail, and more makeup on than Shelby Winehouse (and that girl was a walking makeup sample). I knew it was Annette.

Gloria went on. "He's probably just telling you he's the richest kid on the lake because... you know how boys are around you, Nettie. They'll say anything."

Annette laughed. "You think?" She smiled even broader, her penciled-on beauty mark cracked a little with her facial muscles. A boy looked her up and down and she looked back.

"Please," Gloria said, squeezing her cousin's hand tighter.

"Stop being such a wet rag tonight, Gloria. Gosh. Have I ever left you anywhere?" She turned her head to the side in a coy kind of way. "Okay, maybe I have, but I won't go off with anyone tonight." She held up three fingers on her right hand. "I solemnly swear I won't have any fun at all tonight. I promise."

Gloria didn't respond and Annette pulled her onto the dance floor, almost bumping into a tall, muscular boy in a plaid shirt. He smiled at Annette and she batted her false eyelashes back at him.

"You're the girls from California, huh?" he asked.

She grabbed onto Gloria's arm. "Los Angeles."

He pointed to Nettie. "You were hanging around with my friend Freddie earlier, huh?"

"Well, I'm certainly not married to him," Nettie replied, taking a step closer to the boy. "If that's what you're asking."

"Have you seen him?"

"Who?" Nettie asked.

The boy rolled his eyes, and I suddenly recognized him from

the way his forehead crinkled when he was annoyed. Myles Donovan, looking vaguely similar to his promotional photos around town. There was one at the gym and another in the grocery store. He owned half this town and you couldn't go many places without feeling like he was following you.

He brought out a comb from the back pocket of his jeans and combed his hair a little. "You wanna dance?' he asked.

He licked his lips and Nettie leaned into Gloria, grabbing her arm. "Isn't he the cutest? The cutest. To die for."

"I thought you were just telling me the other boy was the cutest?"

"Can't they both be?"

Gloria talked to me. "Annette was a little bit of a flirt. She hadn't always been that way. It was only after she started dyeing her hair last summer. Everyone told her she looked like Jayne Mansfield and she'd been nonstop ever since."

Myles and Annette went off together to the middle of the dance floor, and Gloria danced by herself for a while, snapping her fingers awkwardly before she backed her way off to the outskirts of the crowd again. I listened in on some of the conversations going on around us, while trying to recognize people.

"We might have to sell the lake house," a girl in loose-fitting jeans cuffed at the bottom said. "My parents are so mad they could kill."

"They're not the only ones," another girl replied.

I tried to hear more from the girls by our side, but Gloria began talking to me in her head. "If I were back in California, I would just have grabbed one of my friends and made her dance with me, you know? But I didn't know anyone here." Her voice was sad. This was a tough memory for her.

"I get it," I said. "I've spent a fair share of my life being an outsider too."

After straightening out her polka-dotted blouse, she stomped over to the punch bowl and grabbed a dixie cup from the stack in front of it, plunking the ladle into the bowl. A group of about four girls passed the table, stopping long enough to give Gloria the curled-lip once-over like she was trash then laughed to themselves and left.

"She always does this. Brings me someplace where I don't know anyone, and I don't fit in, and then she goes off with some boy. I know she only brings me along so her mom'll let her go."

Some of the punch spilled onto the plastic tablecloth. She didn't even notice.

A short, thin brunette in a pale blue dress and thick horn-rimmed glasses leaned into her. I knew it was Mrs. Nebitt even before I read the name tag on her conservative cardigan that said, "Deborah."

"I suggest you drink from the other punch bowl," Mrs. Nebitt said, motioning with her head to a bowl of orange liquid at the other end of the table. "This one has added ingredients." She winked.

Gloria had already filled her cup with punch. She smiled at the woman and downed the punch in front of her. "Thanks for the warning," she said then filled the cup up again.

Next to the punch bowl was a tip jar with a sign that read, "Help build Landover's first public library."

Mrs. Nebitt waddled off to warn someone else about the punch, and Gloria looked around. "I think that girl thought I was 14 or something. I'm 18. I'm old enough to drink in this state. Not in California, but in Wisconsin, sure. Or, at least, that's what Nettie told me." She took a sip of what smelled like Pine-Sol and tasted even worse. It burned our throat a little. "It's awful, though."

She walked over to a group of boys dressed in jeans and t-shirts, stacking dixie cups on a table off to the side of the dance floor. The pyramid was taller than the kids, and a chubby boy stood on a chair with a cup in his shaky hand, reaching up to the top.

"Ain't that a bite. He's gonna make it," one of the bystander's said.

"Nope, never," another kid replied.

"You're going down, fat boy," said the first. Everyone laughed. The chubby boy's face grew red and his hand even shakier.

"You can do it," Gloria told the boy with the cup in his hand.

He looked down, saw who it was who had talked to him, and curled his lip at her. "Get lost, out-of-towner," he said. "Troll."

The other boys laughed their approval.

She went back to talking to me, her voice lower now. "I didn't know any of these kids, and when you look like Kathy from Father Knows Best instead of Marilyn Monroe, nobody wants to know you too much either. At least the boys didn't."

She bumped the table on purpose when she moved past the group and all the cups fell, clattering over the table and onto the floor. A hush fell over the group and they turned to Gloria.

"Oh, you're cruisin' for a bruisin', huh?" the thick-necked teenage boy said, eyebrows furrowed. He jumped down from his chair with a loud thud and strutted after her. Gloria took off, fast-walking through the crowd, pushing by kids. He grabbed her arm, yanking her back. "Hey. What's your problem?" he said.

She pulled away. Looking only at her feet, she walked quickly toward one of the side doors.

He threw his cup at her but missed, and she turned to face him. I got a good look at his face that time. Clyde Bowman.

"Why don't you go home? Out-of-towner," he yelled. "Loser."

She pushed open the door to the outside, not really trying to connect with anyone anymore, her heart racing. "I just wanted to go home," she said. All along the outside of the dance hall kids were making out, leaning up against the wooden frame of the building. Mildred rushed around from couple to couple, trying to break them up while smelling their drinks, her puffy pink dress bobbing from side to side.

"If you don't stop, you'll have to leave," she kept saying to each couple.

They treated her like a substitute teacher. There, but without any real authority. She could only just beg them to be good.

Gloria's nose stuffed up and her eyes welled into tears. A couple kids who were hanging out throwing rocks into a nearby tree laughed and pointed at her. She pretended not to notice, and ran out to the lake to sit by the water's edge. She curled herself into a ball and rocked back and forth.

A gentle breeze blew through her hair, bringing up the smells of a barbecue somewhere. "I couldn't leave her," she explained to me. "I didn't want to be here. I didn't fit in like she did, but I couldn't leave her."

For a few minutes, I just sat there with her. I didn't ask her to fast forward through these tough moments. I just calmly felt her tears sting her cheeks and her breath quicken as I listened to the thoughts running through her head at the time, thoughts of doing herself in, thoughts that she wouldn't fit in at college either and that she'd never find a boyfriend or a career.

Normal thoughts that just about every teenager feels, but when you're going through them, you're convinced you're the only one in the world who feels that way.

Footsteps came behind her. "Hey. You okay?"

She turned. It was Clyde again. She sniffed back a tear. "Yeah, I'm fine." Her shoulders shook, and she didn't at all seem fine. "I'm leaving. Don't worry."

He sat down next to her. "I'm sorry… you know, for back there and everything. I wasn't going to make that stack anyway. You actually saved me the embarrassment of messing it up myself."

She nodded. "Thanks."

"What's your name? You're one of the girls from California, huh?"

"Gloria," she said.

"I'm Tony," he said, lying. The piece of shit. I knew where this was going.

He put his sweaty thick arm around her and I thought I was going to hurl. He smelled like he used Velveeta as cologne. And I tried to get Gloria's memory to slap his face, but I had no control over the way things were going to go tonight. I shuddered thinking about the possibilities.

Gloria sobbed even harder, and he pulled her into him with his mouth open and his eyes closed. His thick tongue touched her mouth, my mouth, just as she turned at the last second and bolted up. Thank God. Leaving him sitting in the dirt, she ran back over to the party.

He didn't go after her. "Like I wanted you anyway, troll," he said. "I heard the ugly friend was always the easiest."

"That was the closest I got to fitting in that night,' she said to me.

"That was a little too close if you ask me. There are some places in life you do not want to fit in."

She laughed.

I went on. "He was lying about his name too. That's Clyde Bowman back there."

"When you're an out-of-towner, boys think they can get away with a lot."

Nettie rushed up to us on her way out the door. "I just kissed the cutest boy ever," she said, twirling a strand of her hair around a fingertip.

"Congrats," Gloria replied, sarcastically. "The boy from the dance floor?"

"Oh no, that boy was a real dud," she replied. "But he helped me find the other one. The one from before. I kissed him in a closet. Can you believe it? I never do that."

Gloria talked to me in her head. "She always did that."

Nettie went on. "And while we were, you know, getting to know each other in the closet, which I still can't believe I did, the door swung open and one of the chaperones walked in on us. I just about died, right there. Died."

"I'm glad you didn't die," Gloria said.

"It was that weird college girl who was going around trying to warn everyone about the punch, like anyone cared. When she opened that door, she just started yelling. Man, the girl went bananas. I think she was upset that Freddie was drunk. Like he was the only one drunk." She sighed. "I was just telling her to mind her own business when Freddie puked."

The girls walked along the lake as they talked. "Anyway, punch-girl and the other chaperones are breaking up the party now. I think because of the puke."

"That's probably for the best," Gloria said. "I just want to go home, anyway. It's late and I'm tired. Maybe you'll meet that boy again sometime. We're still here a few more days."

Nettie didn't seem to hear a word Gloria said. She grabbed her hand and swung it wildly as they walked. The night air chilled Gloria's cheek, and it finally felt like she could breathe again. Nettie hadn't even noticed that Gloria's eyes were swollen from crying. She just went on and on about what a magical night this had been. She was sure this boy, once he sobered up, was going to be madly in love with her. She needed to know more about him. She only knew he was a recent grad like them, and he was one of the richest boys on the lake. She said it was like a page out of Cinderella.

I could hear Mildred's loud gravelly voice above everyone else's. "Thanks for coming. But you heard Debbie and Horace, dance is over. Out! Scram!"

Kids groaned and meandered out of the dance hall, making their way along the lake and the parking lot, getting into their cars or their boats to go home. Little Richard stopped playing and the sounds of engines replaced Tutti Frutti, echoing through the night.

"Come on," Nettie said, grabbing Gloria by the arm and

pulling her into a nearby bush. "It's one of those nights you never want to end. You know, the kind where you feel pretty and loved and like the whole world is hanging on your every word. Don't you just adore those nights? Like you could do anything or be anyone. Nothing can stop you on a night like this."

Gloria bit her lip, allowing herself to be pulled into the bushes.

When Gloria spoke to me again, her voice was very weak, defeated almost. "I should've told her the truth. I'd never known a night like the one she was describing. I never felt pretty or loved. I felt like Nettie Jerome's frog cousin. That's the way I lived, and that's the way I died too."

The branches surrounding our face smelled thick and earthy as we peeked through them. Three boys staggered out from the dance hall arm and arm toward a very large boat docked at the country club; the two boys on the outer sides seemed to be holding up the one in the middle, almost dragging him.

"What happened to Freddie?" a man on the yacht yelled out into the night. "Is he drunk? You have got to be kidding me. I told Ernst to make sure that didn't happen."

The older man continued yelling as the boys dragged their friend onboard. "His dad's not gonna like this one. Let me have a quick word with these so-called chaperones."

"Come on," Nettie said when the older man had gone off to talk to someone at the party and the kids had made their way onboard. She tugged Gloria out of the bushes and over to the boat. "They're gonna be jazzed to have us at their party."

Gloria ran along with her cousin. "This is a bad idea, Nettie. This doesn't seem like a party. That man is angry."

"Stop it," Nettie said, pulling hard on Gloria's arm, pain shot all the way to our shoulder. "You're being a bore again. You promised me you'd stop doing that. Besides, that's the boy I kissed. He'll vouch for us. You watch."

CHAPTER 8

OUTSIDERS

*I*t was dark and hot, and Nettie kept elbowing me in the chin every time she turned to peek out of the small closet we were hiding in. Gloria had been forced to squat at an awkward angle to get the door even remotely closed. It smelled like pine needles and stale beef jerky and when someone came into the room and sneezed, Gloria's nose tickled too.

After sneaking onboard, Nettie had motioned for Gloria to go down to the lower level while everyone was still boarding on top. There were two bedrooms. They checked both, picked the larger of the two, and then found the largest closet there, which wasn't very large.

But it must've been a pretty good hiding spot. People had come into the room three times so far, and no one ever mentioned seeing a crazy blonde peeking out of the closet.

"What're we gonna do?" Gloria asked when the bedroom went silent again.

"Same as I told you before. When it sounds like the party's in full swing, we'll pop up to the deck and join in. They won't even know we're not supposed to be here. You know how it is with parties. Who knows how anyone got there or who's officially invited?"

"This isn't a party," Gloria said. "This is a private get-together."

The voices were back, again. Someone was in the room. Sweat trickled down Gloria's temple.

"Okay, in about 15 minutes, we'll start the music," a man said.

"Got it," a kid answered.

"Grab the bags and beer from the cabinet and let's start this party."

They left again.

"Did you hear that? Beer… and a party," Nettie whispered. "They're probably just driving far enough out so homeowners won't hear them. It's late."

A few minutes later, as soon as they heard Jerry Lee Lewis blaring from the speakers on the main deck, Nettie pushed open the door and motioned for Gloria to follow her out. "Come on," she said, under her breath. She opened her purse and popped out a compact. Looking at herself in the tiny mirror, she ran a finger under an eyelid. "What is with you today?" She swiped her face with the puff and pouted on some lipstick.

"My mom's gonna worry about me. That's all," Gloria said, straightening out the lining of her skirt.

"My mom too." Nettie rolled her eyes. "But let's worry about moms later, and stop acting like moms now, okay, mom?" She playfully elbowed Gloria, handing her the lipstick and her compact. Gloria reluctantly put some makeup on.

"And fix your hair too," she snapped.

Nettie inspected Gloria's face when she'd finished. She pushed Gloria's cute brunette bob this way and that, finger-combing it. "I think you're a doll," she said, making Gloria's heart race.

"You're just saying that."

"I've always thought it. You're definitely the cute one, and you don't even need a dye job."

When the girls were done primping, Nettie pulled Gloria up the narrow staircase that led to the deck with Gloria shaking her head *no* the whole way.

"Just be cool for once in your life," Nettie said. "Talk to people. Don't be a..."

"I'll try not to be a wet rag," Gloria said before Nettie could say it.

"You're not a wet rag, okay?" She adjusted her bra and opened the door to the deck. "I'm sorry I said that before. Let's go have fun."

But as soon as Gloria saw what was going on upstairs, her stomach flopped and her heart sank into her throat.

We could only see their backs as they faced the lake and reached over the edge of the boat, laughing and talking. I tried to count the people there, check their clothing against the people I'd seen at the party, but it was dark and I couldn't tell anything for sure. I heard a large splash over the side while *Whole Lotta Shakin Goin On* played in the background, which was followed by whoops and laughter. "Holy crap. That sunk fast," somebody yelled as they reached over the side of the boat.

Someone else was in the middle of pouring two beer cans into the water then threw the empty cans in with it.

"This is a pretty weird party, Net," Gloria whispered.

"I've been to weirder," Nettie replied, adjusting her dress and sashaying forward. Gloria backed away, eyeing the life preserver on the wall by the stairs, already thinking about jumping. Something didn't seem right.

"Getting the fish drunk so you can take advantage of them?" Nettie teased as she strutted across the boat. She stopped at the group. "Remember me?"

"Oh shit," one of the boys said when he turned around and saw Nettie. The older man, who had been leaning over the side of the boat, turned around to see what was going on. His pale face got three shades paler in the light of the boat and the moon. He chucked the beer bottle he was holding into the lake and charged full speed at Nettie. She fell hard against the boat deck, her head hit the side of the metal rail on her way down.

"Ohmygosh, ohmygosh," one of the boys said.

The one I knew was Myles pointed at Gloria, who was still standing by the stairs. "There's another one," he shouted to his friends and charged at her. Gloria screamed and turned. She tugged the life preserver off the wall, but her hands fumbled and wouldn't work right. Myles yanked it from her grasp and smacked her hard across the face with it. Pain shot through my jaw and down my neck as I felt everything Gloria had felt that night. Punch after punch landed on our nose and eyes, each one felt more numb than the last, less painful as it went on. I fell to the floor of the boat and crawled along the planks, begging for my life. "We didn't see anything," Gloria said, her voice muffled. "We don't know who you are. We won't tell. We don't even know what's going on here." I tasted iron as she talked. She was bleeding a lot.

My eyes had swollen shut, and I couldn't see who was doing what anymore. But the boys were all screaming now.

"Shut-up," an older man hissed through what sounded like gritted teeth. "Just everyone shut up and calm down." He hoisted me over his shoulder with ease as I had little resistance left in me now. Wind shot over my wounds, the pain almost a numb constant throbbing. "They won't survive."

The cold hard water hit me like I'd been thrown onto cement. It whooshed around my ears, spilling into my lungs, making them burn. I spun around, down was up and up was down. I had no idea how to get to the surface. Darkness consumed my every sense and I knew my end was coming soon. Somehow, my body floated upward enough for me to get a sense of which way to swim. My thoughts were Gloria's as I coughed my way above the water, surprised I was breathing, surprised they'd let me off the boat. I looked around for Nettie.

"Nettie!" I yelled over the boys still screaming from the boat. I had no idea what they were saying. I could really only hear my own breathing now, panting hard along the surface of the lake.

Nettie didn't respond and my eyes were too swollen to see much. I swam a little farther out and yelled her name again, gulping in a huge mouth of what smelled like sewer water.

"Gloria," she said, her voice slurred and low. I swam toward it. Nettie's beautiful Marilyn Monroe face was puffed out in odd places and already darkened with bruises. Her hair stuck to her head in matted, wet clumps, mascara streaming into the blood that dripped from her scalp. "I'm so sorry," she said when I reached her.

"It's okay," Gloria told her. "We're alive. That's the only thing that matters. We're okay."

"We're not okay."

"We're gonna be. We can swim back to shore…"

"I can't swim that far." She was crying now.

"I can," Gloria said. "And you can too. I'll help you. We'll take it one stroke at a time, got it? I won't leave your side."

Nettie took a few strokes and stopped to cry again.

"Float on your back when you get tired," Gloria said, pulling herself onto her back. "Like this."

Nettie flopped over, coughing up water, gurgling. "We're never going to make it."

"You just need to take your mind off of it. Remember that song your mom taught us when you fell off your bike in kindergarten? The one about never giving up?"

Hysterical sobs came from Nettie's direction. She slapped the water hard. "Stop it, Gloria. We're going to die. I'm not singing about it."

The sound of a boat approaching caught Gloria's attention and she turned herself back over. "Look, I'm afraid too. But there are two boats now. I think one's the police," she said, with tearful joy in her voice.

"Oh please let it be the police," Nettie gurgled back, her head barely above the water.

"It is! It's the police." With all the energy she had left, Gloria kicked above the surface, enough to scream and wave her arms about. "Somebody probably called about the screaming, and they came to investigate. We need to get their attention."

The engine cut out on both boats, and for a minute, it was quiet, still, calm. "They tried to kill us." Gloria yelled and waved her hands around until a bright light shone right on her. "Over here! Save us! Please!"

She blinked into the light. It stung her swollen eyes and she couldn't really see. The sound of an engine turning on again filled the night, growing louder and louder, faster too. Gloria squinted against the light. It was headed right in the girls' direction.

"What are they doing? They're going too fast." The light got brighter. Gloria waved her arms around a little more frantically. "Stop!" she screamed, her voice high-pitched, desperate.

She grabbed her cousin around the neck, and kicked as hard as she could with achy legs, trying to swim off to the side and avoid the boat. "It's not sto…"

Oddly, I heard it first. A loud cracking sound I knew was probably my head followed instantly by darkness.

CHAPTER 9

SYMPATHY PAINS

he hardest part was always dying. Over and over again. It was all I could think about when I snapped back to life in my living room, gasping like I was still under water.

It never seemed logical that one second there was life and hope, and the next, there simply wasn't anymore. A snap of a finger, a blink of an eye. And even though I always knew the moment was coming, it didn't make it seem right. I wondered if that was how I was going to feel when my time came. Even though I tried to tell myself these channelings were preparing me for my own final moment, I knew they weren't. It was never going to seem right.

I got up, my face still stinging a little with the sympathy pains that came from living through someone else's violent death. I staggered over to the credenza in the back, to my notebook where I would write everything I could remember while it was still fresh in my memory. I checked my face in the reflection of one of the silver bowls displayed along the back wall, fully expecting to see bloody swollen gashes.

I was fine, even though fine was far from what I was feeling.

I made myself remember everything I could — the people

involved, the oddities of the night — even though I wanted to forget every last one of them. I had a job to do here.

Myles Donovan was the one who'd beaten Gloria senseless, him and his dad, and his dad had thrown Gloria overboard. I knew from my research that Myles's dad had died a long time ago, but Myles was still here. The 80-year-old powerhouse who owned much of Landover County. And that old man was going down.

I scribbled as fast as my hands would go, trying to remember who else had been onboard, who the other kids had been, but once Gloria had been spotted at the "party," things had gone ape, as she would say, and not in a good way. I wrote my questions out one after another, circling the biggest one I had. Why?

Why were they dumping things over the side of the boat? Pouring beers out? There was definitely more to this story than the part I'd just lived through. And I was going to figure it out, and a way to connect it to Myles Donovan.

My phone rang and I lost all concentration.

Rosalie didn't even let me say "hello."

"Where the hell have you been?" she yelled. "I've been trying to call you for more than a damn hour. You will never believe who came by my shop today, not to buy anything, of course. But to try to tell me you'd made an agreement with her to do another seance."

I didn't answer her.

"Satan," she began in the overly dramatic tone she seemed to reserve for Paula Henkel moments. "Please, for the love of our friendship and everything decent and good in life, do not tell me Satan is spewing out truth."

"It's true," I said, looking through my cabinet for the ibuprofen, and some crackers. Something, anything to snack on. I was starving. "But admit it. We made a ton of money last time and we could sure use a ton of money right now. What're you gonna do, cut my hours to less than nothing? But honestly, if you won't do the seance with me, I'm doing it by myself because I need the money."

She didn't respond.

"Dr. Dog said the Purple Pony's not doing very well," I added.

"What's it to him?" She spatted back.

"That's not exactly denying it."

I opened my ibuprofen and went to the sink for water, downing my pills. The water tasted good, like I was dying of thirst almost. I took another gulp and another, wiping the back of my mouth with the edge of my sweater. I leaned against the kitchen island, and looked outside. It was already dark. I must've been channeling for hours. "Okay, you think about it," I finally said, sick of the awkward silence. "But I just lived that boater's death in a channeling."

"Oh no," she said, like I'd just told her I kicked a puppy on my way out from robbing an orphanage. "How long?"

"What time is it?" I asked

"Almost 9:15, and the fact you had to ask me that means you were channeling for way too long."

"Only about an hour," I interrupted because I didn't want her to worry, even though I was pretty sure it had been afternoon when I'd started.

I rubbed my jaw and temples as I talked. "It was no accident. I know who did it. And they're going down. Myles Donovan."

"And now, in addition to crazy, you've gone and flipped your lid too." Her voice rose beyond concern, bordering on freaking out. "I am about to turn 60. I have heard about that accident since I was a kid. The papers, the people, the whole town has the same story. What do you have except an old ghost's memory that says otherwise? Because it seems to me you are forgetting the tread-cautiously part."

She was right. "I don't have any evidence yet," I admitted.

"Is that what you're hoping to do with this seance? Get another standing ovation? Not gonna happen with this one.

Besides, Myles Donovan is gonna die soon anyway. He's gotta be close to 80. No sense in stirring the pot."

I opened the cabinet and pulled out a large drinking glass, filled it all the way up with tap water, and chugged. "Just finish setting up the seance," I said in between sips. "The truth about this accident is going to come out, so we might as well make money from it."

"So you're saying you're going to be foolhardy no matter what I say."

"Yep."

Rosalie didn't say anything after that, and we sat in silence until I finally interrupted it. "I can't care if there's not enough evidence to convict anyone and I sure as hell don't care if that old man dies before he's convicted. His reputation, dead or alive, will suffer. Gloria and her cousin at least deserve that."

"I'm just wondering if I deserve it," Rosalie said. "The last thing I need is Myles Donovan gunning for me."

I downed my water, remembering how skunky and rancid the lake had tasted, how it felt in my lungs. I couldn't help but wonder just what kind of hot water I was about to land in by stirring this particular pot. I took a deep breath and reminded myself it had to be stirred.

I knew I wouldn't see Gloria again for a few days while she rested. It was hard on her to relive that night too. But I couldn't wait to tell her how brave she'd been. She always seemed so timid and unsure of herself. She was the one who held Nettie together and figured out a plan. She was the one who'd tried to do the right thing all along. Her family deserved to know that about her too.

I got off the phone with Rosalie, the details of the channeling still crawling through my head like worms in a garden, disgusting yet there for a purpose.

The girls had obviously stumbled onto something they weren't supposed to see, something Bill Donovan was involved in. And something he'd enlisted his teenage son and his friends to help him carry out.

I knew the newspapers weren't going to be very helpful on this one. *Was there anything truthful printed there?*

One of the articles clearly said Mr. Donovan and Mr. Linder had been asleep below deck. That wasn't true. I knew because I'd been there, hiding down below, until I was thrown overboard by one of the allegedly sleeping men, which also happened to be the only older man I saw that night.

The police investigation. The newspaper. They all seemed to be going along with the same narrative the Donovans had created.

I tried to think back to the channeling. Was it really the police boat that had run the girls over?

I decided to pay the local boating shop a visit tomorrow to see what they could tell me. It was a long shot, but maybe they kept records from that time period that would indicate if Myles Donovan had taken his boat in for repairs.

But then I remembered it was winter. Would anyone even be there?

CHAPTER 10

MAKING A SPLASH

*B*efore heading out the next day, I tried to call my mother again. But the woman who lectured nonstop about the common courtesies of answering phones and returning messages wasn't picking up or returning my messages.

I swallowed my worry, grabbed my purse, and headed down to the Knobby Creek Boating Company.

There were several boating service companies on the lake now, but Knobby Creek seemed to be the oldest. It was also the creepiest. And it wasn't just the rundown wooden warehouse that looked straight out of a slaughterhouse movie. I couldn't get over the two weird statues of old fishermen in overalls that greeted customers on a bench by the front door. Because nothing says good service like stuffed people watching you.

With flaky, orangish-green "skin," these men hadn't aged well either. Their chipped off noses were almost nonexistent and the old-fashioned gasoline attendant hats they wore sported logos that were so faded, the KC almost looked like rusted, severed baby legs. Or maybe the logo was supposed to look that way. It might have been an anchor, who knew?

I took a photo of the men before trudging past them, noticing a bright red "open" sign.

Was that for real?

Sure enough, I swung the door open to a small souvenir shop that smelled like boarded-up motor oil mixed with Ben Gay.

A thick older man with a bushy white mustache and an argyle sweater moseyed in from the back when he heard me come in. "Mornin'," he said. His smile wasn't customer-friendly, like you'd expect from a place with smiling dummies out front.

Behind the man was a large chalkboard with the prices and services for boat rentals and storage fees. The store was also full of summer stuff not even on clearance yet: Long, one-piece swimsuits, inflatable inner tubes, water guns, along with some fishing gear, tackle, and brightly colored bait. Rosalie wasn't the only one in Landover with delusions of a more prosperous season.

"Surprised to see you open," I said. He didn't smile, didn't elaborate. He just nodded slowly.

"Something I can do you for?" he asked.

"Information," I replied then chuckled. I knew that was not what any business on the lake wanted to hear, especially not in winter. "How old's this boating company?"

"We opened April 3, 1944," a shaky voice from behind me said, making me jump. I turned to see an old man who looked remarkably similar to the two out front. Only, this one was talking.

He had to be in his 90s, thin and without many teeth, rocking in a chair by the only window. "I had just returned from the war…"

"Dad, go back to your Popular Mechanics."

The old man searched his lap, resting his hand on the magnifying glass sitting on top of his magazine. After licking a shaky finger, he opened the magazine up.

"What kind of information you looking for?" the younger of the two older men asked.

"I want to know about the boating accident from 1957."

"Nineteen-fifty-seven. I would've been five at the time, so I cannot help you." He motioned toward the older man. "And don't even think 'bout askin' my dad. He's senile and won't remember."

I ignored him, mostly directing my attention to the supposedly senile man in the rocking chair pretending to read Popular Mechanics with a magnifying glass. "He seems fine to me. Do you remember Bill Donovan, sir? Or the boat wreck from 1957?"

"We don't keep records that old. And we don't share stuff with… out-of-towners," the younger man hollered for no reason.

"Out-of-towner? I live here."

"I don't know ya."

"Okay," I said, turning back to the man in the rocker. "Maybe you remember something."

He looked up at the ceiling like he was trying. "Bill Donovan had a lot of fine boats. I worked on all of 'em."

"I thought I told you to leave him alone," his son snapped at me.

I went to the rack of overpriced, floral swimsuits with humungous cups stitched into the lining. "Oh you have swimsuits," I said, like it wasn't the middle of winter and these were cute.

"Knock yourself out," the man replied, watching my every move. I checked my cellphone. I was going to have to leave for work soon, and this was going nowhere.

Jackson appeared by my side and I was never more thankful to see him.

"Oh my," he said, looking around the store. "I'd forgotten how quaint this place was. And by quaint, of course I mean if the movie *Deliverance* had a gift shop. I made the mistake of coming in here once when I was in my twenties. I'm not much of a boating person, but I came in with a friend."

"You have friends?" I said, forgetting I was being watched. I quickly put my cell phone up to my ear and acted like I was on the phone with someone while I browsed. "Could you work your magic?" I said, to my phone.

Jackson didn't answer me. He was too busy turning his lip up at the long swimsuit I was holding against my body. "I hear it's all the rage to look 40 pounds heavier and about 20 years older," he said, which made me think seriously about buying it, just to have a swimsuit I could wear in the shower that my ex apparently hated. I looked at the price tag. $169.

Ohmygod, these people were psychos.

I laughed into my cellphone. "I just need you to work your magic, that's all. You know," I motioned around the store.

"Cause a distraction," he said. "That's all I am to you now."

"Pretty much," I replied.

He rolled his eyes but went over to the back of the room, in the corner by the magazine racks. "This is actually a pleasure. When I came into this store more than 30 years ago, they wouldn't serve me because I wasn't dressed properly. Surprisingly discriminating for a place that sells plastic flip flops. My Italian sandals probably cost more than this entire shack …" He threw a magazine across the room. It smacked the back wall, knocking the decorative anchor down. "This same man called me a bum."

The guy looked up from the cash register. "What the… What the hell is wrong with you?"

"I didn't do anything," I said. "But wow, that was freaky. Is this place haunted?"

Another magazine flew across the room. This time, it went in the opposite direction and flew by the man's reddening face.

"Let it all out, rich boy," I whispered into my phone. The whole magazine rack toppled over and the man in the argyle sweater stormed across the room to see what was going on. Quickly, I pulled one of the articles I'd printed at the library out of my purse, smoothed it out, and held it up for the old man in the rocking chair to see. I approached him while his son tried to control the cyclone of overpriced crap circling the store as my ex-husband went for the fishing stuff now.

"I'd like to know as much about this night as you can remember," I said.

He put his magnifying glass over the article. "I know that boat," he said, voice loud and perky. I shushed him. "Bill Donovan's Vanderflint 300." He pointed at the paper. "That was a beaut of a yacht. I serviced it myself."

"So he took it here for repairs?" I asked quickly, trying to get as much information as I could in as little time as possible.

"All the time. Well, when it needed something." He smiled at the fluorescent lights above our heads. "We were the only shop on the lake back then. Still the best. Serviced everything but the government vessels. They had their own people."

"What about right after the accident in 1957? Did he take it here around that time? July of 1957. And did you know the Linders? What about them?"

"Out!" his son said, pointing at me, even though I clearly had nothing to do with the flip flop smacking his cheek right now. Still, I didn't argue the point, just went for the door.

"I'll never know how you made this mess, but I ought to call the police."

"I'm sure you have cameras. If you call the police, I want to see the recordings. I didn't have anything to do with this mess, and you know it." I motioned around the store on my way out. "This place is obviously haunted, by a ghost… who probably likes expensive sandals and hates being called a bum."

I left. I hadn't found out much, but it was at least a start. The weird fishermen statues watched my every move as I made my way out to my car.

Once I got in, I looked up the Vanderflint 300 on my cell phone while my car warmed up.

"That was fun," Jackson said by my side. "We should do that more often."

I nodded even though I was more interested in the yachting article I'd just found.

The Vanderbilt 300 was the epitome of sailing luxury when it arrived on the scene in 1955. Owners could accommodate up to six guests comfortably with two cabins below and a lounge area that converted into a bed.

"Two," I said to the ghost who was still reminiscing about that time when he trashed a quaint souvenir shop on the lake, like it was already a part of his *glory days*. "There were only two cabins below. Just like I thought. Nettie and Gloria checked both of them before hiding in the master suite. So I can conclusively say Mr. Linder was not on board that yacht. I never saw him."

"At least not alive," Jackson chimed in from the passenger's seat.

He had a point. And there had been a very large splash just before we interrupted the party.

CHAPTER 11

STRANGE

$\mathcal{M}$ ildred smacked her gums a lot during our conversation the next morning when I finally got in touch with her from my landline at Gate House. I didn't know what the sound was at first. I thought she might've been kissing the phone.

I told her I'd uncovered stuff about the accident that made me know for sure it wasn't an accident. She smacked her gums.

I told her I knew she'd been chaperoning the dance with Mrs. Nebitt and I wanted information about it. More smacking. At least I knew the woman was alive and hadn't keeled over from the conversation. She sure wasn't saying too much. Parker had been right.

"How did you know I was a chaperone?" she finally asked, suspiciously.

Mildred was one of the few people in life I could tell the truth to. A couple months ago, when I took a bunch of self-published books from her garage to paste in retractions about a suicide that was really a murder, Mildred told me she knew I was different, and that I was helping a ghost.

"Parker told me," I replied. "But I'm also helping one of the ghosts from the accident. Gloria Thomas. Gloria told me she saw you there in a cute pink dress." That was only sort of a lie. I didn't mention the part where I knew what she was wearing firsthand because I had channeled with the ghost to relive her memories. Some things crossed the line of what was considered acceptably crazy.

"I wasn't wearing pink. I hate pink," she said.

She had been. She just wasn't remembering right.

I continued. "If you can, I'd like a list of as many people as you can remember who were there that night. And if you still keep in contact with any of them, I'd love to get their story. I'm also trying to find out more about the Linders. Did you know them?"

There was a long pause before she answered. "I only kind of knew the Linders. They were nice enough, I guess. They kind of thought they owned the town, though. Them and the Donovans. Rich, and spoiled, and strange. I knew Eric better than Freddie. But neither very well. The rich stayed with the rich, you know? Strange family."

"You keep saying strange. How strange?"

Gum smacking followed.

I took a deep breath. "It would really help if you could be more specific. Strange as in 'eats a little paste' or strange as in 'hides in the bushes so they can ambush cats to shave for fur quilts.'"

"Let's just say it wasn't the good kind of strange."

I did not know which of my examples was the good kind.

She lowered her voice. "You know my dad was the caretaker at the country club, right? Well, one time, when I was around ten, I walked in on Eric and his brother outside one of the caretaker's sheds." She paused to smack her gums. "Eric was chasing his little brother around with a saw. Thing was, Eric didn't seem angry. He was just laughing, saying the punishment needed to fit the crime and he was simply and matter-of-factly going to chop Freddie to pieces. I think Freddie tore up one of Eric's baseball cards or something. They were always doing strange stuff like that."

"I was hoping for paste eating," I said.

"My dad made sure all the sheds were locked after that." Mildred paused for a second. "You know what?" she finally said. "If I find my old diary from that year, I can get back to you about who was there that night. I guess I can give you a list of people to contact."

I salivated a little, knowing she had a diary from that year. Every part of me needed to see it, but I also knew if I asked for something so bold, she might shy away from even giving me the list of names.

I tried to choose my words wisely. "Is there any way you could, maybe, take some photos of those diary entries for me?" I asked. "You could omit anything too personal or painful," I added.

A full 20 seconds of periodical smacking followed.

"Mildred, you weren't the one who killed those people. You know that, right?"

"Of course I do, but it still tears me apart, even now." She paused. "Debbie and I didn't talk for years after that night."

"Years?" I repeated.

I needed to see those diary pages.

CHAPTER 12

WARTS AND ALL

*F*ive parking spaces. That's all there were in the Landover County Public Library's lot. Still, I never had any problems finding one. Sitting in my car the next day, I watched Mrs. Nebitt watching me. I didn't even motion for her to open the door. I knew she wasn't about to let me in even one minute early. Our friendship only went so far, and that woman was a rule-follower. I used the time to text Justin. We hadn't spoken in days. I honestly wasn't sure what to say.

Hey, just wanted to see how things were going. Give me a call when you can!

I regretted it as soon as I hit *send*. It screamed needy and desperate, especially with that stupid exclamation point at the end. What was I thinking?

I quickly scrolled over to Facebook before I obsessed any more about the intricacies of punctuation, and looked to see if I could find June Marie Thomas. There were three of them. I clicked on the first one. A young blonde in a bikini taking tequila shots in the Bahamas. I moved on to the second. June Thomas Gilman. The woman didn't have a photo, but she lived in Glendale, CA. I decided to take a chance and sent her a private message:

Not sure you're the June Thomas I'm looking for. If you used to have a sister named Gloria, please get back to me. Thanks!

Once again, I agonized over the exclamation point a full minute after sending the message. At least I hadn't mentioned what I wanted to talk about. I've found that revealing my crazy had to be done delicately in life, a lot like how they say frogs should be boiled. Apparently, frogs don't realize they're dying if you start out with cold water and slowly boil it. Not that I boil a lot of frogs. But the point is, that's the way revealing my crazy had to be done. Just a smidgen at a time, so people wouldn't realize I was boiling them.

At exactly 9:30, Mrs. Nebitt waddled over to the front of the library in her coat and boots, and unlocked the glass door. And I could only picture the young woman from the channeling, with her horn-rimmed glasses and hair in short puffy curls. I smiled at her when I came inside, staring at her, still picturing it.

"Is there something wrong today?" she asked, pursing her lips.

The library's heat rattled on above us. Strange to think that just a few days ago in my channeling, it had been summer and this library had been in its planning phases. "I was just wondering if the library had any puppets I could use for the story time I'm doing next week."

"Puppets?" she asked in such a startled tone I wondered if I'd accidentally asked for severed heads.

"Parker Blueberg says there should be puppets at story time."

"Then Parker Blueberg should bring puppets to his story time. We do not have the funds for puppets. We are a library. We have money for books, and microfilm, and that's about all."

I could tell by her gigantic, yellowing computer monitor that she was probably telling the truth about that one. "I'll see what I can scrounge up on my own. I think old socks still work as puppets, right?"

She didn't answer. "I posted story time on the online calendar for Monday. Should I mention the old socks you'll be dazzling us with?"

I ignored her sarcasm, and decided to get started on my research. Like usual, she followed me to the periodicals section because she didn't trust anyone but trained professionals with degrees in library science to do research correctly. I turned to her. "I heard you and Mildred didn't talk for years after the night of the boating accident."

Her jaw moved back and forth under her saggy skin, and her brow furrowed. "Why on earth did you just ask me that? That came out of nowhere."

Perhaps I was boiling my frog too quickly here.

"It just came up when I talked to Mildred." I laughed like something was funny. "I mean, I know I shouldn't pry..."

"Then it begs the question, why are you prying?"

"Come on, Mrs. Nebitt. You know I'm writing a book and I'm doing a chapter on the boating accident. You have a little part in that history. And I think it's important to know what happened, warts and all."

"Enjoy your warts," she said, stopping at the huge, metal microfilm drawers. She tapped the cabinet and turned around. And I could hardly believe it. She walked right back to her computer and clacked away at her keyboard, like she was suddenly way too busy to care about the welfare of this library.

"I sure hope I don't mess things up over here," I yelled. She didn't even shush me. Must've had her hearing aid turned down again.

I rummaged loudly through the drawer like I was tearing it apart, eventually pulling out a few boxes. I looked over at the woman behind the desk. She wasn't even watching me. Good. That meant I didn't need to follow her "one box at a time" rule.

I pulled out boxes from 1955, 1956, and the last part of 1957. Carrying three at a time so she might not notice, I brought them to my desk and hid them under the big purse I'd begun carrying to hold all my research. I had ten microfilm boxes, a record at this library. I was sure.

I scanned through one from 1956 first, looking for anything that seemed strange or relevant. I spotted the couple I was searching for first in an article in the society section. Dwight Linder was a tall, thin man with greasy dark hair and glasses. His wife had the kind of perfectly plucked eyebrows and straight-out-of-vogue makeup that made me want to dig the woman up and ask her how she pulled the look off. She looked profession-ally cute in every photo. I looked down at my sweatshirt. I needed to step it up.

There were lots of photos of the Linders, with the Donovans, with the Petertons, by themselves, all at fancy-smancy fundraisers and campaign parties, such beautiful people, smiling over their champagne glasses. Apparently, Mr. Linder had been a real estate investor and a financial planner, his wife a philan-thropist. The Donovans and the Linders looked like they'd been good friends.

It just seemed impossible that the loud splash I heard that night was Bill Donovan enlisting a group of teenagers to help him dump his good friend's body over the side of a boat. I could totally see him paying a couple of strangers to do that, but lugging dead friends around himself seemed way out of character.

They had to be staging the deaths. It was the only thing that made sense. After searching the rest of the reel and finding noth-ing, I rewound the microfilm from 1956 and carefully placed it back in its container, craning my neck to see the front desk again. Mrs. Nebitt was still busy pretending to be busy.

I set up one of the reels from 1957, several months before the accident, and continued my search with the society pages. I was hoping to see if Bill Donovan looked at all upset with his friend,

Dwight. I couldn't find even one photo of the Linders in the society section. There were a couple of the Donovans, but the parties didn't seem nearly as full or swanky.

"Exactly how many boxes do you have there?" a stern voice said by my side, making me jump into the heavy peppermint breath that was already smacking my neck.

I screamed.

Mrs. Nebitt shushed me. Her usual scowl had the undertones of suspicion and disappointment this time. She snatched my purse off the table and the hidden stack of about six boxes toppled over.

"This is why this section needs to be supervised," she said, making a tsk-ing noise while scooping up three of the boxes. She waddled over to the cabinets with them.

"I was going to put them back when I was done," I called after her.

She shushed me again without turning around. I got the feeling I was about to be the first person on record to ever get kicked out of a library for quietly doing research.

"I'm mostly interested in the Linders, and their drowning," I said when she came back and looked like she was going to continue her lecture. It worked. She opened her mouth like she was prepared to scold me about the boxes then waddled away without saying a word.

I opened the box labeled *Landover Gazette July - September 1957* while Mrs. Nebitt straightened up the metal cabinet. I'd already checked through this reel, but I must've missed the part where the remains had been found.

The only article I found about their deaths was when the search officially ended. It basically assumed they were dead. No bodies. No proof.

The search for one of Landover's most famous residents and his son was called off yesterday after more than three weeks. Dwight Lender, 48, and his 18-year-old son, Frederick, were last seen on July 20 on a boat owned by family friend and business partner, Bill Donovan.

Dwight Linder, a financial planner at Feldman Martin, was also a volunteer fireman for the county of Landover and a deacon at Potter Grove Methodist. However, Mr. Linder was probably best known for his grandparents' pioneering efforts to bring Landover Country Club to completion in the early 1900s.

"This is a deep lake with lots of rocks and weeds," a spokesperson for the Landover County Medical Examiner said. "It's common for bodies not to resurface right away. The lungs compress and the person sinks, but as decomposition sets in, it could fill with enough gas to resurface again."

"It's probably also common for a body not to surface if the person is wearing a pair of cement shoes," I thought as I scanned the gruesome article detailing the logistics of bodies decomposing.

The last part of the article broke my heart.

Frederick Linder was headed to Yale University where he planned to follow in his father's footsteps to become a financial planner and a real estate mogul.

He, like Gloria and Nettie, had been robbed of that if he really was dead. And none of it was their fault. I looked up. Mrs. Nebitt was still standing by the cabinets.

"Whatever happened to the Linders? Mrs. Linder and Eric? Did you know them?"

My phone dinged loudly from my purse, and she glared at me, but I could tell there was relief behind the glare. I'd given her an excuse not to talk about the accident.

I turned down my phone's volume and checked to see if it was Justin who'd texted me back. It had been June.

Yes, I am that June. How do I know you?

I just about fell out of my seat. Here she was. A real, live connection to Gloria, and easier to find than I thought. Thank you, Facebook.

I quickly messaged her back: *I am writing a story on the boating accident from 1957. I have reason to believe it wasn't an accident and that information has been covered up. I would like to get the family's perspective. Could we talk sometime?*

I left her both my numbers then waited for her to call me. Nothing. After a minute of me staring at a blank phone, cursing in my mother's voice that nobody had common-courtesy phone etiquette anymore, I texted Justin.

We need to talk about our relationship.

I sat with my finger over the send button for probably a good 30 seconds before saying "screw it" to myself and sending it off. He replied almost immediately.

Good idea.

I really wasn't expecting that reaction, and so quickly too. I stared at his words a second. Were we breaking up? Another text came in while I stared.

Dinner tomorrow at my place?

I texted back a "yes" with way too many exclamation points. This was going to end in one of two ways. The same way it had 12 years ago or with amazing make-up sex. Of course I was hoping for the latter, which I decided he must've been hoping for too. It had to be why he'd suggested dinner at his place. But like most things in life, I could also have been reading way too much into it.

Later that evening, when I finally got home after work, Gloria and Jackson were already waiting for me in the living room. I was surprised to see Gloria so soon. Most ghosts needed at least a week after a channeling to materialize again. She was nearly transparent, though. So I could tell she was still very weak.

"We had a long talk," Jackson said, in the fatherly voice he knew I hated. "And we've decided. Some things just aren't worth the effort. Gloria knows what happened that night and who did it, and that's enough."

"You've decided?" I replied, my voice even snippier than I'd intended. "That's nice of you. What about me? Don't I have a say in this?"

Jackson went to open his mouth, but I cut him off.

"And here's the weirdest part. I'm the only one of the three of us with an earthly life left to lose, and I'm the only one brave enough to do this?"

"That's the point." Gloria sat down on the settee, the red fabric taking over her color now. Her voice was so low I could barely hear it. "I don't want what happened to me to happen to you or anyone else. I was able to remember that night in the channeling. Thanks for that. It's enough. I don't need justice for my murder."

I sat down beside her.

"This investigation just seems to be a little more dangerous than we thought," Jackson added. "Myles and Bill Donovan did this, but it might be too dangerous and tricky to prove it."

I stared at the ceiling, unwilling to let them know they had a very good point.

Gloria sat forward. "I'll still do the channeling to take you to the memories I have from the summer of 1954, don't worry. You know, when I saw the weird birds."

I coughed on my own spit. "I didn't know you actually saw the weird birds in person."

Her voice was mumbled. It was like listening to someone whispering. And unfortunately, I wasn't sure I was catching everything she was saying.

"Nettie and I were 15 at the time. I'll never forget it." Her voice cut out here and there. "My aunt was an amateur bird watch… She was the first one to see them and point them out when we were walking along the lake. She had no… what kind of birds they were. Ugliest things… ever seen. Beaks that looked like thick… We saw the girl… attacked. And we saw the hero dog, too."

The hero dog?

I almost fell off the couch and landed on Rex who was sleeping at my feet. A couple months ago, in an article from 1954, a young woman was attacked by birds while walking through the woods but was saved by a hero dog… that looked just like my dog, down to the little scar on his nose.

I knew it was a crazy idea but something told me if I just got a glimpse of that famous bird dog up close, I'd know for sure if it was Rex.

I took her up on her offer and told her how impressed I was with her bravery that night.

"You weren't Nettie Jerome's frog cousin. Not at all. You were strong and quick-thinking. You did everything you could have."

She smiled. "It was good to remember, in a way."

"And, I disagree that this is too tricky or dangerous. The people responsible should be held accountable. Plus, your family has a right to know what happened. I found your sister, by the way."

Her face brightened to almost full color. She turned to Jackson then back to me. "June? What's she like? How's she doing?"

"I haven't been able to talk to her yet," I admitted. "I left my number. So we'll see. But I lived that night with you, Gloria. That was a brutal attack. Your family deserves to know the truth, and the people involved shouldn't get away with it."

Jackson shook his head at me.

"I'm done treading cautiously." I continued, this time to my ex. "You always told me to go with my gut when it came to ending this curse. And I think a huge part of it involves uncovering the secrets of this town, and making things right."

It was a lie. I actually had no idea how to end this curse, but it shut my ex-husband up for once. Gloria disappeared, and he didn't say a word the rest of the night.

Note to self: Mention that curse more often.

CHAPTER 13

My mother was less than apologetic when I finally got a hold of her later that weekend, making me realize, as we both aged, there was a bit of a role reversal going on in our relationship.

"I've been trying to reach you for a week. A week. I was worried sick," I said.

"Brenda and I flew into Cabo for a few days, spur of the moment. She owns a timeshare there and you know how expensive cell phone coverage is in Mexico."

I paced the dining room as I talked. "No, Mom. I actually have no idea. I don't go to Mexico. You don't go to Mexico. We're not a spur-of-the-moment, go-to-Mexico kind of a family. We're a plan-things-out-for-years kind, and then decide it's actually not a good idea."

"I don't like your tone. Should I call back when you remember how to talk to your mother?"

I ignored her. "Stop evading my questions. That's a big spur-of-the-moment thing to do. Don't you think you should have called and told me about it?"

She didn't answer.

Apparently, I was getting the silent treatment now. I went on. "And Brenda is over a lot." I stopped myself from telling her that Brenda was a bad influence, but she clearly was. "I noticed she's even on your answering machine now."

"Of course she is. She lives here."

The awkward pause between us grew longer as I tried to process this new conversation I was having with my mother. Our conversations usually went something like this: *Hello, Carly, I'm very bored with my life, so I called to pry into yours. When can I expect grandchildren? I've been eyeing a pair of light blue stretchy pants on clearance in the grandmother section of Macy's...*

Whatever this new conversation was, it was unchartered territory. My mother was no longer my mother anymore. She had secrets. She went to Cabo. She had her own life.

"So, Brenda is living there now? What does that even mean? Are you guys... I mean, is there something you want to tell me?"

"Are you asking if I'm a lesbian?"

I plopped down at the dining room table. "No, I mean... Well, since you brought it up, are you? Actually, don't answer that. I know you'd tell me if you were."

"Because gay people must announce to straight people that they are gay."

"That's not it. We used to share stuff..."

"Well then, I must've missed your big coming-out-straight announcement."

"Okay, stop," I said. "It's not a big deal if you are."

Her slight country accent was back. She got that a lot when she was angry. "Brenda and I are friends who enjoy each other's company. End of story. I realized you had a very good point when you left in such a huff to head back to Wisconsin. I, too, only have one life to live and I get to live it my way. Life is too short to worry about how others see you. You have no control over that anyway. Be happy..."

I let my mind wander while my mother tap danced on her

soapbox. I didn't need to listen. I was the one who wrote that speech when I left Indianapolis. No doubt once she was finished, she'd somehow figure out a way to ask how close to marriage and kids I was.

But she didn't, and after a while, I got sick of hearing about margaritas and how cold Brenda was in Mexico even though it was 75.

"Look, Mom, I've gotta…" My eyesight flickered. It was like I was blinking when I wasn't. I closed my eyes, a little worried about myself. But I knew from past episodes, it would go away in a second.

"And you know how I get after I've had more than one mai tai," my mother said, like I actually did know or care. She certainly liked to talk about drinking more than she used to. Brenda was her Nettie in life.

I opened my eyes. The flickering was gone, but the room spun a little and I felt a headache coming on. I grabbed the table to steady myself and got up, then walked to the living room to lie down on the couch. The temperature felt like it had suddenly dropped by about twenty degrees. I snatched my super soft throw blanket from the back of the settee on my way by and draped myself in it. "I have to go, Mom." I mumbled into the phone through chattering teeth. I plopped on the sofa, almost missing the cushions.

"But I haven't even told you the part about the worm. I drank a to-kill-ya worm."

"Tequila," I corrected her pronunciation.

"I'm pretty sure it was trying to kill me." She chuckled. "I didn't really drink it, but Brenda tried to dare me."

I said good-bye to my mother and pinched the bridge of my nose to help the flickering a little. After another minute, just when the throbbing made it seem like my head might explode, it stopped. Everything was normal again.

I was just thinking that maybe another channeling wasn't

such a good idea when I heard a loud thud in the hallway that led to the basement.

"Rex," I called, looking around the living room. It was quiet, way too quiet. And I was surprised to hear a quiver in my voice as I yelled his name. He was an old dog (supposedly) and my mind went to the worst case scenario. Of course, Jackson was nowhere to be found. When I needed him, he never materialized, but try to fool around on the couch with your boyfriend, and there he was, critiquing things.

I stepped out onto the veranda without even grabbing my coat, almost slipping on the ice. "Rex?" I called. The sun was barely visible through the clouds. The wind smacked my face, making my nose water. I went back in and was just about to check upstairs when I heard something by the second staircase down the hall again. The only staircase in the house that led down.

"Jackson," I called, slowly walking down the hall toward the noise. "Rex." No one answered. I knew where the noise was coming from, even though I didn't want to admit it to myself. The basement.

I'd only ever been down in the basement twice the whole time I lived at Gate House, and that included the first time I lived there, when I was married to Jackson for seven years.

I listened by the door and heard a definite loud thump coming from down there. Even though logically I knew it couldn't have been Rex, I still went back to the kitchen and grabbed the key for the basement out of the key cabinet. I also grabbed one of the mace canisters I kept in strategic places around the house ever since the incident with the stripper murders.

I flicked on my flashlight app on my phone, one of the only things it was good for because cell phone reception was pretty much nonexistent at Gate House then swung open the door at the back of the hall.

To strangers, the door appeared to lead to a very small closet. I knelt down on the floorboards, running my hands along the planks to feel for the keyhole. After unlocking it and finding the almost-hidden handhold, I lifted up the trap door and an instant smell of must and mold floated around me from the dank basement underneath.

"Rex," I called into the dark pit coming off my floor, but it sounded more like a whisper. I shined my light around the walls and the pitted concrete stairs that led down. I didn't see a light switch, something I probably should already have located in the house I owned.

I stopped myself. *What in the hell was I about to do?* Rex wasn't down in this pit of secrets.

Still, I felt compelled to check. Something made me think I should go down there to make sure.

The banister swayed under my very light touch. Slowly, I inched my way to the bottom of the stairs, my eyes darting left and right like I was in a horror movie.

"Rex!" I shouted, my voice echoing off the walls of the basement.

I didn't hear anything, which was not surprising. How was my dog going to get down here, anyway? Unless someone or something brought him down here.

It was pitch black in the basement, despite the tiny window along the top of one of the walls. And it was freezing. I looked around for a light, willing my eyes to adjust to the darkness, willing warmth to my body. I coughed on some dust floating around in my beam of light.

I remembered there was a lightbulb hanging from the middle of the room somewhere, and I somehow got myself to move forward to look for it. Each step felt like it could be my last. The string overhead swept over my face and I screamed like I'd been stabbed in the head before realizing what it was. I pulled the light on, but my flashlight was actually better at illuminating the room.

The basement was entirely done in bricks, with strange archways that were oddly decorative for something so unfinished. Birds with stuff in their mouths adorned each archway, maybe a stick or a snake or a bone. I shined my flashlight against the back wall where a couple bookshelves had been stored, then I moved toward the old 1950s refrigerator in the corner that I was never, ever going to open.

I looked around for my dog, but there weren't many places to hide here. A washing machine and dryer were off to the side, where Mrs. Harpton probably did my laundry twice a week. Bless her heart. If she hadn't done it, my options would've been come down here and do it myself or go dirty. And we all know which option I would have chosen if cornered to do so.

"Rex?"

No one answered.

"Not funny, Jackson," I said, like every other victim in a horror movie, right before they discover the mysterious noise was not, in fact, their friend playing a trick on them.

The lone rocking chair at the back of the room rocked back and forth even though no one was in it like it was taunting me. I almost bolted up the stairs, but I reminded myself I was a strong medium… who dealt with ghosts all the time. It probably wasn't Rex down here, but whoever it was obviously had something to tell me, and I should take the time to listen.

"Hello. Who's there?" I asked. "I am open to your message." I rolled my eyes at my own cheesy words.

A chill passed through my shoulder, with almost slicing precision. And it didn't feel friendly. I turned quickly with the intention to run back up the stairs and abandon whatever stupid impulse brought me down here in the first place but my legs wouldn't move, despite the fact my brain was telling them to get going. I was frozen in my spot. I went to scream, but I also realized I couldn't form sound. It was like sleep paralysis, only I was most definitely awake.

I heard barking at the top of the stairs. Rex. I tried to call for him, but couldn't. He barked again and again, growling now, demanding I answer. And suddenly, my legs, which were still in the middle of trying to run, were given the freedom of movement again and the jolt of unexpected momentum sent me soaring forward awkwardly like a cartoon character. I tripped over my own feet, stumbling onto the concrete floor, hard. "Rex," I said, able to talk now. "I'm down here, boy!" Pain shot up my leg and over to my back as I crawled to a standing position again, hobbling toward the sound of the barks, almost tripping over a book at my feet.

I picked it up, feeling years of grainy dust coating my fingers. Apparently Mrs. Harpton didn't maintain the basement nearly as well as the rest of the house. A fact no one on Earth blamed her for. I quickly wiped off the dust and scanned the title.

A Crooked Mouse

CHAPTER 14

COLLECT THEM ALL

*I*t was one of the missing scrapbooks. I rushed up the stairs with it, fumbling and tripping onto the concrete stairs, which made my still-hurting leg hurt even more. Rex barked wildly the whole way like he was cheering me on now, and I practically launched myself at him. I hugged him tightly, thankful he was okay. I was okay. I quickly shut the basement entrance and locked it, vowing never to go in that creepy place ever again.

I ran back down the hall and over to the living room, practically throwing the scrapbook onto the coffee table before sitting down to examine my leg. Nothing seemed broken. I took one deep breath after another, trying to get my heart to calm down, already. I hadn't died. I was safe. Crisis averted.

As soon as I calmed down, I opened the scrapbook, still puzzled over how I'd found it in the first place. Was that scary episode an indication of how the house was going to show me stuff? Because next time, I was going to politely decline.

But I had to admit, I was happy to have another scrapbook. My third one in what I was starting to call the "Crooked Collection." I had a feeling the house was encouraging me to collect them all, like incredibly sad Happy Meal toys.

I wasn't sure what was going to happen once I had them all, but I kind of guessed that maybe I'd be able to lift the curse that had been plaguing Gate House and possibly other families in Landover County for generations. The scrapbooks seemed to go along with an old nursery rhyme:

There was a crooked man, and he walked a crooked mile
He found a crooked sixpence upon a crooked stile
He bought a crooked cat, which caught a crooked mouse,
And they all lived together in a little crooked house

So far I'd found the ones titled: *A Crooked Man, A Crooked Stile,* and now *A Crooked Mouse.*

It was pretty obvious to me that Henry Bowman, Jackson's great grandfather, had to be the crooked man. He'd built his fortune in New York off a chain of brothels, even putting the prostitutes' unplanned children to work producing clothing and such for his business. I also guessed that the money he earned from that had to be the crooked sixpence in the rhyme. The crooked stiles were a little trickier. I guessed they were somehow this house. The manor had twists and turns, fireplaces without chimneys, and doors that went into walls. There seemed to be many crooked stiles that allowed spirits to come and go as they pleased but prevented living beings from following them. The stiles also could have been the deaths in Potter Grove that didn't happen the way they were said to have, like their "stiles" leading into the afterlife were crooked.

And whatever was in this book was going to lead me to the crooked mouse. I had no idea what that meant, but I couldn't wait to find out. Kind of.

After checking my watch, I realized I only had about half an hour before I had to leave for my three-hour shift at work, which seemed almost like a waste to drive all the way down there for that amount of time. But Justin was going to get off early so we could talk about our relationship after my shift. I didn't want to end things like last time. We were both adults now. We should discuss whatever it was going on with our relationship together, maturely.

Every part of me wanted to fake sick and back out of dinner, though.

I turned to the first page of the scrapbook, my fingers still chalky with the dust from that room.

It was an 8 x 10 photo of Henry Bowman and his family. Henry was an easy man to recognize. He looked a lot like Theodore Roosevelt, same round glasses and bushy mustache. He was standing with his wife and their four children, each staring into the camera like they were afraid to blink or smile. Wide, blank stares.

Ethel was one of the three girls. I had no idea which one, though. They all looked pretty much the same, with height being their only difference.

Judging by the age of Earl, the youngest who I knew was born in 1900, I guessed the photo was from around 1903-ish. The children were all holding something. The three older girls, each in frilly white dresses and hair in curls, held toys in their hands: one had a teddy bear, one held a wooden bird, and the third girl had a stuffed lion-dog-looking thing in one hand and that creepy doll that looked like me in the other. I shuddered when I saw that one. The reason Jackson called me Carly doll. The doll that was still in the nursery upstairs.

But Earl, a toddler dressed in dark shorts and a dark sweater, was carrying something brown and furry. It was limp in his hand, drooping out of his fist in a furry, slumped mass.

One of the corners of the photo was folded over on its edge, and I could see there was writing underneath. Carefully, I pulled the tape off and turned the fragile photo over.

"Christmas 1903. Earl killed a mouse for Papa" it said on the back. Earl was Jackson and Caleb's shared grandfather. I put the photo back and moved on, wondering now just how disgustingly literal this scrapbook was going to be when it came to catching crooked mice.

Thankfully, the next page was a letter.

My Dearest Eliza,

I have made appropriate transportation arrangements following your release from jail. Gate House is near completion and I await your arrival with breathless anticipation. I do hope you won't hold your predicament against me. You left me no other choice.

Yours Truly,

HB

Jail? Had Henry Bowman had her arrested? For what?

I skipped ahead, looking for answers. But there weren't any more letters, only old black-and-white photos that looked like they were from the early 1900s or before.

Some of the pages had the word "Signs" at the top of them. Apparently, the first "sign" was a photo of a glass figurine bird, very similar to a photo in another scrapbook. Back of a woman's head as she read through her notes next to the figurine.

Under that photo was one of a person wearing a dark cloak and an old plague mask, the kind that resembled a cross between a gas mask and a bird costume. Another picture in the "signs" pages was of bear skins, eyeless and haunting, staked along a fence, three of them. Another photo had a severed animal foot adorned in jewelry.

They were all very weird and I had no idea what any of them meant or what catching a crooked mouse had to do with them all.

I turned the page, unsure if the rest of these photos were still signs or not, and what signs they were even talking about. I stared at the last page, hoping the photos didn't mean anything.

It was one of bones again, but they were laid out like a puzzle on the floor, similar to what they do in museums when they're trying to recreate an animal's skeleton. It was definitely a bird. I could tell by its long bendy arms and beak-like skeleton. But it must've been a hoax. A woman in a long black dress and stockings laid down next to the bones, her face obscured by her arm. The bird-bone puzzle was as tall as she was, and four times as thick.

Its caption said. "Last one. Never again."

Most the rumors in Potter Grove were turning out to be true. Bear shapeshifters, growling birds that probably wanted to kill you… I guessed the shapeshifter wars I'd heard about were probably true too. Supposedly, the wars went on in Potter Grove between the birds and the bears a long time ago. Bears eventually won. But there seemed to be an underlying feeling that it wasn't over yet.

After looking at my cell phone clock, I grabbed my keys and put out the timer-released dog bowl that I was only allowed to use on special occasions according to my house agreement. Hanging out with my boyfriend after work was a special occasion as far as I was concerned. Or at least I hoped it was going to be.

"See you tomorrow, Rex," I said.

CHAPTER 15

ROTTEN FRUIT

*I*t smelled like someone had mixed a vat of wood varnish with some dirty diapers and rotting, fermenting tangerines. Apparently, Rosalie had given up on having customers, ever. I followed the odor into the back room of the Purple Pony. Chopped-up leaves, stems, roots, and flowers were strewn all over the floor along with some dirt and what looked like it could have been blood, but I decided it was best not to ask.

Rosalie looked up from the bowl she was mixing and smiled, caked-on dirt around her cheeks.

"I'm doing you a favor," she said.

"Smells like it."

"You'll get used to that. It's mostly just the one ingredient. Angelica root. I used a lot of it." She wiped her nose with the back of her sleeve and her lip curled. "Maybe too much. I found that recipe I was telling you about."

She motioned to the long strands hanging off the book shelf on the far end of the room where mesh packets had been tied to long ribbons, dripping with something red, probably what I had originally thought was blood. And still wasn't sure.

She rubbed her red-tinged hands together. "I'm making you little sachets to put in your pockets, too."

"So I can smell like I've crapped my pants wherever I go… This favor is too kind."

"Don't be crazy. You want your privacy, right? I've finally found a recipe that will give you that."

"Yes, I'm pretty sure you have." I knew where she was going with this, even though there was no way I was going along. She'd been searching for a recipe to ward off ghosts from certain spots in my house, like the bathroom and my bedroom, places I wanted more privacy.

"I want privacy from ghosts. Not every living thing ever."

She was still talking and didn't hear me. "You should probably hang, oh I don't know, maybe five to seven strands along the entrances to any room you and Justin want a little privacy in. So you don't always have to go to his place." She winked. "Use odd numbers and space them about a quarter inch apart, making sure they don't touch."

"I will be a very lonely girl if I put those things up at my house."

"Precisely," she said like I was saying something positive. "And when you don't want spirits to travel with you, slip a few sachets in your pockets."

I knew she was just trying to help me be normal.

"Thank you, Rosalie," I said, kissing her on her cheek. "I will definitely try them out to see if they help my relationship." I touched one of the dripping wet strands, and pulled back a smelly finger full of whatever the red stuff was. I wiped it on one of the rags on her desk. My eyes were starting to sting from the pungent fumes being produced in the back room. "If only we could open a window without freezing to death."

"The smell'll get better in a few days as they dry." She continued stirring the plant goop in her bowl. Her eyes were red and watery too. "I probably shouldn't have mixed this batch up in winter, huh? It's a little much with the doors closed and the heat blaring."

The wind chimes on the front door clanged indicating we had a customer and Rosalie and I both froze. It'd been so long we'd forgotten what to do when that happened.

Paula Henkel's military-commanding voice yelled from the storeroom. "Ohmygod, she's killed her. I knew this day would come. Hurry, Carly, I'll help you hide the body."

Rosalie's eyebrows furrowed as she yelled back. "I know Paula Henkel did not just say that. She knows she'd be the first one Carly murders in my store. Isn't that right, Carly?"

I didn't answer and she lowered her voice. "Go see what she wants before I kill her myself."

I pointed my red-tinged finger at her. "Be nice and no cussing. We've got to do business with that woman. And we need the money more than she does."

We already negotiated and signed the paperwork days ago. Tickets had been printed. We were good to go. Still Paula Henkel's face was pinched up and her thick arms folded as she leaned against the check-out counter.

"Rosalie's working on a recipe for warding off ghosts," I said when I saw her. I waved my hand in front of my nose, like that was doing something to alleviate the smell. "How's the seance coming along?"

"I haven't sold a single ticket. Not even one, and I know it cannot be my marketing. I have advertising up at all my usual spots: the library, the gym, the grocery, all over the place. I thought you said this boating-accident story would be a hit in this town."

"I thought it would be."

"I'm calling the seance off. We need to cut our losses. Just pay me half the print job on the tickets, and we'll call it even." She stuck her hand out like she expected me to open the cash register.

We both knew it was empty, or darn near it. "Let's wait to see if things pick up. I'll ask around. See what's going on."

Paula turned toward the door in a huff. "I should've known that's what you'd say. I'm giving you two days. That's it. If you don't hear from me, consider the seance cancelled. I can't even get the librarian to come for free. And that woman is desperate for freebies."

"I'm sure it'll pick up," I said, trying to make my voice as reassuring as possible. But, honestly, I wasn't even buying my fake optimism.

JUSTIN'S APARTMENT was small and beige, almost the complete opposite of my spacious Victorian with the different colored wallpaper in each room. My place also never smelled this good either, like some sort of basil and garlic sauce. A definite "million steps up" from the Purple Pony I'd just left.

The man could cook. He was gorgeous, and sweet, and I liked the crinkle around his eyes when he let himself smile naturally. He had everything going for him. I shouldn't be pushing him away.

Why did I always push away the nice guys, and marry the Jacksons?

I rolled my linguine around my fork as we sat at the small table that took up most of his dining room, staring at each other.

He looked good tonight. He was wearing the light gray button-down shirt I loved on him because it showed off his broad shoulders. I wondered if he'd worn it on purpose. A man who wanted to break up probably wouldn't wear the shirt he knew was my favorite, or at least I hoped he wouldn't. I was wearing one of his favorites too, my skinny black jeans and soft blue sweater.

It was quiet at first with only the sound of the exhaust fan humming from the kitchen and our forks scraping along our plates. I took another bite of the shrimp scampi.

"I need this recipe," I said, like I cooked. Sauce plopped along my lip from an unruly piece of linguine, and I quickly wiped it away with my finger, looking up to see if he noticed how messy I was.

He only stared at his plate. "You can take some home if you want. There's plenty."

"Thanks." I hated just how acquaintance-sounding our conversation felt to me right now. I almost asked if he thought it was going to snow again tonight when, instead, I blurted out the obvious. "Are we breaking up?"

He raised an eyebrow at me.

I didn't give him time to answer. "I mean it was nice that we gave this relationship a second chance because I always hated how things ended last time. I'm sorry for that, by the way. Don't know if I ever apologized. And I'm sorry for snapping at you in the car the other day. You hate trash duty. I should've known that…"

"Do you want to break up?" he said, interrupting my ramble.

The million-dollar question. I stared at him a second. "No," I finally replied, with certainty. "But, you should probably know I work with ghosts now. I help them solve their murder cases."

He half-chuckled.

"I know you think that's strange. And it is strange, but I can't change it. Or myself. I'm not going to compromise any part of me anymore. And now that you know that…"

I paused for him to tell me it was okay, but he didn't. He only chewed. His apartment seemed particularly bright, the fluorescent lights contrasting the darkness from the dining room window. I circled the air with my fork. "Well…" I said.

"Well, what?"

"It's your turn. Do you want to break up with the strange woman who works with ghosts?" I asked, putting the fork in my mouth, realizing it didn't have anything on it.

"Of course not. I didn't want to break up twelve years ago either. Just because people disagree with each other doesn't mean people give up on each other."

Ouch. That one hurt. He seemed to sense that, and went on. "I really wish you'd stop snooping, that's all. This isn't about trash duty or ghosts. Things can get serious."

"Well, you can stop worrying. We're probably about to call off the seance anyway. I heard from Paula Henkel that we haven't sold a single ticket. Not even one."

"The town's afraid," he said, mouth half-full of shrimp. "Myles Donovan's a lot of people's boss's boss's boss. Not to mention two mayors are involved here and the police department likely too."

"But if we stand up collectively to this bullying, then their bullying can't work."

A smile escaped his lips. "I don't think you know how bullying works. This is the kind of intimidation that doesn't technically exist. People just know not to rock the boat. Nobody's actually being threatened."

I bit on the tip of my empty fork. He was right.

He slid his chair closer to mine. "But the fact nobody's willing to come to your seance says you're onto something worth fighting for here. And if there's one person in this town who can get people to collectively fight… for something they don't even know they should be fighting for… you're that stubborn person."

I jumped up and threw my arms around his neck, kissing his scratchy cheek, quickly moving down to his lips. Soft and thick, and garlic-smelling. I sat on his lap and kissed him some more. Sometimes all a girl wants is someone who believes her stubbornness is worth it.

Justin's phone rang, an odd sort of ringtone, and he reached in his pocket. "I have to take this," he said, practically pushing me off of him. I scrunched my lips up and went back to my linguine, pretending to be interested in eating when all I really wanted to know was who in the hell was on the other end that was so important right now.

All he said was, "Okay, got it. Thanks."

Two minutes later, we were walking through his parking lot out to my car, my teeth chattering from the bitter wind blowing around us as I swung my plastic bag full of leftovers. My consolation prize. So much for makeup sex.

Like usual, I searched through the trees of the Dead Forest as we passed by it to get to my car. A chill went up my spine and it wasn't because of the wind. I pulled my jacket in closer.

"You okay?" Justin asked, because the Dead Forest didn't bother him. He believed the town's Wikipedia page when it said the Dead Forest got its name because the soil was too acidic to grow crops anywhere near it.

That poor man lived in denial.

One of Justin's neighbors stumbled toward us, holding his shoulder. I recognized the pale blonde man as the guy down the hall on Justin's floor.

"Justin," he said as he passed. He stopped and looked me over, watching as I hopped from one foot to the next, trying to stay warm. He was only wearing a thin jacket, but he didn't even look cold. But then, neither did Justin and he wasn't wearing a jacket at all.

"We haven't met," the man said, holding out a hand. His voice dripped with sexuality and his nostrils flared a little.

Justin pulled me in closer before I could shake his hand. "And you're not meeting now," he replied, making me take a step back by how oddly protective my boyfriend was being all of the sudden. First with Parker, now with this guy. Didn't he trust me?

The man nodded to me. "If you ever want to speak for yourself, I'm just down the hall from your police protection over here. Name's Knox. I have handcuffs too."

Justin pulled me along to my car, stopping just in front of it to give me one last kiss, as his neighbor made his way inside.

"Your apartment complex is so... interesting," I said when we came up for air.

"It's cheap and clean, and most people are afraid to live so close to the forest. But that also means it attracts the kind of people who aren't afraid to live so close to the forest."

I looked at the spindly trees swaying menacingly behind him, like giant finger bones, wagging a final warning to stay out. I didn't need any warnings, thank you very much.

He turned around. "It's all a rumor," he said, shaking his head. "But I'm thankful for it. I get almost free rent."

We kissed good-bye again and I drove off through the parking lot, watching Justin in my rearview mirror standing right in front of the forest, staring at it. He wasn't afraid of anything, all right. I was just about to pull out onto the main road when my vision went blurry and dark again. The white spots were back. I pulled over to the side of the parking lot so I could close my eyes and pinch the bridge of my nose, the only things that seemed to help when these episodes came on.

After about a minute, I opened my eyes again, my vision back to normal, even though my heart still raced. I took a deep breath and looked in my rearview mirror again, wondering if Justin had noticed me off to the side of the parking lot and was worried. He hadn't.

I only knew this because I saw him, clear as day, slowly walking into the forest.

Or was I hallucinating again? I swung my car around so fast I almost hit the dumpster by the parking lot's entrance. But I needed to know.

I pulled into a spot right by the edge of the forest, exactly where I thought I saw Justin entering, and waited while I peeked at every shadow in the trees. Ten minutes later, I decided I was insane. There was no way a man in just a dress shirt went anywhere but back inside.

What was wrong with me nowadays?

CHAPTER 16

JUST TELLING STORIES

*C*rs. Nebitt turned her nose up at the box of socks I set on the counter next to her computer just before story time the next morning. She pursed her lips, white hair blowing softly from the heat sputtering out of a nearby vent. "I see you were serious about the socks."

I didn't answer her. I adjusted my leggings so they'd sit right under my boots. Even though I'd tried my hardest to look professionally cute that morning, nothing had worked in my favor. My curls frizzed, my eyeliner smeared into what looked like dark smudge streaks along my eyelids, and I couldn't find anything to wear except my go-to winter outfit, an oversized sweatshirt and black leggings. I was pretty far from professional or cute. But in my defense, I hadn't had much sleep last night. I could only think about the hallucinations I'd been having lately, and how they were getting worse.

Mrs. Nebitt continued. "Do you know what books you'll be reading, or do you need my help in selecting some?"

"I'm going to start off with *If You Give a Mouse a Cookie*," I said. I rummaged through my box of socks and pulled out a tan one with googly eyes glued to the front of it. It hung sadly in my hand like a vintage photo of a toddler holding roadkill.

"What is that?"

"It's a mouse. I couldn't spend too much money on this either. The library isn't the only one with limited funds around here."

I stretched the sock over my hand and moved its mouth around. Mrs. Nebitt rolled her eyes, and I could see her point. Its cardboard cut-out ears were unevenly spaced and one was falling off a little. "I don't need puppets," I said, taking it off and tossing it into my box of props. "Do you have any instruments? We could do a musical theme."

The door opened and Lil Mil shot into the library like someone had yelled, "Go."

"I heard there's gonna be games and puppets and hula hoops and singing," the little girl said in a gruff voice, pulling her pink hood down to reveal a mass of dark curly hair.

I turned to Mrs. Nebitt. She chuckled under her breath. "Have fun," she said.

Parker wasn't too far behind his little girl. He flashed me a smile when he came in carrying Benjamin. "Kids are excited. Can you tell? Thanks for doing this."

I had no idea what I'd signed up for. I grabbed a stack of printer paper from under the cabinet and Mrs. Nebitt glared at me through her coke-bottle glasses like she was mentally counting the stack.

"C'mon. How much is paper? The library's gotta contribute something." I grabbed a handful of the tiny pencils people used to write call numbers with too.

The walls shook and the floor rumbled under my feet as the sound of NASCAR filled the library. Low, thunderous, revved-up engine noises were followed by laughter and hooting.

Mrs. Nebitt threw me a scowl like story time had been my idea.

We both walked to the large windows at the front of the

building and watched Shelby and her twins struggle to climb out of a large black pick-up truck that took up the entire lot. Bobby, her fiancé, jumped out to help her, his puffy dark hair seemed to morph into his eyebrows, kind of like Satan and Raggedy Ann had a love child. He handed Shelby their humungous baby.

Shelby's hair was still pink, matching the accents in her 50's-style wool coat. She sashayed across the parking lot, her four-year-old twins leading the way.

Opening the door for Shelby, I was instantly greeted with the stench of exhaust, and I took an extra-long inhale, hoping the fumes would help me get through this story time.

"Bobby's brothers are using my car again today," Shelby said as she went inside.

"They still driving you crazy?"

She looked at me like that was the dumbest question I could've asked. Everyone knew her Christmas visitors were still visiting, and it was almost February. Four adults and five kids living in a three-bedroom apartment.

"Every night's a beer fest. They don't work. They don't chip in with the housework. I'm putting my foot down tonight. Mark my words. Either they go, or I do."

"I've only been telling you to do that since New Year's," I said. "That's almost two months of frat parties."

I grabbed my box of puppets from off the counter and headed over to the kids area.

"They got a laundromat here?" Shelby asked when she saw my socks. I didn't answer her.

The kids ran around, tagging each other, swinging their coats around like weapons.

I dragged a small plastic blue chair over to the center of the room and sat down. "Okay, everyone" I called, my voice cracking with every syllable. I tried to bring it back to normal. They could probably sense fear. "Come sit down. Story time is about to start."

Lil Mil put her arm around my shoulder and peeked at the

book in my hand. "It's the mouse with the cookie again, you guys," she announced to the group like we'd had millions of story times together and this was always the story.

"That's your favorite book, Lil Mil," Parker said. "Sit down."

"And, it has puppets this time," I said, nodding to Parker and Shelby who were sitting next to each other on chairs. I pulled out my tan sock and the circle shape I'd cut out of cardboard. Shelby threw her hand over her mouth like she was holding in laughter when she saw me breaking out my props. I ignored her. "Who would like to give the mouse this cookie?"

"Ew. That's a smelly sock and a dirty, old piece of cardboard," one of Shelby's four-year-olds said. A whoosh of cold blew through the library when the door opened. I looked up from my sock, wondering who else was coming to join my story time. A gorgeous blonde with salon-style highlights and a cute, fur-trimmed jacket sauntered in, holding the hand of an equally stylish four-year-old blonde girl.

Mrs. Nebitt looked at them then quickly went back to her computer, almost like she recognized the woman, even though I had no idea who she was.

The woman told her daughter to sit down quietly then smiled at me. "Sorry we're late," she said, taking a chair and moving it over to Shelby. I could smell her expensive perfume from my rickety child's chair in the front of the circle. She introduced herself to Shelby and Parker and I leaned over to hear.

Her little girl dutifully went over and sat down next to Lil Mil. They talked for all of three seconds before Lil Mil put her arm around the girl and announced to the group that this was Clarisse, her bestest friend in the whole world.

"You are so pretty," Lil Mil went on, poking the cheek of her new best friend. "I'm gonna show you how to do a fake burp later on."

Parker's face went red and he said something to the girl's mother.

I was losing my audience and I hadn't even started yet. I quickly slipped the sock puppet on my left hand because I needed my right one to hold the book, but it was awkward and uncomfortable. And the puppet just kind of flopped there until its ear came off in the middle of the story and the kids all laughed and took turns throwing it at me. Thankfully, they had terrible aim.

I tried to pay attention, do things like I'd planned to do them, but all I could think about was that weird forest yesterday and how I'd been almost one-hundred-percent sure Justin had gone into it. But now that I was thinking about it, I was almost one-hundred-percent sure he couldn't have.

The cardboard ear smacked my forehead and I snatched it away before the kids could grab it again.

After I'd read two books, I was ready for a nap. No wonder preschool had those. Obviously, they were for the adults.

I told the kids to sit at a table and draw out their favorite parts of the stories, but not to worry about mistakes. Mistakes were okay in my book, which was why I'd brought these cool, stubby pencils that didn't even have erasers. Then, I handed out the printer paper that Mrs. Nebitt was probably going to dock me for.

"Is this fun or what?" Shelby said to her sons.

They didn't even bother to answer "or what."

I pulled my friend aside. "Who's that?" I asked, pointing to the mysterious woman.

"Her name's Lila. She just moved to Landover. Isn't she cute? She looks like she likes makeup." Shelby was always looking for new clients.

"And it looks like she has plenty of money for a big ole pile of it," I added.

I tossed my pathetic socks back in their box and trudged over to the front desk like a woman defeated.

"Well, how did it go," Mrs. Nebitt asked. "Were your puppets the success you were hoping they'd be?"

"And now we know why I'm not a teacher," I said. "I'm exhausted and I only did half an hour. You can do the next story time, thanks. I'm done."

We both looked at each other for at least half a minute without saying a word. She finally spoke. "Perhaps, we can come to an agreement. If I locate real puppets, crayons, paper, and…" she paused to inhale deeply, "instruments, will you continue with the story times?"

"Once a month, tops," I said and we shook on it.

The library's counter was full of fliers: one for the opening of the new French restaurant complete with coupons. Another for half-off a spin class at Donovan's gym. The obligatory tax forms all libraries had to have this time of year. But there was something pretty obviously missing from the countertop. "Where's the advertisement for the upcoming seance?"

Mrs. Nebitt was looking at her computer monitor, apparently too engrossed in whatever librarians looked at back there.

I wasn't giving up that easily. "Are you even selling tickets?"

She turned her hearing aid up. "I'm sorry. Tickets for what?"

"The seance."

"I haven't sold any. Sorry. I took down the flier because I heard it's been cancelled."

"No. Not yet. Put the flier back up."

She looked around, like she was being followed or something, then lowered her voice. "It's not like Paula's paying for this advertising. This is a library, not the Gazette."

I thought that statement over for a second. The Landover Gazette might be interested in the seance, seeing how the old owners were instrumental in the cover-up.

Parker came over to us. "We need more paper," he sang then turned to me. "Great story time. The kids loved it."

"They loved the part where they threw a cardboard mouse ear at me."

He laughed. "So that's what that was. I thought it was another cookie." He pointed to the flier about the gym, the one taking up the library's prime real estate spot for fliers. "First class is free. You should stop by. I happen to know the instructor." He pointed to himself.

"Congratulations," I said.

Mrs. Nebitt handed him a small stack of printer paper and he went to walk off with it, but stopped himself. "It's funny how life works. The blonde over there's Lila Donovan. She's new to the lake too. When I met her at her family's grocery store, I told her all about the library's story time and she told me all about the new spin class her grandfather's gym needed an instructor for. Isn't that something? And now, her daughter and my daughter are hitting it off." He walked away.

It was something, all right. A little too much of something.

"Did you know she was Myles Donovan's granddaughter?" I asked Mrs. Nebitt, but she wasn't behind the counter anymore. She was halfway to the kids section, a pretty fast waddler when she wanted to be.

I grabbed my box and headed out. "I'll get you another flier about the seance later today," I yelled back to the librarian. She didn't even shush me.

On my way out, I paused at the humungous photo hanging above the copiers, opened my purse, and pulled out the articles I'd printed of the old society pages. They were around the same time, so I hoped to identify some people.

I stared from the articles to the blown-up photo of the ribbon-cutting ceremony and back again. I was able to conclusively identify Mayor Peterton, the only squatty man with a bushy mustache, so he was pretty easy to pick out. I was also able to identify some of the board members of the country club.

And... that's when I noticed a little half-covered sign right by the library that looked like it said "tle Construction," as in Wittle Construction. That was a pretty big coincidence even in this small town since Mayor Darren Wittle also happened to be onboard the boat that killed Gloria. I made a mental note to pay the good mayor a visit, which was something I'd been meaning to do anyway.

The blurry man standing by the sign looked familiar too. I was pretty sure it was Bill Donovan, but I couldn't say for sure. And like a punch in the gut, it hit me. I stumbled back almost bumping into the large glass window behind me, my boots slipping a little on the plastic tiled flooring. The tip jar at the dance.

No wonder that woman was acting weird and didn't want a free ticket to the seance even though she loves freebies. No wonder she and Mildred hadn't talked for years after the accident.

This library, my quiet little sanctuary I'd known and loved for years, had been built on hush money. From that accident. Mrs. Nebitt was probably part of the cover-up, having been paid a library to shut up about something.

I now questioned whether Lila Donovan was really here at my story time to hear *If You Give a Mouse a Cookie* or if this had all been some sort of bizarre, unspoken intimidation tactic. Mrs. Nebitt had known who that woman was as soon as she'd walked in. I could tell by how quickly she'd pretended not to know her.

Lila was probably here to make sure Mrs. Nebitt didn't go to my seance or give me information. She was probably also hoping the librarian would go straight to Mildred to tell her she needed to tread cautiously too.

A large part of me wanted to rush back over there and confront them all with this, to see if I was right. But instead, I walked out to my car. Justin had been right. This was the kind of intimidation that nobody said out loud. Yet, everyone felt it.

One thing I did know, I needed to get to Mildred first to convince her to share her diary before Mrs. Nebitt convinced her she needed to be afraid.

That diary might be the concrete evidence I needed to catch this crooked mouse. It might be my cookie.

CHAPTER 17

I tried to keep my voice calm as I sat in my car, leaving a message for Mildred. "Just wanted to see if you had a chance to look for that diary yet. Call me when you find it." I somehow refrained from adding *before you call Mrs. Nebitt or anyone else.* "I'd really like to get one of the chaperone's perspectives on that dance."

I turned the heater on full blast and called the Purple Pony next. I was supposed to start work in an hour, but I had a better idea. "I think I know how to get more people to buy tickets to this seance. I'm going to the Landover Gazette," I said to Rosalie as soon as she answered, like she would instantly be impressed with my idea.

"What the hell are you talking about?" She only cussed when she was mad, and she was mad a lot lately. "I don't even want to do the seance anymore. I was up all last night thanking my lucky stars that I don't have to work with Satan again."

"I know you don't mean that," I said.

"The nerve of her, coming in here, asking us to pony up money for printing tickets. I'm gonna need to see a receipt, that's what I should've told her..."

I didn't let her finish. "Okay. If it comes to that, we will definitely get a receipt. But let's all try to make money first. I need it. You need it…"

"I don't need it."

I coughed. "Okay, but everyone else does. I have an idea."

"You already told me," she said. "You're gonna buy a newspaper ad."

I laughed. "I don't have money for that. But I think they might give us coverage for free."

There was a long pause, so I continued. "The reporters who covered the accident back in 1957 did a horrible job. Inaccuracies everywhere. Misspellings. Biased, directional reporting intended to persuade an audience, instead of just presenting facts. I think they were in on the cover-up." I paused for a gasp. I didn't get one.

I went on. "But the paper switched ownership in 1993. I bet the new owners would love to help uncover things. Don't you think? Run a scoop on their own paper. Maybe help me find out the truth about that night, so I can nail the murderers."

Once again, crickets.

"Well?"

"I think you have a wonderful imagination. But this is not going to play out like you think it will."

"I have to try, anyway."

I could still hear Rosalie's heavy sigh in my head twenty minutes later as I stood outside the small, two-story brick building that housed the newspaper. I took a deep breath, reminding myself that Rosalie was wrong. These people weren't the same owners who covered up Gloria's death. They would be thrilled to help.

A little bell chimed my entry when I opened the front door. The place smelled like ink and chocolate chip cookies. I looked around, mostly for the cookies. All that talk about mice with cookies was making me want one.

Five desks of various sizes were crammed around the room, each about as cluttered as Rosalie's, except Rosalie's was still cluttered with bloody leaf cuttings right now.

A young, auburn-haired woman sat in front of a police scanner. She took off her headset when she saw me come in.

"Hi. Are you here to see the Herndons? You're early."

"No. No one's expecting me. I'm here to see whoever's in charge, though."

"The Herndons. They own the paper. I'm just an intern from LU. Lynette."

"Landover University. My alma mater. English grad."

"Journalism." She nodded politely. "Go Bears," she said, raising a fist.

I raised my fist too, like I'd known we were the Bears.

"There's Mrs. Herndon now." She pointed toward the backroom where a squatty middle-aged blonde in a bright red sweater and a colorful, flowered accent scarf hustled through the doorway, carrying a plate of cookies. She looked startled to see me. "Can I help you?" she asked, wiping crumbs from her chest.

I introduced myself, making sure to mention that my dead ex-husband's great aunt used to own this place.

"Well, isn't that something?" she said in a tone that made me know it really wasn't.

"Jackson Bowman," I continued.

She smiled like I'd said Jeffrey Dahmer then motioned to the intern who was staring at us with wild, interested eyes. "Lynette, I hope you're not missing important police activity. You have to be the one to make the most of your time here," she said sternly.

The intern put her headset back on, or pretended to. I had a feeling a stranger walking into the newspaper office was a little more interesting than anything the police were doing around here.

"So, what can I help you with?" Mrs. Herndon asked, setting the cookie plate down on her desk without offering me one.

I tried to ignore my stomach rumble while faking some confidence. "I think I have a story you might be interested in."

"Another murder at Gate House?" she asked.

I shot back. "He was innocent, you know."

She put her hands on her hips and gave my sweatshirt and leggings a suspicious once-over, making me kick myself for not spending more time trying to look professionally cute this morning like I'd planned to.

I swallowed and continued. "I know this is going to sound strange, but I'm a medium. I work at the Purple Pony," I began. Her plastered-on smile went from polite to condescending. She sat down in front of her computer, and I felt my nervous facial tic coming back. I was losing my faked confidence. "I'm also a writer, writing a book about ghosts. You know, the ones here in Landover. I have a seance planned about the boating accident that happened in 1957, which was not really an accident…"

She was clicking her keyboard now. "We don't cover seances, sorry. That's not real news."

I resisted the urge to point out how chili contests usually made the headlines around here. "I'm not asking you to cover the seance, but there is a bigger story here. The newspaper's coverage of the boating accident back then. Or lack of. I believe it was part of a much larger cover-up."

She didn't say anything.

"I know it seems unbelievable now because I'm sure you are an honest and trustworthy owner of this newspaper. But, if you look in the archives about the accident, I'm positive you will see the newspaper might not always have been."

"Okay, thank you," she said while I stood there.

She kept typing like she expected me to leave. When I didn't, she added a very sharp, "Thank you, again, for the tip. I will jot it down. Have a good day."

"If you're not interested in the angle, maybe I could just go through your archives myself to see if there's anything I missed at the library. It was almost like they were doing bad reporting on purpose… using journalism as a weapon."

She pressed her lips together so forcefully they drained of color. "You come in here and insult this publication, saying it helped to cover up a murder… that wasn't even a murder. It was an unfortunate accident."

Jackson appeared next to her, leaning against her desk, mocking her outrage with a puppet hand, minus the sock. "My, my. You would think dropping the Bowman name would have more clout than this," he said, making me smile. A part of me was happy Jackson was here. The other part couldn't believe he'd been traveling on me the entire day and I hadn't even noticed. I needed those stinky sachets asap.

He went on. "But then, I suppose I know why she's so upset. This is Grace, my distant cousin. She and her husband, Dan, own the paper now. They had to buy it for fair market value from her grandmother, that great aunt I was telling you about, because she wouldn't give it to them. Aunt Ethel. Lovely woman."

I knew by now that whenever my ex said *lovely woman,* he meant anything but. He said that a lot about my mother.

"Okay, so now I get it," I said to the woman whose neck veins were bulging. "Your grandmother was part of the cover-up, most likely. I'm sorry you had to find that out from me, but that doesn't mean you can't make things right."

"Get out now," she said through gritted teeth. "Or I will call the police. You've been asked plenty of times."

I yanked the door open and left. A chilly wind punched me in the face as I made my way over to my car. I was now late for my shift, and that was time I wouldn't get paid for. And it had been for nothing. I couldn't afford to cut my own hours.

I looked back at the newspaper. I could see Grace's red sweater between the slats of the blinds. She was watching me at the window. It was all I could do not to one-finger salute her. She was just as lovely as her grandmother.

I turned on my car and waited for the heat to kick in just as a beautiful blonde strutted over to the front door of the newspaper. Grace had been watching for someone, all right, but it hadn't been me. Lila Donovan. At least now I knew who the cookies were for.

CHAPTER 18

WHITTLING AWAY

"He can't see you, Carly Mae. He's very busy," Mayor Wittle's executive assistant said the next day before I even had a chance to say "hello" or explain myself. She'd obviously known I was coming.

The lobby was nice, larger than I thought it'd be with American flags and eagle seals as part of its decor. Green velvet curtains covered the one window.

The woman behind the small mahogany desk was an acquaintance of mine who used to work at the Spoony River back in the day. A thin woman around forty with a large head and stringy jet black hair. It was strange to see her in a nice pantsuit instead of a pink 50s outfit.

"Kelly Leone," I said like we were long lost besties. I gave her a hug and asked how she was doing.

She told me all about how her oldest was just about to attend Landover University and her youngest was learning drums. "The neighbors wanna rip his arms off, of course."

She looked me up and down. "I heard you were… interesting now," she said, making me drop my smile. It was like a person couldn't talk to ghosts anymore without getting labeled.

I laughed like she was joking. "Everyone's interesting, right?"

"Right." She curled her lip. "You don't really think dead people talk to you, though, do you?" She lowered her voice. "I'm only asking because Mayor Wittle told me you're crazy now. You know, like Tina."

She was talking about a mutual friend with schizophrenia. And I could tell by the way she was practically whispering that she wasn't at all comfortable talking about her. She went on. "You seem normal to me, though."

"I am normal."

"The mayor's not. Not anymore, he's not. He's been acting crazy. Needy too. He said if I saw you that I should definitely not let you in to see him. He says you only want to talk about your new dead friends."

Mayor Wittle opened his door, peeked out, and shut the door again.

"Looks pretty busy, huh?" Kelly said, motioning with her large head at the now-closed door. She winked at me. "He's busy making more work for me, that's what he's busy with."

I moved toward his office which was at the back of the lobby, but hesitated at the door.

"Oh, it don't lock," she said then went back to scrolling on Facebook. "Good seeing you, Carly Mae. And if that crazy old man asks how you got in, tell him I tried. He knows I don't really try. How'm I supposed to keep people from coming in there?"

The mayor's office was only a little bigger than my walk-in closet at Gate House and just as boring. A photo of his construction company sat proudly on the wall alongside the one of him taking the oath of office. There were also a few family photos and some of the many construction jobs his family's business had tackled over the years, from the 1940s and up.

In one of the black-and-white photos, the mayor stood arm and arm with five large men, each one looked like a body builder compared to him, including the older man by his side. Broad shoulders, full heads of hair. Kind of like if Bill Nye the Science Guy posed with the Thunder from Down Under.

I pointed to the photo. "The original crew of Wittle Construction?" I asked. "Beautiful family. Your dad and brothers?"

He nodded a nervous yes. "Now my sons and nephews have taken over." He fiddled nervously with his bow tie, his wispy gray combover flopping into his eyes with each movement. He looked over at the large stack of papers sitting on his desk like he was remembering he should look busy. He sat down in front of them and picked them up. "Carly Mae, Kelly should have told you. I am very busy, and I do not have time to see you today."

"How about tomorrow?"

He shook his head. "I'm very busy." he said, holding up one of the papers, like it was proof of that. He checked his humungous watch next, probably in case the paper wasn't proof enough. The thing looked more like a compass attached to his wrist than a watch. I wondered if it was just for his "I am busy" show.

He never looked at me. "I know you think it's normal to talk to dead people. But it's not normal. And it's a waste of time and money to bring up that old accident."

"So, you know why I'm here?"

"Of course. I heard about the seance. Everybody has. Vern was right. You're only doing this 'cause you're desperate to make a buck at the Purple Pony."

"Tell me what you remember about the accident."

He shook his head. "Ohmygosh. You talk like it was yesterday. I don't remember anything. Nobody does. Looks like you'll have to get all your information from your ghosts this time. I'm not helping you drum up old stories so you can pretend later that the ghosts told you them. I know how seances work. They're all fake."

He straightened out the stack of papers, his hands shaking. I wondered if it was a condition or nerves.

"Your family built the library, huh," I asked.

"Yes." He pointed to the black-and-white photo on the wall behind him of a bulldozer and a dirt lot. "Very proud of that one."

"Who paid for it?"

"I don't know."

"The Donovans?"

"Stop asking me questions. I don't have to answer, you know?"

"How much did you get for the job?"

He looked at his papers. "I don't think we charged much. It was for a good cause."

"Hush money?" I asked.

I sat down in the chair across from him and crossed my legs like I had all the time in the world.

He motioned toward the photo. "I don't know what you're talking about. We're a construction company. We make bids. We're given plans, and we follow 'em. Plain and simple."

"Did you know the Linders? Did your family buy into the investment?"

"Of course I did. I mean, of course I knew the Linders, but no about the investment." He wiped the sweat from his receding hairline with the back of his sleeve. "Freddie was my friend, and his death was a shock to us all. We're still not over it. I'm sorry the girls got involved." He looked down at his feet.

I had a feeling if anyone was going to crack, it was going to be this guy. He always seemed like the nervous type who liked to talk but tried not to say too much. So, all I really needed to do was get that last part to change.

"What do you mean you're sorry the girls got involved?"

"I mean with Freddie and drinking and swimming after dark…"

I leaned across the desk and lowered my voice. "I already know how those girls died, Mayor Wittle, so you can drop the act. My ghost friends told me they were on the Donovan boat being beaten up and thrown overboard."

His lip quivered as he snapped his chicken neck toward the door. "Kelly!"

"I want to know why."

"Kelly!"

Kelly poked her large head into the room. "What the hell is it now?"

"Please escort Ms. Taylor out. I told you sh… sh…she's crazy."

She motioned for me to follow her. "Come on, Carly Mae." She leaned into me as we were leaving and lowered her voice. "*Ms. Taylor*. Honestly. He's the one acting crazy. Calling me in here to *escort Ms. Taylor out*. Acting like Rockefeller all of the sudden. I swear if that man wants caviar for lunch, I'm knockin' him out myself."

CHAPTER 19

PAGES FROM HISTORY

*M*ildred finally called me back a couple days later. I was right in the middle of figuring out how to hang Rosalie's stinky strands along my bedroom and bathroom door frames, (which included a lot of swearing because hanging weird strands isn't as easy as it sounds), when the phone rang. I jumped down from the chair I was balancing on to welcome the break.

"You were right," the gruff voice on the other end said when I answered. "I found my diary and I was wearing pink that night. How on earth did you know that?"

"I told you. Gloria."

"The ghost," she said, like she halfway didn't believe it.

"Yes."

"If there was any doubt in my mind before, it's gone now. I didn't remember my pink phase. Used to wear a pink flower in my hair when I water-skied too, apparently, so my mom could tell me from the other skiers. Funny the things you forget. Debbie wore blue…"

I listened for any traces that Mrs. Nebitt had beaten me to the punch here, and that Mildred was now too afraid to talk to me, but she didn't seem any more reluctant than usual.

I searched the room while we chatted. "Hold on. Let me find my recorder."

There was a long pause where I heard her smacking her gums again. "I don't want to be recorded."

"It's just for my research. We'll only record the things you're okay with…"

"I'm not okay with recording anything."

I ran my hand over my face. It smelled like dirty diapers from the strands I'd been hanging. "Is this about you and Mrs. Nebitt? What happened with you two anyway?"

She didn't answer.

"Let me guess. It has something to do with the library."

Her voice was louder than I'd expected, and I pulled the phone away from my ear. "My father bent over backwards to get us those jobs chaperoning that night. He was very liked and respected at that country club. Best groundskeeper around. He took such good care of that place, the people there, and us. But after Debbie and I were blamed for the accident, the Donovans had the board fire my father. And you know who my family blamed? Me."

I gasped. "I hadn't known he'd been fired. That's a big deal."

"Damn straight it was…"

I thought about Parker. I didn't think being fired would be too much of a big deal for the guy, seeing how he had just been hired, but he was so happy about being employed.

She went on. "Debbie knew the truth about that night, too. She knew we did our best to keep those kids from that punch bowl. That Myles Donovan had been the one to spike it in the first place. That punch tasted just like my dad's moonshine. Plus, Myles all but demanded I let him do it."

"What on earth are you talking about?"

"My dad liked to make moonshine and most the rich folk

liked to drink it, too. Oh, I know they probably thought it was quaint or kitschy or however they liked to describe the poor, working-class folk when they thought we weren't listening…"

My mind went to my own ex-husband and the way he described the Knobby Creek.

She went on. "My dad never asked for a dime for his moonshine, either. Mainly because he liked all the compliments he got, people saying he was a genius for infusing his moonshine with stuff like juniper so it tasted like gin, or cayenne so it had a bit of a kick. He kept a lot of that moonshine in the woodcutting shed, and Myles made me hand over the key to that shed about a week before the dance. I knew why. Debbie was there, too. She knew why."

I didn't say anything. I just sat and listened as the woman ranted.

"I tried to get Debbie to go with me to the board, to the police, maybe even to the newspaper to tell the truth. There were inconsistencies in everybody's story." She paused for a minute. "You know I've spent most my life trying to forget that night, and reading it over in my diary was a little bit painful."

"I'm sorry," I said. I was tempted to ask if she just wanted to hand over the diary to make things easier for her. But I knew that would never happen.

Mildred's voice was softer after her pause, slower too. "Debbie called me out of the blue the other day to tell me Parker got a job working for Donovan gym. She told me about your investigation too." She started to smack her gums again, but stopped mid-smack. "She said she just wanted me to know, as a friend. You know what I think?"

"What?"

"I think you should call me when you find that recorder. I might have a few select passages to read yet."

I never ransacked my house faster looking for something.

I DECIDED I shouldn't interrupt her as she read each entry into my speakerphone. But it was really hard not to, especially with entries like this one, written the day before the accident:

"July 19, 1957,

"Dear Diary, I am so mad I could scream. The woodcutting shed burned down this morning with all of Daddy's moonshine in it, and I know why. I should tell someone. I should. But I can't.

"I've never seen Daddy so upset. He used every curse word in the book about a hundred times. I feel so heartbroken for him. All his hard work.

"And it's all because Freddie and Myles were mad at me. I saw Freddie sneaking out of the shed last night. So I confronted him. I know. Dumb move. I don't know what I was expecting, but I was mad.

"He denied getting moonshine and even had the nerve to say no one else was in that shed, but I could hear Myles sneezing on the other side of the door. Freddie must think I'm stupid.

"And this time, they've gone too far. Apparently, those two killed a deer off-season. Freddie admitted it. He didn't even care. He said it was an accident, that he was just shooting at cans and trees, but who knows? I told him he didn't own this country club and he needed to stop acting like it, just because his family's rich and one of the town's founders. I told him I'd had enough. I was going to tell on him, to his father and the board.

"And then the shed burned down. I guess he showed me."

"Wow, Mildred," I said. "So, the good ole boys club already knew how to intimidate people and shut them up, even as teenagers." I suddenly remembered I was still recording, and made a mental note to take my comment out.

"You wanna know what really burns my butt?" She didn't give me time to respond. "That was the last time I saw Freddie. I looked for him at the dance because I was getting up enough nerve to confront him about that shed and the fire, but I never saw him."

Could it be because Freddie and his father were already dead? Or already in the Caribbean?

"I tried to tell that to the board when they went to fire my father. I never saw Freddie at the party, much less getting drunk. I tried to get Debbie to tell them that too. But she said she couldn't remember. That she might've seen Freddie there."

I gulped. This was why they didn't talk for years.

"Next thing I know, town's getting that library she always wanted. I think she'd saved all of 150 dollars before the generous, anonymous donors stepped in. They broke ground pretty much right after the accident."

My stomach sank. It was true. The library had been built on lies. Mildred's shaky voice echoed through the room. "She was going to be my maid of honor that fall. But I couldn't. I rescinded the offer and uninvited her to my wedding." Her voice broke when she said that last part.

"Wow. I'm sorry. How'd you two ever make up?"

"It's a long story, but when Debbie's husband got sick, I guess we both decided life was too short. We were different people then, too."

I'd heard Mr. Nebitt passed away in the 1990s from cancer, which meant Mildred and Mrs. Nebitt hadn't spoken from 1957 t0 199o-something. Those women could hold a serious grudge.

"I should read you the stuff I wrote when I got home from the dance. Hold on," she said. I could hear her turning pages.

"And boy was Mr. Donovan mad. He grabbed my arm after the dance and twisted it. He said he had a boat full of drunken teenagers now. And that his friend Mr. Linder was especially mad about how drunk Freddie was. He said if anything happened to them it was my fault for being a poor chaperone."

I interrupted her. "So, after establishing that Freddie Linder was at the dance, even though you say he wasn't, and establishing that he had drunken teenagers on his boat, even though he probably didn't, Mr. Donovan even went so far as to imply that something terrible might happen, which it did. That's pretty suspicious."

Mildred stopped reading. "You know what? Benny wants to check up on Parker anyway. Boy's in his thirties, but he still treats him like he's seven. When's this seance?"

I told her all the details, except the most important one: that it had been canceled, or I was assuming so. My two days had passed, and no tickets had been sold.

"And the whole town's really showing up? I heard you had a lot of people last time."

"Mmmm-hmmm," I lied again. "All the locals. All of them... us," I corrected myself, forgetting for a second that I was a local.

"I'll be there with my diary. There are things that need to be said all over again, in person. My dad's reputation still matters to me."

As soon as we hung up, I threw my head back into the cushions of my couch and closed my eyes.

How on earth was I going to get the seance going again, and the whole town to show up?

As soon as I opened my eyes, I realized Gloria was hovering by the fireplace. I could tell by her vibrant coloring that she was more than ready for our second channeling. I wondered if I was.

I gave her the one-minute sign. "After dinner and a shower," I said, dreading the whole routine I had to go through to shower, which still included a swimsuit. I needed to figure out how to hang Rosalie's stinky strands, and fast.

CHAPTER 20

BIRDS OF A FEATHER

*A*fter finishing the freezer-burned pizza I found wedged behind the ice cube bin and the discolored frozen vegetables I threw in just to say I was eating healthy, I made a fire and plopped onto the couch cushions in front of it. It was only 9:30, but with my pajamas on, it felt like midnight. I tucked my feet under the throw and waited for Gloria to materialize again, allowing my eyes to close and my brain to relax until she did.

Was I awake enough to do this channeling tonight? I was about to see the birds up close, see the things that had terrorized this town. I needed to concentrate.

Jackson appeared by my side. "You don't have to do this. I know you've been having eyesight flickering problems and dizziness."

"I can handle it," I said. I didn't tell him that I was also having hallucinations. And that I kind of liked it.

"You need to take care of yourself in order to be strong against this curse. That eyesight problem you're experiencing is a sign that something's not right."

"Thanks for the warning," I said in much the same way Gloria had to Mrs. Nebitt just before she guzzled the punch in 1957. "I'm well aware of the consequences, Dad."

Gloria appeared. "If you want to do this some other time, that's totally fine. No rush. I have all the time in the world."

"I don't," I said. "I have a seance coming up a week from Saturday and I need you there, too, as well rested as you can be." I turned to Jackson. "I've already decided. After the upcoming seance, I'm taking a break from channelings and seances. At least a full month. I hate to admit it, but you're right. Connecting with the other world is having a toll on me. I need to start eating better, getting more sleep, maybe find a good therapist or use my new gym membership…"

"Spin classes sounding good, huh?" Jackson asked.

"Please stop with that," I said. "You want to cause a rift between Justin and me. And it's not going to work this time. I'm not a stupid, impressionable girl anymore, and you… you're not even a person." I turned to Gloria. "I'm ready."

I closed my eyes and let my mind go blank. The clock in the dining room ticked in the background and I tried to focus on it and my breathing. Tick. Tick. Tick. Inhale. Exhale.

I never even felt her entering this time. I opened my eyes when the ticking of the clock finally turned to something tapping against a glass somewhere. The air felt warm now, humid and stagnant. Hot, actually. Didn't they have air conditioning in the 1950s?

I was in a dark green accented bedroom with pale white furniture and orange shag carpet. I shuffled over to the window where a little gray bird thumped the glass again and again.

"Hello there," Gloria said to the bird. "You birds sure are strange on the lake this year. Why is that, huh?"

The bird tapped out an answer onto the glass, making Gloria giggle.

Gloria's window overlooked the lake. An already loud motor

got louder in the background as a couple of speedboats whooshed by.

She touched the window and the bird flew over to greet her hand. It must've been close to a hundred degrees outside. A chubby brunette bounced in from the hall, wearing a bright red swimsuit and carrying a striped beach bag. "Come on," she said. "My dad said we can watch the ski show."

I looked at the 15-year-old in front of me, round face, freckles, braces, no makeup. I barely recognized her. Nettie, before her Marilyn Monroe phase. "I bet there's gonna be a lot of boys there." She let out a little squeal and held up her bag. "I brought makeup. We can put it on in the boat. Come on. Hurry."

Pulling Nettie into the bedroom, Gloria pointed toward the little bird still sitting at the window. "You have to see this, Nettie. I think this bird is trying to communicate with me. I feel like Cinderella. Watch."

Nettie scrunched her face. "You're acting like weirder-ella. Stop noticing birds like my mother and go get dressed. You're starting to worry me. Of course there are birds. They're all over the place. Geez."

Nettie left after telling Gloria to hurry.

Gloria pulled open a drawer and riffled through the neatly folded pants and shirts until she found the largest floral swimsuit I'd ever seen out. Thick and heavy, the suit made the $169 one at the Knobby Creek look like a controversial Sports Illustrated cover. "This awful thing was my mother's old suit," she said to me. "I was too busy with finals and didn't have time to get a new one. So now, I've gotta make due."

She locked the door before slipping out of her clothes and into the suit. It was just as scratchy and heavy as it looked. She stared at herself in the mirror and I was amazed at how different she looked than she did three years later at the dance. She was shorter and thinner. Her hair hung flat and lifeless, her face free of makeup.

She puffed out her chest and turned to the side. The awful bright green and red flowers seemed to hang off her almost non-existent curves like they were trying to slink away from a bad idea.

Gloria took a deep breath and walked out into the hallway where Nettie quickly fell into a long, hard laugh, stumbling against the back wall. She made a twirling motion with her finger and Gloria spun around to show her the droopy butt part too. "Okay, good one. Now go take off your mom's swimsuit and get dressed into your real one, you goof. And be quick about it."

"My mom's making me wear this one," Gloria said.

Nettie yanked Gloria down the hall by the arm, the carpet scratched at our bare feet. She practically threw me into her room, which was small and bright yellow with the same shag carpet as the hall. Without speaking, she yanked a gray hard plastic suitcase from under her bed, plopped it onto the mattress and unlatched it. There were only a few items in there.

"My secret stash," Nettie said, pulling out a black bikini with its sales tags still on. It was large compared to the bikinis of today, but very small compared to what Gloria had on. She snatched it and hid it behind her back.

"You're not serious," she said.

"Our mothers don't have to know everything we do, you know?" Nettie winked.

Gloria's heart raced. I could tell partly because she was thrilled and excited and partly because she was so nervous she was going to puke.

Nettie went on. "When it comes to moms, you gotta start them out slow, like boiling a frog. This summer, a bikini. Makeup by fall, that we don't have to sneak. And by next summer, they'll be ready for us to get a dye job." Nettie's smile was broad, already straight from her braces.

As Gloria got dressed, I heard something just outside the window again. This time it sounded like a low growling sound. I wanted Gloria to rush to the window and look, but she didn't seem to notice.

"This trip was different," Gloria said to me in her head as she examined her bikini in the mirror, sucking in her stomach so much her ribs protruded. "I saw a lot of birds, everywhere. Weird ones. Ones that seemed to watch you and try to communicate with you. Others that were large and scary. Nettie's mom said they were probably mutants."

The bikini bottoms were pretty much shorts and the top was a large bra-like thing, but she felt very self-conscious, almost as if she'd rather be wearing her mom's suit; I could tell. Blood rushed to our shared cheeks. She opened the drawer and took out a short striped cover-up that seemed a lot like a long, sleeveless shirt. When we came out, Nettie made us take it off so she could see the suit.

"You look good," she said with a slight tone of jealousy Gloria enjoyed. "Better than I do in it. Man, don't let me eat anything else today. I'm going on diet pills as soon as we get home." She pinched a large chunk of her stomach in her fingers. "Stupid baby fat."

"You look cute," Gloria said, snapping up her cover-up all the way to the top again.

It was a short walk down to the pier where we carefully stepped into a large green pontoon that was tied to the dock. I realized where we were immediately. Just a few houses from Mildred's, around the bend from the country club.

A small, skinny brunette about ten with short cropped hair and freckles ran down the backyard's hill to the dock and over to the boat. "Mom says to take me with you."

I knew the girl had to be June.

Nettie shook her head at her cousin. "Liar. Your mom's playing cards next door, same as my mom. She didn't say anything. Scram. You'll watch the fireworks with them."

The girl stuck out her lip at Gloria. "But I want to see the ski show too."

"Then talk your mom into taking you," Nettie said, backing the boat out.

"Glor-i-a, you always say we'll do stuff and then we never do," June yelled, arms folded. "Us against the world, remember?"

"It's okay, Bug. We'll get 'em next time. I promise," Gloria yelled over the boat engine.

"You always say that," the girl yelled back, kicking her shoe along the planks of the pier.

Gloria talked to me in her head. "That's the part that hurts the most. The night of the accident... I never got a chance to say good-bye to Bug. All she ever wanted was to hang out with me." Her voice trailed off. "We should've done more together."

The pontoon was loud and slow, and we lazily made our way over to the country club with the warm summer breeze blowing lightly along our cheeks. The smell of mud, gas, and pollen surrounded us. The lake was so different. Only a few larger houses even existed, most were modest-sized two-stories. I tried to look over at Mildred's when we passed it, but I could only see where Gloria's eyes went that day, and she was checking the trees.

"There they are. Look," she shouted to Nettie, pointing. I screamed a little in my head as four large black birds with crusty, thick, yellowish white beaks swooped down by the boat. They were huge, bigger than I expected.

One was as big as a large cat, only thinner and mangier looking. And another had a twisted, thick beak with a sharp jagged end.

"My mom can't stop talking about these mutant ravens," Nettie said, pushing the lever on the boat. The motor hummed and picked up speed. "Just don't do anything stupid like feed them."

"Like I want to lose a finger today," Gloria replied, making her cousin smile.

The boat went faster, but not by much, and the birds had no problems keeping up. They were very good flyers, easily maneuvering around with the boat. We were close enough to see the pock marks along their beaks and their cold, dead black eyes that seemed to look straight through Gloria, to me, like they knew I was there.

An especially mangy looking one next to me squawked loudly by my side growing dangerously close to Gloria's face.

She screamed and laughed as the boat went around the bend, heading for the country club at a high speed, losing the birds once again.

The birds did a final inspection of our boat and flew off toward the crowd that was starting to form along the pier.

"Those weren't even the biggest ones," Gloria said to me. "You'll see later."

Oddly, the country club looked largely the same as it did today, except in 1954 it also included a large wooden building to the side that resembled a cross between a warehouse and a barn.

"You remember the dance hall," Gloria said to me in our head when we passed it. A shiver went up my spine as I remembered that night. They would be dead in three short years from this memory. "Over there's the ice cream shop and the record store."

It was like a casual tour of a place I knew well but hardly recognized. Like a page out of Mildred's book, *Landover: Then and Now*.

Much of the water was roped off with buoys. And the piers were mostly outlined with boats and filled with people sitting on lawn chairs, sporting sunglasses, oversized hats, and zinc noses.

Nettie was an expert driver. She easily pulled the boat into a small spot along the dock next to the ice cream shop. "Perfect," she said. "We can get ice cream on the way out." She winked as she tied the boat up. "Don't say it. My diet doesn't start 'til we back."

Nettie pulled off her cover-up, sucking in her stomach and puffing out her chest. "Come on," she said. She tugged on Gloria's shirt-dress as soon as she stepped off the boat. "We can't attract boys without a little bait."

Gloria unbuttoned the first button while Nettie rolled her eyes and strutted through the crowd of people, practically pushing her way through. "At least hurry up, already. We only have until dinner."

Gloria talked to me in her head again. "It was the Fourth of July. We had to meet up with our families at the barbecue so we could all watch the fireworks together."

Nettie's pace was fast and efficient, like she already had everything mapped out and memorized. "They say the best spot is right by the Knobby Creek Boating Company. It's where the local kids hang out."

"I don't know the local kids..." Gloria began with a stammer. "I mean, can't we just hang out by ourselves and watch the show?"

Nettie pulled out two sets of binoculars from her bag and handed one to me. "For the show. And the boys. I think you know which ones I really want you to point out."

An announcer's voice echoed through a loud speaker somewhere. "Welcome to Landover Lake's eighth annual Independence Day Water Ski Show." A smattering of applause and whistles came from the crowd around us. Nettie pulled me up a dirt hill, away from the gas pumps lined up along the water, and up toward the large white service buildings where a group of teenagers stood around, leaning on a couple benches set up there. Some were smoking. Some were drinking from a shared flask.

The Knobby Creek rusty baby-leg anchor logo sat proudly atop the shed, making me realize it was supposed to look that way.

Nettie smiled at one of the boys. He looked at his friends and they laughed a little, elbowing him forward. The boy was tall with slicked-back short hair, jeans, and braces. I didn't recognize him or one other kid. I tried to recognize all the boys in the group. Clyde was there. Myles Donovan and Mayor Wittle too. They had to be the Linders.

They looked us up and down. Nettie puffed her chest out while Gloria fiddled with the top button of her cover-up.

"You girls wanna see something?" the boy asked Nettie.

"No," Gloria said.

Nettie elbowed her. "She's kidding. What is it?"

He cupped his hand over Nettie's ear and whispered into it. She nodded. "No kidding?"

"Let's just watch the show," Gloria chimed in. "We don't need to see anything. Thanks for the offer, though."

About twenty crows swooped down by our faces and over to the bench by the front door of the Knobby Creek just as a thin, tall man in a gray uniform with a matching hat stormed out of the building. He waved a rolled up magazine around at the birds sitting on the bench until they flew away.

"Go on, go!" he yelled over and over. He turned toward the kids and swatted the magazine in the air around them too. "You all are as bad as the birds. Go on, get, unless you're buying something." When he saw Myles, he stopped himself and uncurled the magazine in his hand. It was Popular Mechanics, just like I thought. "Sorry," he said. "I didn't know you kids were with Myles, Freddie, and Eric. How are your parents, boys?"

Gloria turned to the boys and I got a better look at the Linders, two thin kids of varying heights with freckles and side parts.

The man continued. "Sorry, if I scared you all. These birds have been driving me crazy since May. I told my wife I'm gettin' a scarecrow, even though she hates those things, thinks they're uglier than the birds. But I'm getting one anyway." He winked.

"Or two. I talked to a man in Fremont, and I think I've got just the kind of scarecrow this town is gonna love. I'm putting 'em right here on this bench so those mangy birds won't sit here."

Myles turned his head toward his friends, but I could tell they were laughing and making fun of the man.

The man tipped his old-style gasoline hat with the KC logo on it before walking back inside. "Tell your father my retirement thanks him for getting me in on that investment. Your father is a fine man. Yours too, Freddie."

I wondered what investment he was talking about. I needed to know more. I made a mental note to go back to the Knobby Creek because I'd seen firsthand what kind of retirement that man was having. Unless being propped in front of a window with a magnifying glass and a magazine was what he'd been saving for.

A motorboat buzzed by and the crowd by the lake cheered. Gloria moved her attention over to the water skiers gracefully zooming by.

"The Landover Ladies Team," the announcer said, allowing his voice to linger at the end like he knew they were a crowd favorite. All the men and most of the women stood on tiptoes to see the action, oohing and ah-ing.

Ten ladies wearing red, white, and blue swimsuits and tutus zoomed by with American flags mounted on their skis. As soon as the lively band music picked up, they pulled their flags out one by one and waved. I immediately recognized two of the ladies, Mrs. Nebitt and Mildred, only because Mildred told me she always wore a pink ribbon in her hair and Mrs. Nebitt wore a blue one.

"I don't think your friend wants to come with us," the boy said, shaking his head at Nettie like she shouldn't even bother to ask. "She's really into the show." He laughed.

They walked up the hill toward the surrounding patch of woods and Gloria took a deep breath and followed them. I could tell it was more to talk her cousin out of going than it was to see if she could come. Nettie touched the boy's arm and went back down to her cousin.

"Just stay here, Gloria."

Gloria kicked her foot into the dirt like June had at the dock. "Why don't boys ever like me?"

"Oh please," Nettie replied. "Stop being such a dud and they will."

I felt the punch in Gloria's gut. She knew her cousin was leaving her, again.

She ran her hand through Gloria's hair to fix her headband. "They can tell you're too much work," she began. "And boys don't like hard-to-get girls. Not in the summer, they don't. Maybe at school, they'll like the girl who sits off in the corner reading a book and wearing her mom's humungous, awful swimsuit."

"Nobody wears swimsuits to school."

"You know what I'm saying." Nettie bit at her cuticle. "That's fine for long term, when they have more time to get to know a girl. But we're summer girls. We have to be fun."

"I don't want to be fun."

"Then I'll see you later," she turned to go with the boys, but then turned back around. "Whatever you do, don't go home. My parents might be there, and they'll ask where I'm at. But they also could be here. Just... if you see my parents somewhere in the crowd, tell them I went to find a bathroom, okay?"

Gloria nodded. "What's in the woods anyway?"

She rolled her eyes. "Supposedly, a dead body."

CHAPTER 21

COORDINATED ATTACKS

The smell of fuel surrounded Gloria as she searched the beach bag she was carrying for some money or a soda. The sun beat down on her exposed shoulders and her heart raced as she debated what to do next: follow her cousin, go home, or stand around like a weirdo by herself and watch the ski show.

A couple of skiers came by the main pier, and Gloria put the binoculars back over her eyes, apparently choosing the weirdo option.

This time, a woman skier climbed onto the shoulders of the man skiing by her side. I could tell by her pink flower, it was Horace and Mildred, her muscular legs wrapped firmly around his neck. It was hard to believe the little old couple from the lake used to ski like that. Strange how time changed people.

After a second, Gloria threw the binoculars into the bag and stomped up toward the woods where Nettie had gone.

"I should've gone home," she said to me in her head. "It would've been a long walk, but I should've done it. Who knew this was just the beginning of Nettie's stunts?"

She turned back around to scan the crowd for their parents as she walked. I could tell she was half-hoping she'd see them.

It grew darker the deeper she walked into the woods. The sound of music and boats slowly faded into the sounds of cicadas and frogs. Gloria listened for the kids, but didn't hear anything out of the ordinary, except a low growling sound. She gasped, turning her head this way and that, not knowing what was going on. She spun around to head back, stepping on a large, dry twig that caused a cracking sound to interrupt the otherwise calm woods. Loud flapping followed, whooshing past leaves, piercing branches.

"Go away!" A girl screamed, her voice shrill and frightened. Gloria at first thought it was Nettie being attacked by the boys.

"I knew it," she said, running toward the voice, even though every part of her wanted to run in the opposite direction. She put her binoculars on and scanned the area.

A young brunette in a multi-colored pleated skirt darted frantically through the forest, birds diving for her head like she was an unfortunate extra in a Hitchcock movie. She swung her book bag around in windmill fashion, smacking some of the humungous black birds, but none looked even slightly deterred by her efforts. I knew exactly who it was from the article. Bertha somebody-or-rather. I would see the hero dog soon. I couldn't wait.

The hero dog was the one that looked just like my dog. It was a crazy thought, but my dog didn't seem to be aging, so I couldn't help but wonder if he'd been around, not-aging, in the 1950s as well.

Gloria was almost to the girl now, but stopped short when a large black bird flew straight into her face as if it were daring us to go any farther. It swooped up at the last second. Gloria stumbled back, narrowly escaping its thick beak, the smell of rot and mildew swooping up with it.

Tripping over a rock, Gloria landed hard on the ground. A sharp pain shot up our back. She scrambled to her feet, grabbed a large stick on her way up, and swung it above her head like a baseball bat.

The girl I knew to be Bertha was on the ground now too, screaming with the book bag covering her head as the birds pecked her legs and arms. I already knew the girl would survive. The newspaper article said minor injuries.

"Get away!" Gloria screamed. But they weren't like other birds. They didn't respond to loud noises. They seemed laser-focused on their attack.

Gloria's attention turned toward a blur of gold bolting through the bushes and trees beside us. Without stopping or hesitating, the dog snatched one bird after another from off Bertha's legs, easily snapping through bones even though most the birds were about as big as rabbits. He swung the animals around in his jaw, spitting them out as soon as they'd broken into two or gone limp in its clutch. He didn't pause, never looked up. He was equally as focused. The sound of cracking bones and whimpering birds filled the woods. Most the birds gave up and flew off with only a few larger ones remaining.

"Get off my dog," I screamed, but it didn't come out. Gloria's ghost was the only one who could hear me in the channeling.

"How on Earth is that your dog?" she asked me in her head.

"I don't know," I said. "But I see now how Rex got the scar on his nose."

The dog bled profusely from the tip of its nose. And even though Bertha was covered in cuts and bruises herself, she grabbed the dog into her arms after the birds left and held him close as the other kids finally arrived.

"That was crazy," said the boy I recognized as Clyde. "You okay?"

Bertha checked her legs and arms. They were dotted with blood but she nodded.

"My aunt owns the newspaper. They're covering the ski show

right now, but wait'll I tell them about this. You all stay here," he said, running off through the woods. "I'll get help."

Jackson's aunt was on the scene in less than 15 minutes with her photographer. She was a graying stick of a woman around 60 with a sleeveless shirt, a very dark tan, and so much extra skin hanging off her bony arms and legs she looked like she was wearing a Silence-of-the-Lambs skin suit in need of an iron. A dark brown cigarette dangled from the side of her mouth as she finger swept her thin bangs from her forehead. "This the victim?" she asked, pointing to Bertha.

A paramedic also pushed his way through the crowd that was forming and began assessing Bertha's injuries. "Stay still," he told her, opening up his bag.

Gloria stepped back, still trembling from the experience. She turned around and saw Nettie standing there with the boys, and Gloria's eyes filled with tears.

"Oh Nettie," she said, wrapping her arms around her cousin and hugging her. Nettie smelled like pot and cologne.

"It was awful," Gloria whispered into her cousin's ear. "Those birds wanted to kill that girl, and I swear, they wanted to kill me, too, for trying to stop them."

"Were you coming into the woods to spy on me?" Nettie asked.

While Gloria tried to convince her cousin she was just following Bertha's screams, I listened in on the other conversations around me.

"People are already afraid of these damn birds. And we can't afford to lose any more tourists," Aunt Ethel said in a cigarette-induced low voice, probably to her photographer. "Focus on the dog, the hero perspective. Comb the girl's hair and get a close-up of her and the dog. Don't show any of that blood. Not a drop."

Gloria was still trying to placate her cousin, reassure her she wasn't going to say anything. Her attention was nowhere near the dog and the girl, so I couldn't get a close look at the Lab like I wanted to.

"Did the boys really show you a dead body?" Gloria asked.

Nettie's cute hairdo was a disheveled mess and her swimsuit was turned to the side, all wrong. She twisted it right and giggled. "There wasn't a dead body anymore, no. Just the spot where the boys found one a couple weeks ago or something. They're not supposed to say anything about it. You know, so the police can keep some details secret. But they told me because I'm an out-of-towner, so it didn't matter."

"Congratulations," Gloria said.

Nettie continued, oblivious to the sarcasm. "The paper said the man had been split in two, right down the middle, but the boys said the man had actually been decapitated. His head was on one side of a log, body on the other. Can you believe it? Someone sliced his head off."

"I want to leave right now, go back to California," Gloria said. "And never, ever come here again."

"The man was a transient…"

"So?"

"So, that doesn't happen to normal people. Besides, one of the boys said the bum came into some money, some sort of great investment, and a jealous relative did him in. So, it's not like there's a crazy person on the loose."

"This whole place is crazy," Gloria said, looking all around. Her gaze stopped on the police officer who was grilling Bertha on the incident.

"If you don't mind, we'd like you to come down to the station to make an official report, Miss…" the police officer said. His voice was familiar, but I knew there was no way I could possibly have known the man.

"Hawthorne. Bertha Hawthorne. Call me Bertie," she said, still holding onto the dog.

"This is about the same spot ole Richard was found in last

week," the police officer said, and I realized it was the same voice my ex-husband used.

"Mason, you're not suggesting birds did that to Richard, right?" Aunt Ethel said. "Any fool knows a bird couldn't split a man in two. And the last thing we need is for that to get around." She turned to her photographer. "Don't put that connection in there and don't get any of these mangled, dead birds in the shot either."

"But they're huge."

"Exactly. Everybody knows Richie died from one of his drug deals gone wrong. Being split down the middle is what happens when you lose your moral compass," Ethel said loud enough for the crowd around her to hear. A couple people nodded. A few others winked at her.

Ethel had called the sheriff Mason, which I knew was Jackson's father's name. Fortunately, Gloria's attention went to him so I could get a better look at the man I'd never met and didn't know very much about.

Even though I'd seen him in many pictures, he wasn't nearly as tall as I thought he'd be or as thin, and he seemed to have a perpetual hunch in his shoulders and a faraway look. Other than his full beard and mustache, he didn't look very much like my ex-husband at all. And I couldn't help but wonder why Jackson never mentioned his dad had been the sheriff of Landover before.

But the biggest question running through my brain was who was Richard? And what in the hell had split him in two? Was it a drug deal, a jealous relative, or a wild animal? That was definitely one for the research pile.

The paramedic had a cigarette dangling from his mouth as he bandaged Bertha's leg.

Bertha pointed all around as she told Jackson's dad what had happened. "I normally don't cut through the woods," she began. Her brown hair was cut short like Elizabeth Taylor's, her make-up almost as perfect. And after a bird attack. *Was I the only one who could never look polished?* She continued. "I only took the shortcut because I was coming from school…"

"What kind of school is that?" Ethel asked, looking up from her pen and paper.

"Secretarial," the girl said proudly. "Mrs. Hetterman's, the best in the county."

"They have school on the Fourth of July?"

"I get a discount on tuition if I come in and correct papers. It took longer than I thought, and I wanted to catch the whole ski show, so I took the shortcut. I don't know what would've happened if it weren't for this dog," she said, pointing to the Lab still by her side. "He's my hero. I'm calling him Normandy on account of the way he stormed in and saved the day. Like the allies in Normandy."

The dog barked at her and she laughed.

"Sounds like he likes his name," the photographer said, clicking photos.

"And you said crows did this to you?" Jackson's dad asked.

The girl looked up at the trees like they might come back.

"No," Gloria interrupted. She marched over to the sheriff. "They were birds, and some were crows, but some were different, larger and with weird beaks. I saw the whole thing and my aunt's an amateur ornithologist."

"A what?"

"A bird watcher. She says she's never seen anything like them before. We just got in yesterday, but they're all over the lake. They growl."

The wrinkles around Aunt Ethel's eyes grew thicker as her face contorted from a scowl to a smirk. "Growling birds? Ain't that something, sheriff? These kids pulling your leg?" The cigarette fell from her lips, and she stomped it out with her sandal. "I'm not putting any of that crap in my story and I suggest you keep it out of yours too. No sense scaring the town over a kid's joke." She stared at him long and hard, drawing large x's over some of her notes.

Mason ignored his aunt and turned his attention to Bertha and Gloria. "Just tell me exactly what you saw."

"Hey Clyde," someone yelled from the crowd. "Looks like your dumb brother actually believes this crap. Dumbest sheriff ever. That's what my parents say." It was the kid I was guessing was Freddie Linder, elbowing the chubby younger Bowman. Clyde's face grew red under his freckles.

"Sheriff Moron Bowman, that's what they call him," Eric chimed in. "They wonder if you'll ever solve a case."

Mason blinked over and over, looking down at his shiny black shoes and back at his pen again. He looked everywhere but in anyone's eyes. "Young lady, are you sure that's what you heard and saw? I just want the truth."

Gloria nodded profusely. "One-hundred percent. Yes, sir."

"One-hundred percent. Yessss, sirr. I'm a fancy ornithographer, so I know. Those birds growl. Grrrrrrrr," Clyde mocked, and the group burst out laughing. Nettie laughed too.

Gloria's eyes stung and her nose stuffed up. She pushed past the kids while they pointed and laughed at her. She pushed past the group of grown-ups that had formed a circle along the outskirts, studying her with skeptical eyes and hushed whispers.

Nettie was right behind us. I could tell.

"I'm sorry, Gloria. I shouldn't have laughed," she yelled, but Gloria kept running, never even turning around.

The announcer's voice was still projecting in the background from the ski show. "Let's hear it for another fine demonstration of athletic ability and showmanship," he said to the sound of applause. "That concludes the ski show this year, but stick around for the barbecue and fireworks…"

Nettie caught up and pulled on Gloria's arm, apologizing again and again. "We need to keep our stories straight, okay? We both saw the bird attack. We were together watching the ski show when we heard the girl scream. Got it? We need to stick together on this..."

Gloria's head throbbed along her temples, but I couldn't tell if it was Gloria's headache or my own. I closed my eyes, or Gloria did, and let Nettie's whines drift into the background. She was telling us she would never let this happen again. They were going to stick together from now on. She promised.

When I opened my eyes, I was in my own living room. My head still throbbed and I slowly turned my neck this way and that to try to loosen my muscles and relieve my headache.

Jackson hovered nearby, watching me. It was creepy and endearing all at the same time. "I was very worried about you," he said.

"I'm fine," I replied, my voice raspy and dry from channeling for hours without drinking anything. I slowly got up and made my way to the kitchen for some water. My legs moved but I barely felt them. I had no idea how I'd woken from the channeling. That was one area I seriously needed more control over.

"Your great aunt was horrible," I said to my ex as I grabbed a large glass from the cabinet and filled it from the tap. "So was Clyde. Your father seemed all right. Why didn't you tell me he was sheriff of Landover?"

Jackson's transparent face grew slightly paler. "I forgot you'd see that. He wasn't sheriff for very long. Apparently, he quit right around the time of Gloria's accident. Told my mother she could have the baby she always wanted." He framed his chin with the back of his hands. "An adorable son, well worth the wait. And they just lived off the inheritance from then on."

I nodded, looking up at the ceiling. It was strange how Gloria's accident had changed the town, from who the sheriff was to the library being built.

"You should've told me sooner," I said.

Rex ran up to me and stuck his head in my lap as I scribbled.

"And you, young man," I said to my dog, cupping his head in my hand. "You were quite the hero in my channeling."

He walked away like he had no idea what I was talking about.

"Whatever, Normandy," I yelled to him. I turned back to my ex. "The birds were very coordinated in their attack…"

I grabbed my notebook and wrote as I talked, circling *Look up Richard. Decapitated or split in two? Find out about the investment.*

Jackson glanced over my shoulder as I wrote. "Not that I'm your secretary, but someone called and left a message on the answering machine while you were channeling. A university student, works at the paper."

"Lynette," I said, dropping my pencil. I knew she hadn't really been listening to that police scanner. "Go Bears," I said.

CHAPTER 22

DULY NOTED

The next day was one of those days in Wisconsin when the news lectures nonstop about the importance of having an emergency kit in your car in case you get stranded.

I shivered my way into work, scarfing down both granola bars I'd brought with me as emergency rations even though I'd already eaten an early lunch. I wiped the crumbs from my sweatshirt, kicking myself a little for eating rations for no reason. Now if I got stranded, I'd probably have to Donner-party my own arm to survive. I glanced over at my left one. We both knew which one was going down first.

Almost as soon as I arrived, Lynette bounced under the glitter unicorn that adorned the front entrance of the Purple Pony. I could tell immediately she had the kind of positive energy I was going to have to stop myself from wanting to smack out of her.

"I could not believe my luck when you walked into the newspaper office," she said, barely pausing to breathe. "It was like, what do you call that, kismet or something."

Rosalie rushed in from the backroom when the wind chimes clanged.

"Not a customer," I said to her. She limped back. At least she was getting exercise. The doctor was always on her about that.

Lynette looked around the shop. The gemstone section seemed to catch her eye and she sifted through one of the bins as she talked. "Anyway, I've been searching for a story to investigate for this nightmare investigative journalism class I have to take this semester. I was like, 'How do you just make up something to investigate?' And then, there you were."

"There I was," I repeated, wondering briefly if this girl was trying to step in and take credit for my investigative work, something I probably should've been okay with.

She went on. "So, when I overheard you talking about the Gazette's botched reporting job and a possible cover-up on that accident, I looked up the old archives the next day as soon as the Herndons left for lunch. Because they always go out for lunch. Dinner too. They barely work, actually. I searched every file every day until I found something."

I leaned in. "Okay, what'd you find?"

She threw a small, gray notebook onto the counter, and I recognized it immediately. Aunt Ethel's.

THIS PARTICULAR NOTEBOOK covered almost five years of Aunt Ethel's notes, from 1953 to 1958. And trying to sift through the mountain of bad handwriting was too much for me to sneak in during work, but I still tried.

Lynette was making it almost impossible, though. Sitting on a stool by my side, she went on and on about her ridiculously hard classes and how disappointed she was that the seance had been canceled because she really wanted to film it.

"I would've been able to use that footage for two classes. Two. Ohmygod, how amazing would that have been? Investigative journalism and broadcast journalism," she said, her voice rising for added emphasis and enthusiasm. "And it's such an interesting angle, right? The ghosts coming back for revenge."

I nodded. "They're not really coming back for revenge. It's more like closure."

Her face dropped.

"But last time all the windows did get blown out at the bed and breakfast," I said to cheer her up. "And that would've made for some awesome broadcast journalism."

Her face brightened, and I realized I had just used the word *awesome.*

"Unfortunately," I continued. "The town's too afraid to come out for this seance because if they did, it would look like they supported my investigation into the good ole boys club around here." I smoothed in a little post-it note on the page I just found in Ethel's notebook about the split-in-two body in the woods, squealing a little to myself about finding that.

"You could do it for free," Lynette said. "I'll post the seance in the Daily Bear."

I turned my head to the side, no idea what she was talking about.

"Landover University's campus newspaper. It's called the Daily Bear, but we don't release it daily, not sure why it's called that. If I call now, I can make it into the next issue. I'm one of the editors there."

"Do it," I said. "Put the seance in for a week from Saturday, here at the Purple Pony. For free."

Rosalie hobbled into the room, making me realize she'd been listening at the entrance to the back.

"For free?" she said. "You said we were going to make money off this?"

"Good thing you don't need money." I teased her. "But it's great for the long run. We'll be tapping into a whole new local market, one you can use in winter. College students."

"Oh yeah," Lynette said, looking around at the long tie-dye

dresses and vintage clothing. "They'll probably buy tons... and tons of... stuff."

Rosalie twirled one of her dreadlocks around a finger. "I can't do the seance here, for free. Sorry." Her voice was unusually quiet, and her limp extra pronounced as she turned and headed to the backroom again. I'd never seen her act so strange before.

"I'll talk her into it later," I said as soon as she was out of earshot.

Lynette shrugged and looked at her watch. "Well, let me know before seven if you guys change your mind. I've gotta run or I am going to be late to class. And I need to sneak that notebook back into the Herndons' files after that." She held out her hand like she expected me to hand over the notebook, that I'd barely had time to look through because she wouldn't stop talking.

I shook my head so hard and fast I pulled a neck muscle. "I'll return it tomorrow when they're out for dinner. I promise. In the meantime, look for more. There has to be more than this notebook. Look for an article about the Linders. I want to know if their remains washed ashore or if just a couple of shirts and shoes did."

Lynette's face turned almost as red as the highlights in her auburn hair. She bit her lip.

"Don't worry. They'll never know you're doing this," I said in that confident tone I was getting far too good at faking. "Plus, think how amazing this is going to be for your career."

I had no idea how whistleblowing and a seance were going to be amazing for anyone's career, but she seemed to buy it. And as soon as the talkative girl left, I went back to the notebook.

I took a deep breath and leaned over it, finally able to look at the small, black leather notebook in peace, when it occurred to me it really was in peace. I hadn't seen or heard my ex-husband all day. I patted the pocket that held a couple of Rosalie's stinky sachets. Score one for privacy.

Ethel's notebook seemed to be divided into what was put in

the newspaper and what was x'd out. I went to the bird attack first to see what it was she had crossed out that day.

~~Near the same spot as Richard. Bertie Hawthorne, growling birds, thick beaks, fifth bird attack~~

Instead, the notes about the dog had been circled, and even though the headline read "Another Bird Attack in Landover," the article never mentioned that this was the fifth one.

That was a lot of bird attacks.

But the strangest parts of Ethel's notes that day were scribbled almost illegibly into the margins, so I concentrated mostly on those areas. Things like:

Check on cut of R rumor. I KNOW I sent more leads than was paid for. People winking and nodding at me all over the place. He better deliver. Get L to call his friend in DA office. Crime or society pages — D's choice. He already owes me.

I had no idea what that meant. L was probably Lawrence, her husband, and the mayor. D was probably Dwight Linder. R was Richard, most likely, the dead man in the woods. Her code really wasn't hard to decipher, but then it was reflective of the cocky attitude that plagued this whole town, an attitude that almost dared someone to figure things out and say something.

Rosalie hobbled out to check on me. "You can go on home early if you want," she said in a defeated tone. "I can handle things today."

I barely looked up from the notebook. "But I have another hour on my shift," I said, like I was busy and leaving early was a crazy notion.

She sighed and left, and I continued flipping through the notebook, wondering what Dwight Linder owed Ethel.

Crime or society pages?

Did this have to do with the investment the old man from Knobby Creek was talking about?

And what was the Richard rumor she'd been referring to? The one about the drug deal gone wrong or the greedy relative?

I scanned for entries from July 1957 when the accident happened to see if I could find anything on the Linders. But Ethel's notes ended the night before the accident and picked up in December with the best egg-nog recipes. I took a picture of the eggnog recipes for later.

Flipping back over to her notes just before the accident, I looked for anything strange about the shed fire's reporting. There wasn't much about it, but I was excited to see it in there.

Fire erupted just outside the country club, 2:00 a.m. when a worker's shed caught fire. ~~Probably all of Ernst's moonshine. A blowtorch and a welding mask found just inside.~~ *The fire was seen clear across the lake. No injuries or threat to the main structures. Shed is destroyed.* ~~Arson suspected.~~ *Firemen responded promptly. Cause under investigation.*

I bit the end of my fingernail. Every piece of information that could have implicated the good ole boys club had been struck from her notes, of course. Mildred had been right. The fire was started on purpose, to put Mildred in her place and destroy all her father's hard work.

In the light of the fluorescent bulbs overhead, I could just see what looked like an erased message scribbled into the margin of the page, just like before. Aunt Ethel's margin notes were always the hardest part of her notebook to read, little jokes and reminders written in an almost illegible scrawl. But this time it had been erased, making it almost impossible to decipher.

I squinted and tried to concentrate on the faint lines. An "L" maybe... or an "R." I brought my face in closer. Nope, it was definitely a "B." *B wants article on FM. DS driving him crazy. Bury it. A* loud deep cough interrupted my thoughts. Cigar and coffee breath. I screamed and fell off my stool.

Mayor Bowman and Dr. Dog. I'd been so into the notebook I hadn't even heard the wind chimes on the door.

"What in tarnation is that?" the mayor yelled, pointing a thick shaky finger at his aunt's notebook.

I threw the opened notebook into my purse. "Just taking notes on the inventory I need to order," I said. "Someone has to keep this place stocked. We are busy…" I looked around for a stack of papers to prove it, but I didn't have my props ready like Mayor Wittle had.

Mayor Bowman leaned in so close I could see the wild nose hairs protruding from his flared nostrils. Of all the Bowmans, he resembled Henry the most, only the mayor was shorter with a slightly more modern hairdo. Same round glasses, though.

Dr. Dog towered over both of us. I'd forgotten how huge that man was, easily the largest man in Potter Grove. "This place busy?" He laughed. "You think for one second we believe that?"

"I don't care what you and the mayor believe. What do you want?"

I could tell by the mayor's cold stare, he wanted me to break open my purse and prove my lie about the notebook, but he could stare all he wanted. I wasn't intimidated by flaring nostrils or gigantic veterinarians.

I kicked myself for not tossing the notebook in my purse sooner, though, and for not hearing the door. *The one person who would recognize his aunt's notebook…*

Dr. Dog's heavy footfalls echoed through the floorboards as he stomped around the store, scanning the place from ceiling to floor. He took a couple dangly turquoise earring sets from their display cases, shook his head, and put them back.

"Most everything here is done by local artists," I chimed in, like I actually thought he was interested. "Beautiful, huh?"

The mayor's face relaxed when I said that, a smile escaping his thin lips. "I'm just gonna cut to the point, so you don't get your hopes up that you might actually have a customer. Rosalie is behind on her rent. Did you know that? I don't know how you couldn't."

I looked around for Rosalie, but she hadn't run out from the back like she usually did when the door clanged. She must not have heard the wind chimes either.

"So?" I asked. "It's winter. I'm sure she'll make it up when things pick up."

"Dr. Dog's thinking about expanding his business. To this location."

"Location's good, but it's a little small," he said, shaking a package of incense.

I walked over to the veterinarian and snatched the incense from his grasp. "Let me guess who Rosalie's landlord is," I said, gesturing with the box before putting it back on display. "Myles Donovan?"

The mayor didn't answer.

My face grew hot with anger. Rosalie had begun keeping the Purple Pony about five degrees colder than most businesses, but I could feel the sweat threatening my cute curly up-do. I took my cardigan off. "The Purple Pony has been around for decades, and she has quite the following among the wealthy ladies at Landover Lake. I can guarantee if Myles Donovan kicks Rosalie out, the women at the country club will revolt."

"Most of 'em are already pretty revolting," Dr. Dog laughed from across the room.

The mayor chuckled. "It's funny how famous you think you are. I doubt losing the Purple Pony would even make the papers." He tsk-ed. "And to think, I had such high hopes for that seance to help y'all out over here. Such a shame. Heard it got cancelled."

"You heard wrong," Rosalie said, coming out of the backroom. "It's actually going on, for free. Here at the Purple Pony. There's a demand for it, from my new clientele. The college kids."

"The college? Everyone hates the college. They're out-of…" he stopped himself.

"Out-of-towners?" I said through gritted teeth. I took a deep breath. "Yes, most of them are. And so am I. Maybe that's why I'm so interested in an accident that involved a couple of out-of-towners, even though it happened way back when. And that reminds me. I'm actually glad you're here, Mayor Bowman. I have some questions for you about that night. Thank you for saving me the trip in to see you." I strutted across the room to the checkout counter, a new-found confidence in my step.

I grabbed my purse and plopped it on the counter, careful not to let his aunt's notebook out. "Let me just find my recorder. You don't mind if I record your answers, do you?" I said, sifting through my stuff. I looked up when the wind chime clanged again. He and Dr. Dog were gone, for now.

I turned to Rosalie. "When were you going to tell me about the rent?"

She didn't answer, didn't even cuss. She just put her head down and shuffled into the backroom again. I grabbed my phone from my purse and texted Lynette about the seance. This needed to be my best one yet.

CHAPTER 23

A LITTLE BIRD TOLD ME

*O*n my way up Gate Hill, it hit me. *B wants article on FM. DS driving him crazy. Bury it.*

B had to be Bill. I was guessing FM was Feldman Martin. But who or what was DS? Not too many people in life were allowed to drive Bill Donovan crazy.

I put my car into park, flicked on the overhead light, and went back to that page. I glanced up at my gas tank to make sure I had enough gas not to get stranded on Gate Hill, seeing how I no longer had rations.

Then, I checked through every page. Sure enough, in between the egg-nog recipes was an almost complete article about Feldman-Martin, including scribbled notes in the margin that read, "Bury behind the recipes, just before Santa's mall location."

Local Financial Firm to Close Its Doors Early Next Year

After forty years, local brokerage firm Feldmen Marten is going out of business amid allegations of fraud and embezzlement with a scheme some experts are calling reminiscent of Charles Ponzi.

The firm allegedly took money from new clients to pay off earlier investors until too many clients demanded payment and it became apparent that they could not cover the amounts.

"It's devastating to realize you've been a victim," Mrs. Delilah Scott said, of Potter Grove. "You trust people and consider them family."

DS was Delilah Scott, Bill's cousin. The only person allowed to drive Bill crazy over a bad investment, and probably the only reason the article about Feldman Martin had even been written.

Carefully, I inched my car around so I could head back down Gate Hill without getting stuck in the snowbanks around me.

Ten minutes later, I found myself trudging up the front walkway to Delilah Scott's door. I actually had no idea if she was even home. Ninety-year-olds rarely strayed from home, except this one.

Delilah Scott liked to go on safaris to exotic lands when the weather here in Wisconsin didn't suit her tastes. My breath surrounded me in a puffy, frozen cloud as I scanned the snow piling up along her garden boxes. I could not imagine this suiting anyone's tastes.

Delilah's cottage could only have been described as "straight out of a storybook." It was cream colored with dark green accents and a rich chocolate colored roof that made you want to eat it. Or maybe I was the only one who got hungry over roofs. I made a mental note to my growling stomach that I would replenish my emergency car rations as soon as I got home.

I knocked at the door, surprised when it opened. Delilah Scott looked around her front porch when she saw me. "Come on in," she said like she'd been expecting someone else. She motioned for me to hurry inside and offered me tea. The room smelled like vanilla and chamomile, and I couldn't accept the offer fast enough.

I'd only met Delilah a few times, but this was the first time I'd ever been inside her house, which was equally as adorable on the inside, decorated with the kind of handcrafted antiques that were designed to outlive all of us. They were at least a hundred-years strong and just getting stronger.

She motioned for me to sit on one of her claw-footed stuffed chairs that looked a lot like a throne. Her silky turquoise blouse billowed with every movement as she casually peeked around the curtains of her bay window.

I looked around, too, immediately noticing there wasn't a TV, but there were a lot of properly bookmarked books and note-books at every accent table, unlike my books that got dog-eared or left opened on their spines.

"I heard you were investigating the boating accident from the 1950s," she said.

"Yes, the *accident*," I replied, emphasizing the word accident so she'd know I didn't really think it was one. "And, in my research, I keep coming across the Feldman Martin scandal. Can you tell me more about that? I read you were one of the victims."

"It wasn't just me, dear," she began. "Most of the well-to-do in town were taken in by it."

She poured my tea from a shiny silver tea set already sitting on the coffee table, making me wonder if she lived this way, prepared for guests at a moment's notice, or if she'd been expecting someone else when I showed up.

She went on. "Dwight was a friend, and it hurt to have him rob me and my husband. He claimed he was innocent. It was always the firm's fault. They had refused to pay him his owed commissions and they were unduly blaming him for their finan-cial woes. The firm said Dwight had embezzled millions from their clients. There were lawsuits filed and then Dwight Linder had his accident, so we'll never know."

"I assume there was an investigation."

"The firm quietly closed its doors, yes, but as one of the victims, I can tell you we did not receive anything. The whole thing was tainted in speculation, rumor, and sneaky trails of paperwork. I never talked to Bill again. He was the one who told me to trust this."

"Your cousin," I said. *How could this sweet, refined woman be related to the man who beat Gloria to a pulp?* "Did Bill get swindled too?"

She chuckled. "Nobody swindled Bill."

And lived to tell about it... I thought, but didn't say.

"Tell me about the investment."

"By the time my husband and I invested, it was already the talk of the town," she said. "I was actually mad at Bill for not letting us in on it sooner. I obviously regret that."

"You seem to be doing all right," I said, looking around.

"Yes. Thankfully, we were one of the lucky ones who didn't put everything into it. We were all issued promissory notes, some mumbo-jumbo about investing in Eurodollars after the war that were unregulated by the Federal Reserve." She paused to sip her tea. "It was really just a pyramid scheme that went on for years, earlier investors being paid by newer ones. That's all I remember. You'd have to ask someone from Feldman Martin if you want more specifics. "

"Do you know of anyone," I asked. "I'd also like to find out what happened from their end."

She laughed. "May I remind you I am over 90? I doubt too many of us are still around who can tell you much…" she stopped herself. "No, I do know someone. I was surprised to see her when I visited a friend at Landover Assisted Living a couple months ago. Dwight Linder's secretary. Waved to me from across the room as if we were friends. I could've strangled her."

"I'm sure the poor woman had no idea about the firm she worked for," I said.

Delilah pursed her lips. "I don't know about that. She married one of the firm's owners right after the scandal. Tell me that's not suspicious. Name's Bertie Martin. I knew her as Bertie Hawthorne back then."

Somehow, I held in my tea, refusing to do a spit-take all over the thousand-dollar Oriental rug under my feet, mostly because I'd probably be asked to pay for it. Bertie Hawthorne was the girl in the bird attack. I thanked Delilah for the tea then headed out the door.

Glancing over at the last second, I caught the older woman writing something into a notebook on the coffee table, a small glass bird sitting just to the right of her. And my heart flopped into my stomach. From the angle I was standing at, she looked just like the picture of the woman in the scrapbook with the bird figurine, on one of the pages marked "Signs."

She closed the notebook before I could see what she was writing then stood to walk me to the door.

"Interesting figurine," I said, motioning toward the bird. "Funny, there's a picture of one just like it in a scrapbook I found at Gate House."

"I'm sure it only looks similar. This is one of a kind, and has been in my family for generations." She smiled. "I adore crystal sparrows, though, mostly because they symbolize spring. Changes. Things coming to light. And new beginnings to follow. Some people fear change. Almost as if they're afraid to choose sides. Me? I'm having a hard time waiting this winter out."

We walked to the door, and I somehow stopped myself from asking just what in the hell was going on here. Why had she suddenly started talking in some sort of cryptic, poetic riddles? And if that crystal bird was one of a kind, how did she just recreate a photo I had sitting in my scrapbook, down to the angle of the back of her head in relation to the bird and the notes?

I stopped at the door. "I'm glad you were home. I was almost worried you'd be on safari someplace," I said instead of everything else I was thinking.

"I try to go where it's most important to be."

I had no idea how to respond to that.

But I knew where I was heading next.

"Directions to Landover Assisted Living," I said to my phone on my way out to my car. It was already getting dark, and I wondered how long visiting hours lasted.

Just as I headed down Delilah's quaint, tree-lined street, a black SUV passed me, heading toward Delilah's house. I thought about turning around to see if it would pull into her driveway. But I stopped myself. I was acting crazy and paranoid.

People could have guests, and I didn't need to know about them, even when 100-year-old photos were unintentionally recreated and cryptic messages were being tossed around like they were normal conversation.

I did a quick three-point turn and headed back to Delilah's. Something wasn't right and I just wanted to check, but it was too late. The SUV was parked in her driveway, the door to her house just closing.

I shook it off and drove straight home to see the photo in that scrapbook again. I was going crazy. There could be no way one of the 100-year-old photos labeled "signs" in a dead guy's scrapbook was actually something that just happened.

CHAPTER 24

PHOTOGRAPHIC EVIDENCE

*D*ust spilled out from the pages of the scrapbook when I plopped it down on the dining room table, and I held in a sneeze. This thing hadn't been touched in ages.

I almost didn't want to look. The Dead Forest. The weird signs. I was just hallucinating. I needed a break from channeling. It was the only thing that made sense.

Still, I opened right to the pages on signs. There it was. The exact one-of-a-kind sparrow figurine from Delilah's, along with the back of the woman's head. Light, probably gray hair swept neatly into an up-do while the lady in the photo overlooked her notes, wearing what looked like Delilah's same billowy blouse.

I closed the book so hard more dust popped out.

What in the hell was going on?

I opened it back up again. Same photo. Same angle. Leaning over toward the credenza at the back of the room, I was just able to open the drawer and grab my own notebook.

I needed to write down everything that woman said. Every cryptic riddle.

I bit the end of my pencil.

Damn it. Why hadn't I paid more attention?

I took a deep breath. I could do this.

She said something about changes. I remembered that, and new beginnings. And taking sides. And something about sparrows, I think.

I pulled one of the other photos out of the scrapbook and turned it over and over in my fingertips, fully expecting to see "Hello Carly" scrawled on the back now, but completely thankful I didn't. The photo was old and fragile and had that dank smell that old paper sometimes took on. I smoothed it back into its spot, wondering now if this whole thing with Delilah was a fluke or if other cryptic messages were coming my way related to these signs.

Delilah's sudden weirdness had thrown me off my game, but that wasn't going to happen again. If anyone else handed me some sort of weird message, I was going to call them out on it. Ask questions. Be prepared. Shelby Winehouse once told me she didn't think Potter Grove was safe anymore, like things were changing. I felt it too, but I also felt connected to its strangeness.

I spent the rest of the night taking as many photos of Aunt Ethel's notebook as I could. Jackson appeared by my side as I was reviewing them, and I tried to fill him in on everything new about the investigation, but the ghost was even moodier than usual.

"Looks like you've been very busy," he said, his voice dripping in sarcasm. "But were you able to link Myles Donovan to Gloria's murder?"

"Not yet, but I have a feeling if I uncover the cover-up, I'll be able to link everything. And I'm very close." I began filling Jackson in on the stuff he missed, which was mostly that I had his aunt's notebook in my possession.

He didn't even smile.

"That woman took full advantage of the fact she had the power to publish a career-damaging story or sit on one. I think she was taking bribes all over the place. And, I think she was in on the investment. Her notebook is full of lies."

"So, I can tell you're dying for me to ask. How did you get her notebook?"

I turned my head to the side. "Oh yeah. You weren't there." I shrugged. "I guess Rosalie's sachets work."

"I guess so." He crossed his arms.

I sat up. "So that's what this is about. You're upset about the privacy recipe Rosalie gave me." I rolled my eyes. "I've only used the sachets one day. One day. And you can't even handle that."

"Need I remind you, we have an investigation to do together, and I feel like I'm on the outside of it now." His voice had the condescending tone again, the one I hated back when he was my professor in college too.

I egged him on. "You should've been there when Lynette brought in this notebook. Thanks for telling me about her phone call, by the way, not that you're my secretary." I laughed. "I think my mouth dropped to the floor when I saw the notebook. You would've loved it."

He stared at me, the clock in the living room ticking noisily in the background.

I held up the small black journal. "And this thing proves your aunt was close to a lot of scandals in Potter Grove. I bet you'd love to see it."

"Perhaps," he said, with jealous eyes. "But, Ethel is dead. Even if you prove she got away with every pyramid scheme out there, it doesn't implicate Myles Donovan for the murders of these people. Come on, Carly. Focus on what's important."

"Sorry, professor. I no longer care if I get a B."

With Aunt Ethel's notebook in hand, I grabbed my phone and stormed up the stairs, but Jackson was right on my heels. People are so much faster when they're dead.

"I don't need to explain my research to you, but I'm pretty sure staging the Linders' deaths was the only way out of that investment for a lot of people," I said as I ran up the second flight, hurrying down the hall to my room. "Your aunt included. And staging deaths are much easier when you have the police and the press in on it."

"Are you implying my father…" Jackson replied, or tried to. He crossed Rosalie's stinky strands and disappeared mid sentence. I smirked to myself.

I finished my research alone.

I WAITED until I got a text from Lynette that the Herndons had left for dinner before making my way over to the newspaper the next day.

The office was hotter than most people set their heaters, and cleaner than it was before. I pulled my knit hat off as soon as I got in and fanned myself with its cuteness.

"You were right," Lynette said when she looked up from her computer and saw me. She waved me over to her desk, which was just a small, cluttered table off in the corner. "There was more than just the notebook."

She brought up a window on her laptop, peering over her shoulder toward the door. She whispered. "I'm pretty sure they would kill me if they knew I was snooping. These are the pictures the photographer took of the accident in 1957. Only a couple made it into the article."

I pulled a chair over to her desk and sat down. There were ten grainy, black-and-white images on the screen.

Each image looked strikingly similar to the last. Five images of the stretchers being pulled from the lake, a boat being lifted out of the water, a close-up of the beer bottles floating along the shore.

But I noticed something odd. "Look," I said, pointing toward the screen where the photos all went in sequential order

IMG0167 was right next to IMG0168, and on down the line. "Image 173 and image 174 are missing," I said.

Lynette nodded.

I quickly grabbed my phone from out of my purse and took pictures of everything on the screen, trying to guess what the missing pictures could have been from the photos that surrounded them. IMG0172, the image before the missing ones, was a picture of Mason Bowman, sheriff at the time, talking to someone. Unfortunately, I could only see the back of that person's head. Ball cap, about the same height as Mason. IMG0175 was a photo of the boats involved in the accident.

It was hard, even now, to see the old photos of the paramedics with their stretchers, knowing who was under the sheets and how they got there.

Lynette pointed to the screen with her pencil. "I'll text you these photos along with a picture of the article I found about the Linders. Their remains washed ashore in October," she said. "And — huge surprise here — their names were misspelled."

October. That would explain why I hadn't found the article. I'd only looked at reels from before that.

"Remains. Are we talking bodies or clothes?"

"It didn't say. I assume bodies."

"Don't assume anything with this paper." I was really getting annoyed with Aunt Ethel's journalism standards. "Send it to me anyway," I said as I took the liar's notebook from my purse and handed it to Lynette, just as a cold wind shot through the office from an opened door. Because I have that kind of luck.

I looked up and into the eyes of a chubby, balding man in armpit-reaching jeans and a tucked-in polo shirt. "What's going on here? Some sort of party? I thought we said no friends…"

Lynette stuffed the notebook in her pocket.

"She's not a friend, Dan," Grace said from behind him. "She's the medium I was telling you about. The one doing a seance on the old accident. The one who practically called my grandmother a murderer."

I waved to the man. "That's me, minus the murderer part. And, to clarify, I don't think your grandmother was a murderer. She was simply a journalist before ethics were a thing."

Lynette chuckled by my side and Grace scowled at her.

I searched my purse for my hat as I headed toward the door, trying to think on my feet, which was not my strong suit. "Anyway, just forgot my hat the other day. Thankfully, your intern found it. She is a treasure to have around. So helpful."

Judging by the glares on my way out, I wasn't sure they bought it. But at least they hadn't seen the notebook. I smiled to myself as I walked to my car. Maybe my luck was changing.

Sitting in my car outside the newspaper office, I looked over the article Lynette sent me while my car warmed up again. Like the intern said, the article only mentioned remains.

Remains believed to be those of Dwight Linder and his son, Frederick, were discovered just south of the country club late last night when a passerby spotted them along the shore. Mr. Linder and his son were last seen July 20 on a boat owned by family friend and business partner, Bill Donovan.

That was it. I wondered if the article had been buried behind the tips for safe trick-or-treating. I was just about to bring up the photos when a text came in.

For real? You were the one who wanted to try the spin class. Where are you?

It was Justin. I was letting this investigation ruin my relationship again. I texted back. "*On my way. Meet you at your place in 10.*"

CHAPTER 25

SPIN CYCLES

*J*ustin smirked at the receptionist when we checked in at Donovan's gym, like they were sharing a joke. "We're here to learn bike riding," he said.

I couldn't take my eyes off the humungous smiling photo of Myles Donovan placed above the waiting bench in the lobby. It was the same one that stalked you in the hallway of the Grocery Ranch if you ever had to use the bathroom and the one at the main lodge of the country club. A cheesy, promotional, "I'm important because I'm in this suit" photo, mostly there to remind employees they're being watched.

I almost pointed at the smug old man and yelled something about how he was going down, but instead followed Justin into the room the perky receptionist told us to go to.

"Hey, you guys made it," Parker said. He was dressed like he shopped in the Tour-de-France section of Big Five: bright yellow top and tight-fitting spandex biker shorts. "You both ready?" He clapped his hands together.

"Ready?" Justin rolled his eyes. "To ride a pretend bike? Yeah, I think I'm ready. Are you ready, Carly?"

Parker didn't seem to pick up on the macho-sarcasm coming

from my boyfriend, and I wasn't entirely sure whether Justin's bad attitude was directed at me or Parker. He was still on trash duty, and despite the "you're probably onto something big" speech he gave me the other day, I knew he was still pissed.

The spin class was empty except for the two rows of exercise bikes and the three of us. Parker's bike faced us, and when he got on it, Justin leaned in and whisper-yelled, "Is this guy seriously going to show us how to ride a bike?"

I shrugged as hip hop music began to play.

"We're going to keep it slow to begin with," Parker said, cycling away like he was just strolling around a park. "A nice easy pace. Get the heart rate going."

I looked to my side. Justin's "nice easy pace" looked more like a killer was chasing him. Every once in a while, he'd look over at me and roll his eyes, which I couldn't help but think was adorably confusing.

Was he trying to impress me with his bike riding skills or was he working out some anger issues?

"We're just warming up," Parker reminded Justin. "You don't have to go so fast."

Justin half-smiled. "I want this to actually be a workout, dude."

"Okay," Parker said as the music began to pick up. "Then get ready. Let's go." The music went at triple speed and so did our pace, except for Justin's because he was already going pretty fast. Parker woo-hoo-ed and stood up. We followed him. At first it was fine, but after about thirty seconds I was ready to sit back down again. Each pedal felt like a million. My butt hurt, along with part of the back of my thighs where I hadn't even realized I had muscles. Justin was doing even worse than I was.

Sweat poured from his purplish face. He guzzled his water. Parker was barely sweating. "Everyone okay?" he asked, obviously directing his question to the heart-attack by my side.

Justin nodded, puffed out his chest, and picked up the pace again.

"Good. Because that was the beginning round. Let's raise it up a notch. This is why they pay me the big bucks. Because I get results." Parker turned a knob on his bike and Justin and I both followed suit. And suddenly, it felt like we were riding uphill, slower, harder. Parker stood up again and so did I. Justin stopped pedaling and drank some water.

"Do whatever you're comfortable with," Parker said, and Justin glared at him before turning his knob even higher and fast-peddling again.

After about five minutes of this, I was pretty sure my boyfriend was on the verge of death. He was making weird, raspy, gasping noises, kind of like a wild animal with emphysema.

I grabbed the side of my stomach and stopped. "Sorry, Parker," I said. "I'm out of shape, and I have a cramp. I'll need the beginner class from now on."

"This is the beginner class," he replied, still standing as he rode, not even sweating at all. "My advanced class is in half an hour."

"Let's go home," I said to my out-of-shape boyfriend.

Justin stopped pedaling and sucked in another strange-sounding gasp of air. "Only if you're sure you've had enough," he managed to say.

He grabbed my water on the way to the lobby and chugged it down because he'd finished his. Then he turned to wave to Parker, putting his arm around me.

"Impressive job out there, *dude*," Parker yelled to Justin. "You certainly made pretend bike riding into a real workout."

"Be prepared to bench press next time," Justin yelled back as we left. "I want you to know what a real workout feels like."

He turned to me as soon as we were out of earshot. "He was being sarcastic, huh?"

"Oh yeah," I said. "I thought you were pretty impressive, though."

Justin kept a normal pace as we passed the receptionist and some other clients in the parking lot until we reached his truck where he practically collapsed into the passenger's seat, weakly demanding that I drive because he'd pulled something.

"Let's go to Spoony River. I'm starving," he said.

"Exercise and a healthy meal?" I replied. "We're living to a hundred."

I leaned over and gave him a very light kiss on his very sweaty cheek, even though he didn't deserve it. The sun was already setting and dinner sounded good to me too. I pulled across the parking lot as a gorgeous blonde in an expensive black SUV pulled in, blaring Taylor Swift.

"I cannot believe it," I said, taking my foot off the gas and throwing the truck into park. "Lila Donovan's here."

Justin barely opened his eyes from his fetal position in the passenger's seat. "So?"

"So, that's a pretty big coincidence, don't you think? Myles Donovan's granddaughter has been following me all over town since I started snooping into that accident. Or I've been following her. Not sure yet."

"Maybe you should just stop snooping," Justin said. He groaned and rolled over, his seatbelt curled uncomfortably around his thick neck.

"The library. The newspaper. And now this."

I also realized she had probably been the one heading to Delilah's earlier for tea. Delilah's distant cousin, and probably her namesake.

I turned around and watched her park, straining my neck to see if she was even wearing a workout outfit. "I cannot picture that woman breaking a sweat."

She got out of her SUV and sauntered across the parking lot in leggings and a cute coat, a different cute coat than the day at the library. How many cute coats could one incredibly rich person own? I mindlessly fixed my hair, pulling my curls out of their sweaty ponytail and swishing my head around, pieces of frizz sticking to my cheeks. I checked my hair in the mirror, noticing Lila looking over at me. She waved and I ducked into my seat.

"She's watching me," I said.

"Well, you are the only vehicle just sitting in the parking lot, idling by the entrance. She probably thinks she knows you."

I lifted my head up again as she went inside. "Do you think she's going to the advanced spin class?" I asked as I pulled forward toward the exit.

"Probably," Justin replied. "Rich people have time to excel at things like pretend bike riding."

"And did you hear Parker say he was getting paid the big bucks? I bet they're overpaying him so they can control Mildred's family again."

"Carly, you're being very paranoid."

He didn't know the half of it.

I knew I needed to ask him about the forest. It was still playing heavily on my mind. "Speaking of probably just being paranoid," I began. "When I left your apartment the other night, I thought I saw you going into the Dead Forest. Did you?"

He groaned and rolled back over so he was facing me again. "Now, I'm really worried about you. What? Why would I go into the Dead Forest? Why would anyone? I mean, I'm not afraid of it and I don't believe the rumors, but it's also not something I would do. It might be time for you to see someone."

I leaned back in my seat. He was right. Damn it. My phone rang, and I pulled it out of my purse, half wondering if it was really ringing or if I was hallucinating again.

"It's not a good idea to talk on the phone while you're driving," said the police officer beside me.

"I wouldn't be driving, officer, if my boyfriend hadn't pulled something pretending he and Lance Armstrong shared steroids."

The call was from California. Gloria's sister maybe.

My hands fumbled trying to answer it fast enough. "June Gilman? Hi. This is Carly Taylor…" I put her on speaker, and pulled down the road toward Potter Grove and the Spoony River. "This is probably going to be the strangest phone call of your life," I said.

Justin groaned even louder from the passenger's seat, but I ignored him.

Her voice was shaky and I could tell her hearing was a little off. "What's this about again? How do you know Gloria?"

"I'm investigating your sister's death," I yelled, watching my boyfriend turn closer toward the window. "I'm gathering information about a possible cover-up from 60 years ago."

"Who is this now? And what do you want from me?"

Not exactly how I'd pictured things going. I held the phone closer to my mouth. Justin shook his head when he saw how I was driving.

I went back to my conversation. "I'm a medium."

"A what?"

"A person who can connect with ghosts, talk to them, and your sister came to me. Gloria wants you to know the truth about that night. She wants you to know what happened. She loves you and…"

A man's voice shouted from somewhere in June's room. "Mom? Who's that on the phone? You okay?"

I rushed the rest of my message. "I'm going to be exposing the truth next Saturday at a seance at the Landover Bed and Breakfast in Wisconsin. Gloria will be there. I know it's short notice, but if you've got some frequent flier miles…"

"A seance? You want me to go to a seance in Wisconsin a week from today?" she said.

Her son's voice got louder. "Who are you talking to?"

"It's about Gloria," she said to the man. "Some woman is claiming Gloria wants me to go to a seance in Wisconsin. She's a medium."

The man got on the phone. "Hello?" He didn't wait for me to answer. "What is wrong with you? You've made my mother cry. I will never know what kind of a person calls up a vulnerable senior citizen like this, but if you call again, I will alert the authorities. She's not going to a seance."

"But I can prove…"

"I don't care what you can prove, lady. We don't want any."

My face felt hot. "Just tell her Gloria said, 'It's okay, Bug. We'll get 'em next time.'"

"I'm not telling her squat. If you call again, I'm taking this straight to the police."

I hung up the phone and slipped it back into my purse. "Shoot," I said. "I forgot to tell June the location's not at the bed and breakfast anymore." I told Justin about how Paula Henkel had called the seance off but how I was just about to expose everything for free. "Maybe I should call them back."

Justin pointed to the road. "Just take me home," he said. "I'm not feeling up to dinner."

He didn't say a word the rest of the way.

CHAPTER 26

PROS AND CONS

It was already dark when we got back to Justin's. I parked next to my car even though I wasn't ready to leave yet. And I hoped he wasn't ready to let me leave.

I leaned into him. "You want me to pick something up for dinner and bring it back for us? We could vedge out on the couch and see what's on HBO?"

He inhaled deeply like he was going to say something then exhaled without saying anything.

I could tell. This boiling frog was about to jump the pot. He thought my investigation wasn't worth it, and he was right, but I was still doing it.

The engine rumbled and hummed, the only sound in the car other than the disappointment sighs coming from my right.

I looked at my cell phone. "Is it really almost eight? I have to feed Rex and put some dishes away, straighten the living room."

I shut the engine off.

"I think I pulled something in my leg," he said. "I'll probably go to bed early, anyway."

"Are we breaking up?" I asked just before I opened the door.

He looked at me, but he didn't say "no."

I threw the door open.

"There are so many things I like about you…" he began.

"Oh no. This sounds an awful lot like another pros and cons list," I said. "You pulled that crap twelve years ago, and now, here we go. Round two."

His eyes grew large.

Snow fell softly outside and a gush of wind blew in from the opened door. I closed it again so I could rant in comfort. "You didn't know I found that, huh? Twelve years ago. Your little pros and cons list. It was right by your computer, so I'm pretty sure you wanted me to find it. And now, it sounds like you're starting another one."

"If I remember right, twelve years ago," he began. "The only thing on my cons list was that you were a little immature and you liked to pick fights."

"That's not quite the way it was phrased on the piece of paper. I believe the words *childish* and *moody* were used."

"I'm not so sure you'd find a different list now."

I opened the door again and got out, slamming it behind me. I looked back momentarily then kicked myself for doing it because then I knew, he wasn't looking back at me.

I got in my Civic and shivered while it warmed up, watching as Justin walked to his apartment.

He could've at least faked a limp.

THE WHOLE WAY home I tried to get my mind off of Justin. It felt an awful lot like we'd broken up, even though we hadn't officially. He was so confusing to me. On the one hand, he said he liked my crazy. But on the other, he always seemed so upset whenever I talked about it.

And how dare he call me moody and childish? He was the one who was moody and childish, the jack-ass bastard.

Ohmygod. I was making a pros and cons list while being moody and childish.

I decided to concentrate on what the missing images could have been from that night, and why they'd been deleted. Maybe the newspaper didn't want anyone to find out who the sheriff had been talking to, in case anyone ever investigated things.

I turned my car onto Gate Hill, thinking I saw a shadow in the distance. I hit the door locks and looked out at the falling snowflakes, drifting along the darkness. No shadows. Nothing but darkness. I took a deep breath and pinched the bridge of my nose, just in case another episode was starting and I was hallucinating.

"Not a good time for one of those," I said to myself, like timing was the only thing I should be concerned about.

Just as I pulled past the first old, dilapidated gate that was always left open for convenience, I realized there were headlights behind me. Someone was following me. And it was obviously a large vehicle, like a truck.

Justin. He was coming to say he was sorry, not that we were fighting. But it was about time.

I slowed down to let the lights get closer, thinking about the full-on grovel session I was going to make the man go through as soon as he caught up. That was the least he could do after calling me moody and childish.

I quickly texted: "Is that you? Hope you're prepared to apologize." I didn't get a response. We were probably too far into the no-cell-phone-coverage area of the hill for that, though.

When the truck got close enough, I realized it easily towered over my vehicle. Much too big to be Justin's and it also wasn't exactly slowing down like you'd expect oncoming traffic to do. I threw my foot on the gas pedal but it was too late. The truck hit the back of my Civic hard, shooting me forward into my seatbelt. A pain shot up my neck and my teeth smacked together.

Had the good ole boys network lost its flipping mind? How obvious was it going to be if I turned up dead?

And there was my problem, right there. I'd been trying to apply logic to a situation that defied it.

As mad as I was, I needed to do something. I gently turned my car around to head back down the hill to safety, but the truck backed up and blocked my way, like it was daring me to try. It revved its engine, gray exhaust pouring menacingly from around the sides of the black vehicle. I pressed the park button on my hybrid and revved my engine too. Two could play at this game. My car gently hummed, just as pathetic as I thought it'd be. But I needed to let this guy know I was not intimidated. I probably should have been, though. It wasn't going to take much to send my car into a "stranded-without-granola-bars" area of the hill.

We stood there a moment, both of us revving and humming, until I backed up to try to turn around and go up the hill. Even though he was in a truck, I could probably make it up to the house faster because I'd done it so many times. Maybe get a little help from the ghosts at my house and the house itself if I was quick enough.

I heard the roar of the truck's engine again just as I was about to put my car into drive. It crashed into the side of my vehicle, spinning me around. Left was right and right was left, and I suddenly had a flashback of splashing around in the lake, coughing out water, knowing that a human could only tread water for so long.

My final moment was coming if I wasn't careful. But just like Gloria, it wasn't coming without a good fight. My car finally landed in the snowbank, my head smacking against the steering wheel while the taste of blood formed along my bottom lip. I checked my car over. The passenger's side door was dented, but everything else seemed fine. Facing the opposite direction to the truck now, I saw the driver in my mirror, wearing black, face obscured by a dark ski mask.

I tried to pull forward. But my wheels spun helplessly in the snow without moving the car. I pushed harder on the gas.

Crap. Crap. Crap.

I was stranded. All the guy had to do now was drive back down and I'd probably die here. Damn those granola bars.

Just in case leaving me stranded wasn't his plan, I grabbed my coat from the back, the mace from my glove compartment, and the Swiss army knife that probably wasn't going to do much. And waited.

The truck backed up again, but not like it was turning around to leave. I didn't even turn off my car. I unbuckled my seatbelt and took off into the snow, ducking behind a boulder that was sitting nearby. I threw my coat on, zipping it up and readying my mace and my knife. Snow fell all around me as the bitter cold shot through to my bones.

He's going to demolish my car, I know it. Or he's coming after me.

My nose ran and my hands shook as I shivered with my mace, listening to his truck just idling there, taunting me.

My breath puffed out in little clouds in front of me, giving my location away. I tried to slow it down. But I was just getting colder and more hysterical. I sniffed in a tear. This was a game of cat-and-mouse, all right.

And this sicko wanted me to make a move, or freeze to death.

And that's when I heard it. A growling noise.

The noise was low and loud and I turned my head this way and that to try to tell where it was coming from. It didn't sound like the birds from the channeling.

A dark shadow emerged from the other side of my boulder, followed by the largest black bear I'd ever seen. It didn't even hesitate, and neither did I. I threw myself against the rock as it charged past me and over to the truck.

And I realized I had a chance to run back to my nice, warm car.

As soon as my butt hit the seat, I slammed the door shut and locked it, not that bears could open doors. Then I somehow held in my fear-pee, watching as the humungous rodent-like beast scraped the paint and metal of the truck, breaking the side window with what seemed like a mere tap of its paw. A long series of expletives came from the the man in the mask. "What the… I'll kill you," he yelled over and over again in a voice I didn't recognize. The bear opened its jaws, drawing its head closer to the man.

The truck shot backwards in reverse, sliding along the snow as it turned around and took off down the hill without the man killing anyone.

And I let my face fall into my hands. I took one long breath after another, thanking my lucky stars until I remembered that whoever was driving that truck probably wasn't about to call for help for me when he got back down the hill. And I was still stuck in the snow. With a bear. And no rations.

I cursed Rosalie's stinky sachets right now. If I hadn't defiantly stuffed them in my pockets, I might have had some ghost help right now.

"Shouldn't you be hibernating?" I whispered to the bear as I ducked down into my seat, hoping the large animal would forget about me.

No wonder that thing was so angry. We'd either woken it up or it was a shifter, helping me.

Please God let it be a shifter.

My head suddenly smacked against the side of my window, knocking me out of my pity party, as my car lifted on its side then fell back down again.

I screamed then got it together. This could still be a shifter.

Somehow, I got myself to peek out, into the humungous jaws of the angry bear, who didn't at all seem human or like he was helping me. He smacked his side into my window, and I tried to stay calm through the jostling. Maybe this thing would accidentally kill itself while trying to kill me and then I would have a whole bear for rations. Or maybe, it would get tired and leave. There were still many options if you were delusional enough.

Those were the thoughts I clung to, until my Civic let out a sad, metal-crushing noise that let me know it was tagging out of the fight. It was no match for the animal swinging its weight into the side of it, over and over again.

After a minute, the rocking stopped.

I no longer heard a thing. I peeked out the window, my finger on the trigger of the mace the whole time, even though I had no idea if mace worked as bear spray.

The bear was scampering off in the direction it came from.

And I threw my car into drive, surprised that my wheels no longer spun when I put my foot on the gas pedal. I jerked unsteadily forward on wobbly tires. The bear had freed me. I knew for sure it was a shifter now.

"Thank you," I yelled to no one.

As soon as I got home, I swung the veranda door open, and stood in the kitchen a second, enjoying every ounce of relief I was entitled to. I'd escaped death once again, but I couldn't let myself stop for too long. I ran to the phone, not even checking to see if I had any messages. Oddly, I thought about calling my mother first. I stopped mid-dial, reminding myself I was the adult here. And she was probably in Mexico with her Nettie, anyway.

"Potter Grove Police Department," the familiar voice said.

My hand shook and I could barely keep the receiver up to my ear.

"Hi Christine. It's Carly. I need to report a crime," I said, my voice cracking. I told her all about the attempted murder with the truck and the bear smashing out the guy's window. "Look for a truck with a broken window and scratches on the paint."

As soon as I hung up, Jackson was by my side. "What in the world happened?" His faded eyes were large and concerned. It reminded me of the good years we had, how gentle and caring he could be when he tried, even when he was mad at me.

There was a knock on the door and I jumped out of my seat, hyperaware of everything at the moment, my nerves and adrenaline still in high gear. But I was also acutely aware that the guy in the truck could easily have come back. I should've told the police to come here first. I hadn't even heard a vehicle pull up the hill.

"Don't answer it," my ex said.

The knock got louder. "It's me, Justin."

I ran past Jackson and threw open the door, falling into the cold thick arms of my boyfriend.

"You got my text," I said, pulling him inside. I kissed his cheek and his lips. I barely noticed my ex-husband fading into the background. "You were right. Someone just tried to kill me. This investigation isn't worth it."

"No, you're the one who's right," he replied, pulling away. He hobbled over to the sofa.

He took off his jacket and his sweater, revealing spots where bruises were forming along his arm just under the sleeve of his t-shirt. "This town has too many secrets, and it's time we started exposing them."

He looked at me, and I knew. The bruises were right in the spot where the bear had smacked against my car.

CHAPTER 27

I spent most of the night at the police station, filling out a report and trying to describe the truck and the bear, making sure my description of the animal didn't sound a thing like the gorgeous man holding my hand.

Caleb was about as concerned as I thought he'd be, scratching at his dyed-dark goatee while raising a skeptical eyebrow at me. "So, you say a bear saved your life?"

Justin squeezed my hand, and I pulled away. "It sounds crazy, I know."

"It sounds like a joke," Caleb snapped. "You pulling my leg?"

I felt like Gloria when she'd tried to tell the police about the growling birds.

Justin stepped forward. He was about half a foot taller than Caleb, broader too, and he towered over the smallish man. "Carly's Civic is right out front," Justin said. "You can have a look at it yourself if you think she's joking."

"I'll get to that if I think it's worth it," Caleb replied.

"Since when is crime not worth investigating? Probably since you've been having your deputy clean trash cans and file reports," I yelled.

186

Justin pulled me outside before I could say anything else.

"I'm sorry. I'm making things worse," I said.

"Probably." He kissed me. "But thanks for trying to make it right. And I'm sorry for calling you moody and childish."

It was hardly the groveling session I'd been expecting, but I stood on my tiptoes and kissed his cheek anyway. The cold night air was already making me shiver, and I curled into the warmth of his jacket. "And I'm sorry for calling you a confusing, jack-ass bastard. That was in my car later, so you didn't hear it, but I thought you'd want to know."

He took me home, offering to stay with me and help me get a rental car the next day.

"I think you should go to the seance with me," I said as we walked up the steps to my back porch.

"Too weird," he replied.

I leaned in and whispered as close to his ear as I could get. "Now that I know your secrets, you can't pretend mine are the weird ones around here."

"Your secrets are weird."

"Said a talking bear."

He nodded, stomping his large boots onto the mat just outside Gate House. We went inside, and I pulled him straight through the kitchen and the living room and over to the stairs. "Come on. I'm making a pros and cons list. We'll see how you do," I teased. "How's your shoulder?"

"It's fine," he said. I couldn't tell if he was in pain or not.

"That's a pro. Holds up well under pressure." I was on the stair in front of him, yet I was still shorter. I kissed his cheek and made my way to his lips. I knew they'd be scratchy from his not-so-closely-shaved beard. I threw my arms around his neck and he easily lifted me, carrying me up both flights of stairs. If he was in pain, he did a good job of hiding it.

"I'm so glad you're strange like me," I said.

"I don't feel strange."

"We never do."

He stopped at the strands hanging along my bedroom door frame, sniffing and touching them.

"Rosalie's recipe for keeping ghosts out of my room," I said.

"I have to get this recipe," he replied, carrying me through the doorway, closing the door behind us.

I WOKE in his arms the next morning and it felt so good I almost forgot I had a seance to prepare for, and no idea how to prepare for it. Somehow, I needed to find evidence from today that tied Myles Donovan and the rest of his gang to the crime from 1957 in order for Gloria to get her justice. And no one in this town was helping.

But right now, the only thing I cared about was the bear beside me in bed.

"Good morning," I said the moment Justin opened his eyes. "So, how does this superpower of yours work, anyway?"

He blinked several times, his eyes barely focusing. "Wait, what?" He shook himself like he was trying to wake up. "Superpower what?"

"The shifting thing," I replied. "How does it work?"

He sat up along his pillow and I snuggled into him, smelling his neck. I could never explain why, but I always loved smelling his neck. It always made me feel safe and connected to him. Now, I wondered if it was because he smelled like a bear. I took another whiff. Lingering cologne and sweat.

He didn't answer me, so I went on. "Do you need to get angry to change?"

"You mean, like the Hulk?" His voice was curt as he looked at the ceiling. I could tell he didn't want to answer my questions. I wasn't sure why.

"No. I have more control over it than a comic book character. It's painful, yet compelling."

I nodded. It sounded a lot like the way channeling and the curse were to me.

"And how did you even know I was in trouble last night, anyway, Dr. Banner," I asked, sitting up.

"I had a feeling." Justin turned over to face me.

"Like a spidey sense?"

He always looked good in the morning. It was easier for men to rock the tousled, bed-hair look. I wondered if it was even easier for bears. I nervously twisted my frizzed-up curls into a makeshift bun, trying to get there.

I didn't want this new information about him to change things between us. I tried to look comfortable like nothing had changed, even though it had.

He ran a hand through his hair, and I noticed every muscle in his bare chest and arms. "I've been checking this area a lot since you told me about the snowplow incident. When you have a gorgeous, stubborn girlfriend who refuses to carry a gun and likes to stir up trouble in a town that doesn't like to be stirred, you pop in every once in a while to make sure she's okay."

I knew he was looking for a thank-you, but I wasn't feeling it. "I don't need protection," I said.

"I know. I wasn't asking."

I mindlessly ran a finger over his bare chest. It wasn't even hairy like you'd expect a bear shifter to be. "But thank you."

He was right. I probably should've carried a gun, but I didn't really like those. Plus, I had horrible aim. I changed the subject. "So, how many shifters are there? How does this all work? And…" Something came to me. "Is your neighbor a shapeshifter too? Neither of you were cold in the parking lot the night I was over despite the fact you weren't wearing coats. And that weird phone call in the middle of dinner. Was that like your top-secret, superhero call? I bet your whole apartment complex is full of bears, huh? And you all forage in the Dead Forest…"

"What? Now you've gone one-hundred percent out of your mind."

His smile was crooked, his teeth straight. He leaned over and pressed his mouth over mine, stopping my line of questioning with a long kiss. When we came up for air, he said, "One of these days we'll have a long talk about this whole thing. You can ask me questions about shifting and I'll ask you questions about being a medium."

"Deal." That was seriously a no-brainer. I could talk all day about the oddities of being me. I wasn't sure he was ready to hear those oddities, though.

"But we have to get going soon," he said. He got up and I watched him walk across my room to find his clothes and get dressed, muscles rippling like he stepped out of an erotica book. The man certainly did not need a spin class, which was a good thing because the man also did not know how to ride a pretend bike.

And he was right. I still had a seance to plan and a multimillionaire to cook, and slowly, so the frog wouldn't know.

CHAPTER 28

DOUBLE TROUBLE

The rental car made a weird grinding noise every time I turned on the heat. The radio didn't work, and the tires slid even more in the snow than my Civic. But it was cheap, and when cheap is all you can afford, you just drive like a grandma while listening to the beat of your heat grinding. It took me half an hour to get from the car rental place to the Purple Pony.

I knew as soon as I pulled in, Paula Henkel was either buying more snacks at the Bait n' Breath or she was harassing Rosalie. Probably both. Her large white truck took up two spots in the lot, like usual. As soon as I stepped inside, I noticed Lynette was there too.

"Got fired," she said as soon as she saw me.

"Sorry," I replied. "I guess they didn't buy my 'I'm just here because I forgot my hat' lie after all."

She shrugged. "No biggie. I'd rather have it this way. It wasn't like I was getting paid. And it's gonna look amazeballs on my resume when I put down what I was fired for. We've gotta nail that newspaper for covering up the murder and anyone else involved."

She stared at me like I should chime in with how, exactly, we were going to do that.

"Is that what we're all talking about here?" I said, directing my question to Rosalie and Paula Henkel more than Lynette.

"No, not exactly," Rosalie said. "We heard what happened last night on Gate Hill." She adjusted her head scarf. "Are you sure this is worth it?"

"Hell yes," I answered. "The only thing I'm not sure about is what you're doing here, Paula. The seance is at the Purple Pony now, for free. We need to make money and you are no longer getting a cut."

She pursed her lips. "And that's where we have our problem. I didn't know you did that. You should've told…"

Rosalie cut her off. "As soon as Lynette posted the free seance in the university's newspaper, somebody called Paula and bought up every damn ticket." She smiled, probably because she could use the money and was breathing a little easier. "So good news: we're not losing the farm. Bad news: They're either going to let the bed and breakfast sit empty or they're stacking the audience full of people like the Herndons."

"Nope," I corrected her. "The bad news is for whoever bought those tickets. The seance is here now, for free. So, the Donovans or whoever else bought the tickets can sit alone at the bed and breakfast and enjoy their buffet."

"You didn't tell me you changed the seance's location," Paula said, hands on her hips.

"I didn't need to. You told me you were giving me two days, and if I didn't hear from you in those two days, I should consider the seance cancelled. That was a long time ago. I considered it cancelled."

We scowled at each other for half a minute.

"So we have two seances at the same time, different locations," Rosalie said. "And the one with food may or may not have people attending."

I sat down on one of the stools my boss kept at various places around the shop so she could rest her bad hip whenever it acted up on her. "How many free tickets have you given away?" I asked Lynette.

"I just wrote to show up here at eight o'clock like you said. And I can't change that because the next edition of The Daily Bear doesn't go out until next week."

After debating for a while on the best plans, we ultimately agreed to do the seance at the bed and breakfast like originally planned, but to put a note up at the Purple Pony telling people about the location change so they'd know where it was at.

"What if those raggedy tag college kids come and eat all the food someone else paid for?" Paula asked.

I stared at her.

"This is Chez Louie we're talking about. The new fancy restaurant. This isn't Waffle Buffet."

"Rich people hardly eat anything," I said.

"And college kids eat everything and the napkins too, if you let 'em."

"Okay, valid point. If Myles Donovan and the rest of his gang actually show up to claim the dinner tickets, then we'll ask for tickets at the buffet line. Otherwise, the food is free for everyone," I said, reminding Paula that it had already been paid for, and profited from, so she shouldn't care who enjoyed it.

I scrolled through my phone as soon as the dreadful woman left. On the one hand, I needed to impress the college kids with a good seance full of ghosts and spooky stuff so they would become interested enough to want more from the Purple Pony. On the other hand, I needed to blow this case open using evidence and proof, and ghosts were not generally considered factual.

And so far, I really had neither.

"What can you borrow from the media center at LU?" I asked Lynette, an outrageous plan forming in my mind.

Maybe I could at least make this entertaining.

CHAPTER 29

SOMETIMES, FRIENDS TURN

$\mathcal{S}$everal little-old-lady faces peered through the blinds of the large front window, probably to see who was making "all that racket" when I pulled into the parking lot a couple days later in the car I was now calling the preacher, because it was loud and seemed to be demanding money at every turn.

Landover Assisted Living was a beautiful brick building with horizontal parking along a circular driveway and a ridiculous amount of shrubbery separating the parking lot from the walkway. I stumbled through the bushes instead of going around, waving to the faces that were still staring at the woman in the loud car who was so lazy she took awkward shortcuts through snow-covered bushes.

The place was really warm when I got inside, which made the combined smell of incontinence, medicine, and mac n' cheese make my gag reflexes act up.

"I'm here to see Bertha Martin," I said to the woman in scrubs at the front desk.

She pointed to the guest book. "Just sign in."

No ID required. No "Is she expecting you?" They were way too happy to have visitors at this hell hole.

"Bertie is down the main hall to the left, room 106."

I passed by the living room, where 80- and 90-year-olds sat around a large TV or played cards at tables. No wonder they'd been so interested in my car sounds. This place was seriously lacking in entertainment.

Bertie was a woman who could afford a lot of facelifts in life, and decided to purchase every single one of them. Her cheekbones were unusually high and pronounced, more like strange growths protruding under taut skin that seemed to also somehow make her lips seem frog-wide. She adjusted her short, dark wig when she saw me, but it was still askew.

"I thought you were Charlie," she mumbled, wringing her hands together, her long, bony fingers covered in rings.

The room held two beds and two chairs. The older lady sitting on the bed next to Bertha scoffed. "Stop talking about Charlie. He ain't comin'." She turned to me. "She's off her rocker again. Charlie's her son, but he don't come to see her."

"You don't know that," Bertha said.

"The hell I don't. When's the last time he came?"

"Thanksgiving."

"Maybe one of the Thanksgivings before I got here. He and the pilgrims brought you a turkey." She had white hair that almost matched her velour sweatsuit. She shook her head, turning her attention back to me. "Gets dressed for Charlie every single day. He ain't comin'." She was shouting now.

I leaned into Bertha. "Maybe there's a place we can go to have some privacy," I said ignoring her roommate. "My name's Carly Taylor. Delilah Scott sent me. She said you might know about the scandal way back when that involved the firm you used to work at."

"Delilah Scott. She came to visit me the other day."

I nodded. I didn't mention the part where she'd technically

come to see another friend and had originally wanted to strangle Bertha when she saw her waving to her.

Bertha stood up. "There's a computer room nobody uses too much."

We headed over to it. Fluorescent lights buzzed over our heads as we walked, at a pace only slightly faster than not moving at all.

"What do you remember about Dwight Linder?" I asked, taking her arm to help her along.

She smiled up at me. "I got fired because of him. And I got married because of him too. How about that?"

"Sounds like quite a story," I said.

"One of the owners at Feldman-Martin, Samuel Martin, took me out to lunch to see what I knew about Mr. Linder. I didn't know anything. How could I? I was just the secretary, fresh out of secretarial school to boot. It didn't matter. He was there to break the news to me that I was being fired, tell me how sorry he was they had to let me go. But something magical happened." She paused like she was remembering it. "We never had a better time. I was being fired and all I kept thinking about was what a marvelous time I was having at lunch. We married six months later, much to the chagrin of his children who were all older than me."

"That is a story," I said. "I married an older man too."

"Then you know. The problem with falling in love with an older man is there's never enough time for the good times. The age difference robs you of that."

"Nope," I said, shaking my head. "There just weren't enough good times, period. Nothing to do with time robbing me of them."

I thought it was best not to tell her the part where that dead older man and I were now roommates who solved murder cases together in our haunted house. Some things were best left unsaid.

"Sam used to tell me that if he'd met me sooner, it would

never have worked between us. He said he was a different person back then. Things are supposed to happen when they happen in life."

"Plus, years sooner and you would've been a child." I pointed out, then regretted it. I could tell by her expression she liked to remember things her way.

"I can't tell you much about Mr. Linder," she went on. "I never saw anything too much out of the ordinary. Never knew about an investigation until I was being fired because he stuck his hand in the cookie jar."

"How many cookies?"

"Way too many." Bertha smiled through her wide, bright red lips as we turned down another hall. She seemed especially happy to have me there. "I feel like I know you," she kept saying.

Since Bertha was Sam Martin's widow, I knew she was only going to be able to tell me one side of this two-sided argument. She probably believed her husband that Dwight Linder was the guilty one.

"Do you remember any of the names of Mr. Linder's clients, the ones that he allegedly bilked out of money?"

She shook her head. "Only a few. Most of it happened before I got there. In fact, Sam found out later that's why Mr. Linder's old secretary quit. She was tired of people coming in, demanding to know stuff about the investment. Being his secretary was harassment."

"Did you experience this harassment?"

"I wasn't even there a full year, but yes, especially there toward the end. A lot of wealthy, powerful people were very angry. And some not so rich people too. I'll never forget the last day I saw Mr. Linder…"

She pointed to a room and we went inside. It was small and bright with a large desktop computer sitting on a table along with a printer. No one else was in there. She closed the door and gently sat down in the only seat, which was in front of the computer.

"It was the Friday before the accident." She paused to look at the overhead lights. "No, it must've been a Thursday. Mr. Linder always took Fridays off. And he usually left early most days anyway. He'd sneak out and I wouldn't even know it until I'd check on him." She lowered her voice. "Rumor had it, there was a shed at the country club full of moonshine that Mr. Linder took full advantage of, if you know what I mean." She winked awkwardly, her thick mascara sticking a little when she opened her eye again.

She propped her hands over the keyboard in front of her in perfect about-to-type formation. "I wasn't a very good secretary," she said.

"You look like you know what you're doing." I commented, pointing to her hands.

"Typing? Yes. But, I let all sorts of people in to see Mr. Linder, even when he told me he was too busy to see them. But when a teacher comes in with tears in her eyes holding the deed to her house, or the construction worker's kid pulls out a photo of his family… What can you do? I had no idea it was because Mr. Linder was swindling them. I thought they needed Mr. Linder's help."

"Was Bill Donovan one of Mr. Linder's clients? Was he angry too?"

"I'm sure Mr. Linder never swindled Mr. Donovan. They were good friends. Inseparable. Their families went way back. Why I think their grandparents even built the golf course together or something like that."

"Sometimes friends turn on each other."

"Not those two. I used to send birthday cards for all the Donovans. Myles and Freddie were going to go to Yale together. They went on vacations together every year. The Bahamas. Mexico. They'd kill for each other."

"I bet." I thought, but didn't say out loud. I was starting to think the loud splash I heard that night was "evidence" of the drowning, just enough for the corrupt newspaper to report that remains had been found and the Linders declared dead, on page ten behind some recipes.

"But I do know Mr. Donovan was very instrumental in telling people about Mr. Linder's investment. When I first started working there, people would come in and tell me Bill sent them. They wanted that foolproof plan. Foolproof? More like foolhardy. A lot of people lost their retirement because of that investment and a lot more. And poor Sam was blamed."

"Did Mr. Donovan lose credibility because of Mr. Linder?"

"Oh, I'm sure he didn't care too much about that. Just as sure as I know, if Mr. Donovan invested in Mr. Linder's scam, he was one of the lucky ones who got out with money."

"I bet." This time I said it out loud. "Can you tell me anything about a man named Richard? He was a homeless man who died in the woods in 1954, but there were a lot of rumors tied to him and the investment."

She looked at the ceiling. "Nineteen-fifty-four was a couple years before I got to the firm. I do remember the rumors, though, but mostly because Sam liked to talk about them. Apparently, Mr. Linder's career really took off when that man was murdered."

I tried to take mental notes as she talked because it was probably rude to break out a paper and pen at this point. I should have brought my recorder.

"People believed the man was murdered by a greedy relative after he came into money. Or a drug deal gone wrong. Either way, people believed the man had come into some money, from the investment. But Sam always told a different story about that one."

I sat forward in my seat, kicking myself even harder for not bringing the recorder along.

She continued. "He said Richard came into the office,

demanding they make good on his promissory note. He was out of control and angry, yelling like a crazy man. I guess he'd put all his savings into it. Mr. Linder took the man into his office and ultimately convinced Richard to reinvest his money. Not long after that, Richard was dead."

"So… he didn't come into any money?"

She shook her head. "Only on paper, and we all know how good that was. He was one of the first to ask for it, though. Or at least, that's what Sam told me. Of course, at the time, Mr. Linder told everyone that Richard must've needed to liquidate his investment to pay off his drug dealer. And when the drug dealer didn't get paid off, the bum got his head chopped off…"

I remembered the fact that decapitation was a detail the police were keeping to themselves about the homeless man in the woods. Apparently, a few people knew it.

She was still talking. "I think, after everything came out about Mr. Linder, Sam wondered about the drug-dealer story."

"Your husband thought Mr. Linder killed the man?"

She shook her head. "He always wondered, and we'll never know for sure. A lot of things died with Mr. Linder, I'm afraid," she said, adding a frozen half-smile.

"Whatever happened to Dwight's wife and his oldest son?"

"Who knows? After the accident, they didn't stick around for long. Who could blame them? Whole town hated that family, except the Donovans."

"Before I go," I began, smoothing out my cardigan, trying to figure out how to ask her this. "I also wanted to talk to you about something completely unrelated. I read an article about you and a hero dog. Can you tell me about him?"

She stared at the ceiling. "Normandy. It's been a long time since I've thought about him." It was in that instant where I saw the Bertha from 1954, the way her face lit up when she talked about the dog, the twinkle in her eye. It was funny how it's impossible to picture somebody's old-person face when they're young, but you can totally see their young face when they're older. Even through plastic surgery.

"I got to keep that dog after the bird incident."

My eyes bugged. I wasn't expecting that. "How long did he live for?" I said, then realized that was probably the weirdest question I could possibly have asked just then. Plus, I was afraid of the answer. I wasn't prepared to find out my dog wasn't that dog. I was really getting used to the thought that Rex might last forever, that maybe I was his fourth human or something.

"I only had Normandy for about two years. I never really had him, though. He'd get out and patrol the neighborhood. He was a watch dog, such a good protector, watching for those sick birds that kept attacking people. Then, one day, he didn't come home. It was about the time the birds stopped coming around too. I guess someone else needed a hero dog."

"Like me," I thought in my head, but fortunately refrained from saying out loud.

"Some people think the birds are back," I said.

"Oh my." She wrung her hands together again, the sound of her rings clacking against each other were the only noises in our tiny room.

After a minute of silence, I finally told her I had to get going. Her face fell, or it seemed to try to.

"Yes, I think Charlie's coming soon, anyway," she said, looking around.

That's when something inside me must've gone a little crazy because I found myself saying, "I'd like to come visit you, if you don't mind. Maybe once a week on one of the days Charlie's not here."

"He won't mind," she said, her face brightening.

"Maybe I could take you up to Gate House…"

"Gate House?" she said. "So you're a Bowman?"

"No. The old man I married was."

She nodded. "I've heard rumors about that place. Always wanted to see it."

"I think you'll like my dog. He's a lot like Normandy."

I helped her back to her room but paused before opening the door. "It's kind of a coincidence that Mr. Linder had an accident right before he was going to be investigated for securities fraud. Don't you think?" I rolled my eyes. "That man is in the Bahamas and I'm going to prove it."

"I thought that too," she said. "Until just before Halloween that year. I'm afraid Sam and I were called in to identify Mr. Linder's remains. His family was nowhere to be found, and I guess the Donovans had refused to do it. They were just too upset."

She leaned against the door frame, wringing her hands together, clanking her jewelry again. "Sam told me I didn't have to go with him. He could identify Mr. Linder alone, but I insisted on going too. You know what? I honestly wish I hadn't." She lowered her voice, her face growing paler like she was still seeing it. "I'll never forget the cold, sterile smell of that morgue, and the moment they opened that drawer. I thought there'd be more of him. When they pulled back the sheet, it was just his big bloated head."

I held in my scream. "You were sure it was him?"

She nodded. "Unfortunately, yes. They said his head likely got wedged between some of the larger rocks at the bottom of the lake as the body was surfacing, causing it to detach…"

I realized I was curling my lip and holding my breath. I exhaled. "What about Freddie," I asked, louder than I'd meant.

She shrugged. "You know, I don't know. The medical examiner said sometimes bodies don't surface."

THE WHOLE WAY home I tried not to think about it. Linder's

bloated head, and the gruesome way Bertie told me it likely got separated from its body.

But decapitation was too big of a coincidence for me to dismiss that easily, seeing how that was exactly how Richard had died. And Linder had likely done it to him.

I couldn't help but feel back at square one. And the seance was tomorrow. I turned to my empty passenger's seat, once again cursing the stinky sachets in my pockets.

CHAPTER 30

*H*ours before the seance, dressed in my fanciest outfit, I sat crouched in front of my laptop at the dining room table, still trying to figure things out.

I paused the powerpoint presentation and zoomed in on one of the photos on the screen. Mason Bowman was talking to a man in a hat, and I thought I saw something in the sheriff's glasses. I squinted and turned my head. What looked like infant legs curled into an anchor stared back.

I practically fell off my chair. "See that? The Knobby Creek logo," I yelled, pointing to the screen. "That means it couldn't have been the police boat that was damaged in the accident. Knobby Creek doesn't service government boats. There would only have been one reason they were called to the lake that night."

No one responded.

"Jackson, did you hear me?" I said as I looked around the dining room for the ghost I knew was here but wasn't materializing. I hadn't seen him since the night someone attacked me on Gate Hill, and not only did I have a ton of information to tell him about the case, I also kind of missed him.

I would never admit that last part, though.

Catching a glimpse of myself in one of the silver bowls along the shelf in the dining room, I grimaced.

I should've felt powerful in the black designer dress I was wearing. I bought this sucker on clearance last summer with an extra 30-percent-off coupon, and it was, by far, the nicest dress I'd ever owned.

It practically smiled too, when I pulled it out from between my bulky sweaters and wrinkled cardigans in the closet, as if it were saying, "Finally, these tags are coming off."

But I knew I was only wearing it to impress Myles Donovan and the rest of his good ole boys gang. And that rich bastard probably expected everyone to try to impress him with their best clearance-rack stuff, like we were all begging to make the society pages.

I hobbled toward the stairs in the ridiculous heels I had coupled with the dress, my mind wandering to the consequences of simple life choices. The choice of wearing a professionally cute dress or being yourself in jeans and a t-shirt. The choice to allow yourself to drink a to-kill-ya worm and go to Mexico on a whim or stay off the yacht and live.

Gloria appeared. "You look cute," she said.

I smiled my thanks. "I'm changing. Do you ever regret letting Nettie talk you into so many crazy things?"

"I used to," she said, her voice weak, her coloring strong. "I mean, she did ultimately talk me into the night that caused my death, but she also talked me into living a lot more than I would have too."

I refrained from saying that maybe everybody needed a bad influence just as my ex-husband appeared in front of the stairs that I was wobbling toward. And I held in a smile. My bad influence.

"I see your big plan tonight is to bore Myles Donovan into confessing," he said, motioning to my laptop. "Nothing dazzles potential customers and intimidates thugs more than full-page, powerpoint slides."

"I will be presenting evidence, yes," I said. "But I'll also have you and Gloria to jazz things up with flying objects and levitating tables for the seance part."

Jackson shook his head. "Excellent plan, if I were going."

"You can't seriously still be mad about the privacy recipe," I said as I walked past him, catching the side of his elbow as I did. A chill sliced through my shoulder, shocking me a little, and I struggled to regain my balance. "If you'll excuse me, I'm going to change in the *privacy* of my own room," I said, almost twisting my ankle as I hit the first stair. I slipped my shoes off so I could actually make my point without falling on my face.

But when I came back down in my black skinny jeans and sweater, Jackson was nowhere to be found. Gloria hovered by the door.

"Guess it's just us tonight," she said. "You ready?"

I shook my head. "Jackson, I know you're not serious. Stop playing around! Let's go."

No answer.

"We are going to be late."

I only heard his voice. "Oh, now you want me to travel on you. When it's convenient for you. All other times and you've got the fruitcake's ghost repellent in your pocket."

I checked my watch as I grabbed my laptop and gently put it in the backpack I reserved for seance stuff. I didn't have time for the 50-year-old's drama tonight.

"Look, Jackson. I'm sorry. I just wanted more privacy. And truth is, while I do need privacy, I also need you more than I care to admit."

He appeared, arms crossed so I could see every crease in his pretentious jacket. "I'm listening. Go on," he said, like he expected a full-on groveling session.

I bit my lip and somehow got myself to continue. "There have been several times lately where I've regretted not having you around. So, how about we compromise? I only really need the privacy strands along the door frames, and the sachets on important nights with Justin. Other than that, I won't put them in my pocket anymore."

"Because…"

"Certainly not because I missed you if that's what you're getting at," I said.

He smiled. "I missed you too," he replied and disappeared. "Now, let's go. I feel like being a bad influence tonight."

I TOLD Jackson everything on the ride to the bed and breakfast while trying to keep the wheels of my rental from slipping in the ice. My heat had begun making a fun, new "screaming" noise when I turned it on, but that didn't stop me from turning it on all the time.

I turned the heat up a notch then waited to talk until it was done screaming.

"So now, I'm back to square one," I said. "Linder really did die, apparently. But at least now I know why people have been trying so hard to keep this under wraps. Dwight Linder is the murder no one wants to be tied to."

"The others are optional?" Jackson replied.

That's when it hit me. "The shed," I shouted. "It burned down the day before the accident. I bet whoever murdered Linder did it in the shed, then burned everything down to cover their tracks."

"You don't know that for sure," Jackson said.

"Nope. But I don't need to. Not when I'm just looking to trap a mouse."

CHAPTER 31

ALWAYS KNOW YOUR AUDIENCE

*P*aula Henkel rushed around the lobby of her bed and breakfast at breakneck speed, lighting a candle here, directing workers there. The woman was in her element. Her short, spiked, bleach-blonde hair swayed with every movement, making her look a couple inches taller than she was. But Rosalie still towered over her in flats as she sported her "good luck seance dress," which was basically a humungous gray pillow case with moons glued to it.

"Only pass around the hors d'oeuvres if I direct you to, and only to those people I direct you to," Paula said to a waiter when I approached her and Rosalie.

I looked at my watch. It was almost 7:00, the time on the tickets when the buffet started. Lynette was already filming everything, a large camera on one shoulder, press pass dangling from her neck, like that meant something. She'd been the one to print that out for herself.

The dining hall was full of fancy tables with mystic dark scarves draped across the ceiling over them, like a Halloween circus tent.

Dinner guests would be arriving soon, if they were arriving.

The smell of garlic shrimp and the little baby quiches I loved took over my senses, and my stomach rumbled.

"I'm starting to think no one important's showing," Paula said just as the door opened and Lila and Myles walked in, dressed like they were heading to a million-dollar fundraiser instead of a seance.

"I stand corrected."

Lila took her coat off to reveal a long, black, Oscar-worthy dress and her grandfather had on a tux. They ignored the entourage of about five people walking alongside them.

The mayors and their wives walked in next and I got my nervous facial tic again. "You can do this," I reminded myself. "This was what you wanted."

The place was filling up fast, with people I hadn't really expected to show. It felt a little like they were daring me to say anything bad about them "to their faces." Another form of intimidation.

I tried not to think about it and grabbed one of the dinner plates at the buffet while Paula rushed over to every "important" guest, her hand already extended, ready for a handshake like they were royalty. "Welcome. Welcome," she said, her smile strained and phony. "Plenty of food. Chez Louie, you know. Nothing but the finest for my finest guests."

I tried to look away, but Paula pulled my arm to introduce me to Myles and Lila.

"And speaking of the finest. Carly is the finest medium in all of Landover County, probably the whole state of Wisconsin," she said. I could barely shake the man's hand. All I could think about was how we'd already met, face to fist, just a couple weeks ago. I could still taste the blood on my lips after he and his father beat us up.

"Nice to meet you," Myles said. He was in great shape for a man of around 80. He didn't have that arthritic, hunched-over look most men his age sported. But then, the hardest "work" he probably ever had to do was punch a woman 60 years ago.

"I heard you got into a bit of an accident," Myles said. "I do hope you're okay."

He leaned into me and whispered in my ear, his breath hot against my cheek. "I just want to let you know my lawyers are here in case things get libelous for anyone. Anyone. I don't care if every ghost here tells you what they *think* happened that night. You'd better have real proof to back it up. I just want you to keep that in mind. Court can be so expensive." He pointed to two bald men in dark suits sitting at the best table in the house. Obviously his lawyers. "Have you tried the garlic shrimp? You must," he said, moving onto the buffet.

Dan and Grace rushed over from across the room and asked Myles and Lila to pose for a quick photo.

"We stopped running the society section when we bought the paper from Grace's grandmother," I heard Dan explain to the millionaire. "But we're thinking about bringing it back, just for tonight, in special memory of Dwight and Frederick Linder. The Linders and Donovans shared many society photos together."

Myles smiled. "My father would have been proud to hear that." He chuckled. "Maybe he is hearing it. You never know who will show up to a seance."

They all laughed like seances were a joke.

Lynette stepped in beside Dan and filmed them. Grace scowled at her. "What are you doing here?"

"Not surprised you don't know," Lynette said, pointing to her lanyard. "It's called journalism. Look it up."

Dan turned his nose at Lynette, trying to ignore her, but the camera was pretty much right in his face the entire time. He directed his attention to the Donovans. "We just wanted to thank you personally for the invitation," he said to Myles, holding his hand up so his face was shielded from the camera.

Dan's sleeve fell back against his watch, revealing what looked like a long, red scratch peeking out from underneath it.

A bear scratch, maybe?

Could they have seen me give back that notebook?

I excused myself to the coat check so I could text Justin and tell him to check out Dan Herndon as a possible suspect, see if they owned a large, black truck.

That's when I noticed Shelby sitting behind the coat-check counter with a basket full of makeup samples next to her, and my shoulders finally relaxed. I hadn't even noticed I was clinching up until then.

"Thank goodness somebody decent is here," I said. "This place is full of old, rich, and awful."

She nodded. "Three things I hope to be someday."

"So what happened with Bobby and your ultimatum?"

She straightened her makeup samples, her eyes tearing up.

"Nuh-uh," I said. "He chose his brothers?"

"All three of them walked out together about a week ago. I haven't seen him since. He left his own baby. It's why I'm here, working all the jobs I can get. I gotta pay the rent on my own soon."

"He'll be back."

"That's what my parents say," she said. "I'm not so sure I want him back after this."

"I don't blame you," I said. "I'm sorry." I hugged her then offered to get her a plate of food.

She happily accepted. "I left Spoony's so fast to get here, I didn't have time to eat."

I glanced over at the buffet table and knew I'd have to act fast.

The college kids had started trickling in, and things were getting crowded. About twenty people in torn sweatshirts and jeans grabbed plates at the buffet table. "I didn't know there'd be food," one of them said loudly. "Sweet."

Paula tried to tug the plates from their grasps, but hungry

college kids can be pretty strong. "May I see your dinner tickets?" she asked again and again, like that was going to mean something to them.

I rushed over during the commotion to help myself, not even caring that Paula was watching me out of the corner of her eye the entire time. She pushed past the college kids and grabbed my arm, pointing to the second plate in my hand. "At a hundred dollars a person, I cannot afford to feed the coat-check girl."

I shook myself free of her grasp. "This has already been paid for."

"Not by Shelby Winehouse."

"Then you should probably tell that to Lila," I said, pointing to the woman in the perfect up-do who was bouncing over to say "hi" to Shelby. She handed her a full plate of what looked like shrimp, bread, and pasta.

Paula's mouth dropped. "What the..."

"They met at my library story time," I said, matter-of-factly. "So, go ahead. Tell Lila what you just told me. Her lower-class friends shouldn't be eating the good stuff, after Lila's family paid for every single ticket."

Paula stomped off but quickly found her fake smile again when she saw Mayor Bowman and Mayor Wittle with their wives at the buffet table.

Mayor Wittle looked almost the same as he had 60 years ago. He was a lanky, bald man with a bit of a nervous twitch but nothing that really screamed his age. It was funny how that whole group of equally horrible friends had aged the best out of everyone in town. It was true; only the good died young in Landover County. With the exception of my ex-husband, of course.

As if on cue, Jackson appeared next to me. "So, how many windows do you want me to break tonight?" he said.

We both knew he was joking. He didn't have the energy for that kind of ghostly display. Only experienced, well-charged apparitions like our friend the suffragette could manage something so spectacular, which was good. It was a huge sore spot the last time we'd had a seance here, so it was one of the main things Paula made sure we put in the contract, stating in triplicate that the Purple Pony would pay for the windows this time if it happened again.

But then, we had technically cancelled that contract when the tickets hadn't sold.

"Break them all out," I said. "But wait 'til the end, or we'll freeze."

I looked around. It was really getting crowded. One of the waiters brought in more chairs from a back room and Paula was busy making sure paid guests got all the best spots.

At about 8:00, Paula grabbed the handheld mic and introduced the seance by calling out all the distinguished and honored guests she had in the audience, the very ones I was about to call murderers.

"Saved the best for last," she said after introducing the mayors and the sheriff. "Myles Donovan and his absolutely stunning granddaughter, Lila."

They both half-stood and waved to a mostly standing ovation, minus the college kids who had no idea who the man was, except maybe "that creepy old dude on the wall at the gym."

After about ten minutes of Paula spewing out upcoming events at the "historical Landover Bed and Breakfast" and the 20% off coupon you could grab in the back on your way out for locals, she finally dimmed the lights and put the spotlight on the black-clothed table in the middle of the living room, just like last time.

Rosalie, Paula and I all clipped our mics onto our collars, and I began the show, thanking everyone for coming and introducing myself. I explained the items on the table. The spirit bell, the EMF meter, and the crystal ball that was "just for show because I actually didn't know how to use that." The audience only laughed awkwardly at my jokes.

"Tough crowd," Jackson said, as he plunked the spirit bell. Nobody even gasped.

Most of them knew the story I was about to tell and the people who were about to be involved in it — the mayors, the Gazette, and Myles Donovan— and they liked them. Or, they were scared of them. There was very little difference when it came to this town.

"You see, not everyone comes back to the physical world after they die. Only if they are clinging to a person, a place, or an event. Maybe they have something they want to tell you or maybe you have a need to connect with them and they sense that, and come back to tell you they're okay." I looked around at the audience, but spoke to no one in particular. "So at the end, if there's time, we'll see if there are other ghosts here that would like to make their presence known to someone too. But right now, we have a story to tell."

Lynette had been able to check out a projector, so I turned it on.

The senior photos of Nettie and Gloria took up most of the large screen in the dining area of the bed and breakfast.

"More than a hundred dollars a ticket for a powerpoint presentation," Mayor Bowman chuckled loudly from his seat at the table, like he actually paid for stuff.

Jackson shook his head. "Don't mind him, Carly doll. He obviously doesn't know you have an Excel sheet and bar graphs coming up."

I took a deep breath and ignored them both. "As you all know, we're here to tell the real story of the boating accident on July twentieth, 1957 on Partiers Loop, otherwise known as Accident Loop. Only, those girls weren't partiers and this was no accident."

The audience didn't even stir, except for the lawyer next to

Myles, who sat forward, obviously letting me know I needed to tread cautiously.

"First, I'm going to let the ghosts tell their story, and then I'm going to back that up with evidence from today, so it won't at all be libelous." I looked right at Lynette and her camera when I said it then over at the bald lawyers.

That's when I noticed a gorgeous, Marilyn Monroe-looking blonde hovering by an older woman sitting by herself in the back of the room. Nettie was here, and she was right next to a woman I was guessing was June.

The blonde girl looked exactly the same as I remembered her looking from the channeling with the same tight-fitting black dress as the night she died, hair in a high ponytail. She and Gloria both hovered by June, chattering away to one another, probably reconnecting.

"I… I just noticed Annette Jerome is here," I said, to no applause. "Gloria Thomas too."

Myles looked at his Rolex and yawned. The jerk. He was trying to look bored and so were the rest of his gang. They wanted this seance to bomb and for the news of my massacre to make it to the Gazette, the Daily Bear, and the gossip around town.

They could control a lot of narratives in life, but not this one. "I won't bore you with the details, Myles. You know them already, seeing how you and your father beat the girls to a pulp when you discovered them on your yacht then tossed them overboard to die."

The audience gasped. The lawyers sat forward.

"Libel!" A few voices yelled from the crowd.

"How dare you," someone else screamed.

"I see that got your attention," I said, my voice echoing through the mic. "Good. These girls deserve at least that."

CHAPTER 32

THE OPTIONAL MURDERS

*M*yles and Lila stood up to leave, and I casually flipped to my next slide. "Don't go yet. You'll miss the best part. The proof I have. Plus, the whole seance thing with ghosts and stuff. But then, you might just have come tonight to pretend to be offended by it all."

"We've seen enough, thank you," Myles said, taking his grand-daughter's hand. Shelby handed them their coats and Myles opened the front door, only to have it flung closed again, straight from his grasp. Myles grabbed the knob, but couldn't get the door to open. Gloria appeared in front of it.

Dan from the paper stood up. "Let the man go."

A chorus of angry yells from the audience followed.

I looked over at Paula Henkel. She glared back, shaking her head like I was somehow controlling this, probably wondering what her own liability was if the old, rich man didn't get his way.

My voice barely rose above the yelling and I had a mic. "Gloria Thomas is holding the door." I shrugged. "I guess these ghosts have a lot to say to Myles Donovan tonight."

Myles leaned casually against the back wall, coat draped over his arm, and waved to me to go on, probably because at this point, he didn't really have a choice.

The next slide was already on the screen. The ten grainy photos from that night.

"Then, when those 18-year-old girls didn't die fast enough, the Donovan boat located them in the water and purposely ran them over. The police stood by and did nothing."

"Lies from an out-of-towner," I heard from more than one person mumbling in the crowd. "Everybody knows the police ran them over."

"And here's how we know it wasn't the police boat." I showed them the photo of the Knobby Creek logo being reflected in Mason Bowman's glasses. Then, a photo of the dummies in the front of the boating company. "Same hat," I said, explaining that the Knobby Creek didn't service government vessels.

Mayor Wittle wiped the sweat from his brow as he whispered something to Mayor Bowman. Mayor Bowman shot him an angry look.

"And now, we'll talk about why."

I then invited Nettie and Gloria to tell their version of events, relaying everything to the audience as they spoke.

Nettie's voice didn't have that youthful lilt anymore like it did in 1957 as she hovered around the room talking about how she met Freddie and how they snuck onboard the yacht.

"I thought he was the cutest," Nettie said. "I was also thrilled that one of the richest boys on the lake was interested in me."

"Like many people," I said, knowing full well what most of this crowd thought of girls who went out with rich boys. "She was impressed by dumb things like wealth. I was, too, back when I was her age. None of us are the same people we were as teenagers, and I think most of us are pretty thankful we were given the chance to grow out of our dumb phases."

Nettie was a fierce sight to see in her powerful black dress, the rest of her a ghostly white contrast. "We were introduced by that man," she pointed to Myles. "He's older now but I still recognize his spirit. Freddie and I were the reason the chaperone ended the dance early. We made out in a closet, and she said we were drunk…"

"I am wondering if you see Freddie Linder in this room," I said. This was the part I was guessing at.

She looked around, doing a double take. "Why there's Freddie now," she said. She touched Mayor Wittle's cheek, and I could tell he felt her, the cold slicing sensation people receive when brushing up against a powerful ghost.

His face shook and he fell over in his chair a little.

"She is pointing to Mayor Darren Wittle," I said, watching as the mayor's already pale face lost so much color I thought he might pass out.

I put the two images of Mayor Wittle and Freddie Linder's senior pictures side by side on the screen. Both were lanky, dark-haired boys with a penchant for bow ties and side-parts.

"P-lease," one of the lawyers sitting with Myles Donovan yelled to the crowd. "Everyone knows that just because the photos of two men look similar does not mean anything."

"I'm sorry," I said. "This is not a courtroom, so any and all objections will have to shut the hell up."

A few college kids laughed when I said that.

I was playing to my new customer base, and I was loving it. Jeans-and-t-shirt outsiders were my kind of people. "Leave if you want. We'll see if Gloria and Nettie let you. Ghosts can get pretty angry. They've been known to throw things. Break windows."

I looked over at Paula. She had her head in her hands.

Mildred was sitting with her son, Benny, toward the back, and I motioned to her to come forward.

She adjusted her thick cardigan as she took the handheld mic and introduced herself. She held up a small yellow book with flowers on the cover. "My diary," she said, like that would make sense to the crowd. She coughed. "I have been asked to corroborate this story, so I looked over my diary to make sure I got everything right. I was a chaperone at that party in 1957, and I did not see Freddie Linder there." She opened her book. "Let me read straight from a passage…"

"Don't bother," Clyde Bowman yelled from his seat. He stood up, voice so loud he didn't need a mic. "This is nothing new. This has always been Mildred Blueberg's version. It's exactly what she said when she begged the country club not to fire her father. It was a weak argument then and it still is. It's sad how she worries more about her family's reputation than the truth about that night."

"Maybe," I replied, standing so the squatty man would see me clearly from across the table. "She, for one, will fight for her family's reputation. Or did you think that was a trait only admirable in Bowmans?"

He sat back down, swallowing hard to hear his own words used against him.

One of the lawyers took over. "I'm sorry, but it was under Ms. Blueberg's supervision that Frederick Linder got drunk and out of control, went swimming in the dark, and drowned. End of story. To suddenly say he wasn't there is crazy. Plenty of people saw him at that dance, including the other chaperone who walked in on him and Ms. Jerome making out in a closet." He sifted through his notes. "What was her name?"

A voice from the back of the room yelled. "Deborah Ford. Deborah Nebitt now."

I looked over, trying to focus on the parts of the bed and breakfast that were dark. A tuft of white hair bobbed through the crowd. Lynette followed her every step with the camera as she took the handheld mic from Mildred.

Thank goodness that woman really did love a freebie.

"It's true," Mrs. Nebitt said. Her voice was shaky but loud. "My name is Deborah Nebitt. I was the chaperone who walked in on Darren and Annette."

The crowd gasped.

"Yes, I said that correctly. It was not Freddie. When I opened that closet, I got a good look at the young man guzzling punch in the letterman sweater Freddie always wore, his arm around a gorgeous blonde. He turned and tried to pretend to be too drunk to look at me, sneezing and coughing, looking as if he was going to throw up. I knew it was Darren Wittle all along. Even when Myles's father scolded Mildred and me for letting Freddie Linder get too drunk."

Mrs. Nebitt's voice cracked and shook as she looked around the dark room. "Mr. Donovan offered to find a generous donor for the library while also suggesting that it had been dark and chaotic the night of the party, so no one would blame me if I didn't remember things correctly."

She turned to Mildred. "I'm very sorry. I should have corroborated your version of events back then."

"My father would've been fired anyway," Mildred said as the two hugged.

Gloria hovered near me and I gestured toward her. "I don't believe it was a coincidence these girls were involved. I think they were targeted. Because they were out-of-towners. Darren Wittle was supposed to wear Freddie's clothes, find the only two girls at the party who would believe he was Freddie, drink enough punch to pretend to get drunk, and then leave on the Donovan boat. Isn't that right, Mayor Wittle?"

He didn't answer. He only shook.

"But you didn't expect the girls to follow you onboard. And we all know what happened then."

I went on. "You see everyone on the boat was in the middle of staging the deaths of Dwight and Frederick Linder. Dwight was involved in swindling the town out of millions with his bogus investment and was about to be investigated for securities fraud. Bill was helping his good friend out of the mess by helping him out of the country."

I paused long enough to see my new customer base playing on their phones by the buffet. Great.

I continued like they were still interested. I needed to get back to ghosts breaking windows and fast. "And when Nettie and Gloria witnessed these men staging the Linders' deaths on the boat, they were killed. And everyone else covered it up because Bill Donovan wanted them to." I turned toward the lawyer. "That's the end of the story."

The room was silent, until the lawyer stood up. "Well then, I guess we will see you in court."

"Lies. Lies. Lies," Mayor Bowman yelled, loosening the tie that seemed to be strangling his thick neck. "I will sue you for everything you have."

I knew that man already thought he deserved everything I had: the house, the inheritance, probably not the curse, though.

Mayor Wittle staggered through the crowd, smacking chairs on his way from the back of the room, knocking the empty ones over. His face was as vacant as a stuffed fisherman. When he reached me, I backed away and scanned the room for some sort of a weapon.

With shaky hands, he reached for my neck, and I screamed, then realized he was actually reaching for my mic. I breathed a sigh of relief and gave it to him.

"Is Nettie really here? I… I felt her. If she's here, I want her to know I'm sorry," he said, his voice quivering worse than Mildred's had been.

"Sit down, Darren," his wife yelled from her seat. "And for God's sake, shut the hell up."

He didn't seem to hear her. "I know she only made out with me that night 'cause she thought I was the richest kid on the lake…"

My face dropped. I wasn't expecting a confession.

He went on, sputtering each syllable. "I had no idea that… stuff on the boat was going to happen. She knows that, right?"

"Get a hold of yourself, Darren," Myles yelled from across the room.

Darren shot back. "Shut up, Myles. I trusted you. You said nothing was gonna happen. We would all be okay… Then you and your dad beat up the girls, threw them overboard… ran them over with the boat. And then Mr. Linder was actually murdered. Who knew that?"

"No one tells Myles Donovan to shut up," Dan from the paper said. He picked up a chair and lifted it over his head. Caleb got up, arms folded over his police uniform, and Dan put the chair back down again.

Mayor Wittle continued. "We were supposed to be staging deaths. That's it. Freddie's and Mr. Linder's… I didn't know there was a real murder…" His voice cracked as he talked. "I never knew…"

I leaned over Rosalie so my voice would pick up through her mic since I wasn't wearing one anymore. "Actually," I said. "I think you did know, Mayor Wittle."

The college kids at the buffet stopped eating and playing on their phones and looked over.

Rosalie yanked her mic off her seance dress and handed it to me so fast part of a moon pulled off of its seam. "Damn," she said, her voice ringing out before I took over. "Damn. Damn. Damn."

CHAPTER 33

A MURDER SO QUAINT

The room seemed extra quiet to me now. I had no idea what libel entailed or how to defend myself against it in court, but I knew I had to do what was right.

I put the mic up to my mouth and continued. "At least one person onboard the Donovan yacht that night knew there was more than staging going on, and I think that person was you."

The crowd gasped.

Mayor Wittle went on. "I don't know what you're talking about. Did your ghosts tell you that?" He chuckled to the crowd like they were suddenly going to be on his side.

"They didn't need to. But I will take some ghostly help to cue up Mildred's diary entry to the day the shed burned down."

I waited. Nothing happened, but everybody's heads turned this way and that to see if I was off my rocker.

I covered my mic and yelled for Jackson under my breath.

He was rolling his eyes when he appeared. "Honestly, the things I do for you. Mildred's right there with her diary. She could easily read it herself…"

I sent the lazy ghost mental daggers until he picked up the recorder and hovered on the table with it, half-heartedly moving it this way and that in front of him, kind of like a sign spinner five minutes before quitting time. "Oooooh," he said like anyone could hear him. "No strings."

It was enough to get the college kids' attention, though. One dropped his plate of garlic shrimp when he looked up and saw the recorder dancing across the table over to the mic stand.

Jackson pushed "play" once he got there, and Mildred's voice shot out through the mic, the same entry about the shed as before.

> "He denied getting moonshine and even had the nerve to say no one else was in that shed, but I could hear Myles sneezing on the other side of the door. Freddie must think I'm stupid.
>
> "And this time, they've gone too far. Apparently, those two killed a deer off-season. Freddie admitted it. He didn't even care. He said it was an accident, that he was just shooting at cans and trees, but who knows? I told him he doesn't own this country club so he needed to stop acting like it, just because he's rich and his family was one of the founders. I told him I'd had enough. I was going to tell on him.
>
> "And then the shed burned down. I guess he showed me."

Jackson clicked the recorder off and I took over. "Hours before the shed burned down, there was something bloody inside it. According to Ethel Peterton's notes, the only things recovered from that shed after it burned were a metal welder's mask, a blow torch and some tools, including an ax."

I clicked on the photo of that page of her notebook on my laptop and it appeared on the screen. "As you can see, arson was suspected."

"I knew you had that notebook," Grace said, hitting her husband's bear scratch.

I ignored her. "And, Mayor Wittle, your family had access to welding equipment. Isn't that right?"

"A… a lot of people did," he replied.

"But how many do you suppose also had a weird allergy to pine? That was you that night, not Myles, sneezing in the shed. Mildred's father infused his moonshine with juniper, so you were allergic to the stuff you were supposed to be getting drunk off of. That's why you were sneezing in the closet the night of the party too. You and Freddie killed Mr. Linder in the shed then burned it down to cover your tracks. Later on, you threw his head into the lake as proof of the drowning. Why not? You were already staging the death. Freddie's body was never recovered because Freddie was in the Bahamas by the time his father's remains were discovered…"

Mayor Wittle didn't say anything, wasn't cracking like I wanted him to, so I went on. I steadied my eyes on his. "You killed Dwight Linder. Because you thought you deserved better. You deserved to be a part of the rich circle, and I'm guessing you might have thought you were even born into it."

I checked through the photos on my laptop, clicking on the one I took from Mayor Wittle's office of him and his family. "Funny. You don't really look like a Wittle. But you look an awful lot like Freddie and Eric Linder."

I didn't let him respond yet. "You killed him because you thought you deserved to be an insider and one of the richest boys on the lake, and you weren't."

Mr. Wittle shook his head. "No…no. It wasn't like that. I told Myles about it. He knows. It was Freddie. He killed his dad."

I sat back down in my chair, exhausted. I knew that mouse would crack eventually. I didn't know it'd take so many cookies to get him there, though. I handed Rosalie her mic and whispered that I was done. I didn't hear applause. Rosalie had been right. There was no standing ovation this time. The town hadn't rallied around me to hear the truth. It was like they didn't care. Or didn't believe it.

"Thank you all for coming," my boss said. "But that concludes the seance."

Her voice was barely audible over the pandemonium erupting around us.

Mayor Wittle was still confessing. "Freddie said his dad already had everything set up. The plane tickets, fake IDs, offshore accounts. They didn't need him anymore, and he wasn't a good man. He threatened Mrs. Linder with an ax…"

"Shut up," Mayor Bowman yelled as he tackled the other 80-year-old mayor, wrestling the mic from his hands while the Donovans tried to open the front door once more, their lawyers right behind them.

Dan picked up his chair, but this time, Caleb couldn't stop him. It soared past the fighting mayors and crashed against one of the windows.

The glass cracked, little pieces clanking along the hardwood by our feet.

"We will not be paying for that," Rosalie said calmly into her mic. "That was clearly a living human who did that."

Cold wind streamed steadily through the now broken parts of the window. Paula stood up. "Sheriff Bowman, handle this, please."

Caleb seemed almost frozen, unsure of what to do to get the peace. They were all his friends and family. He bent down to take Mayor Wittle by the arm, but the two older men were still wrestling, egged on by yelling and hooting outsiders. The college kids had circled the aging fighters like they were watching a mosh pit form at a Barry Manilow concert.

Nettie raised her arms out by her side and two chairs rose with them. The chairs flew across the room at the same time. One smacked Myles across the side of his shoulder. The other chair landed squarely by Mayor Wittle's feet.

With a swirl of her hand, Gloria wrapped one of the mystic scarves from the ceiling around Mayor Bowman's leg and yanked him out of his dog pile with Mayor Wittle. The thick man rose into the air by his leg, screaming and kicking the whole time. Then she released him so he landed hard against the floorboards.

"Tell Tony that's from the troll friend," she said. I didn't even try to tell him. I no longer had a mic, and it was too loud anyway. Smoke drifted around me, and things got instantly quiet.

Someone was burning sage.

I've never heard Paula's voice louder, and I've heard that woman get pretty loud. It practically vibrated off the walls. "Enough! If you are living, go home now or you will be arrested. This party is over. And if you are dead, I have burning sage. I'm not dealing with any more broken windows or chairs or anything else tonight."

I wondered if she was mad enough to turn polar bear. I looked for Hulk-like signs as she waved the bundle of sage all around the living room. Ghosts disappeared right and left.

Slowly, I walked over to her. "And you said you didn't believe in any of this sage-burning hocus pocus…"

"Still don't," she replied, the house quieter now. "But it's cold enough."

"For a polar bear?"

"That was your last seance at my place," she said, staring me right in the eyes, making me regret my big mouth.

I sat down and cupped my head in my hands, regretting a lot of things as I listened to people complain about the seance on their way out.

"I've never been to a party where old people fought before," one of the college kids said.

"I totally saw the strings when that recorder floated above the table," another chimed in.

"And when the chairs flew around. Lame."

So much for a new customer base. It was my worst seance yet, if it could even have been considered a seance. It was more like an interrogation mixed with a senior-citizen brawl. The Purple

Pony was never going to make money until summer rolled around again.

A very light, smattering of applause came from a dark corner in the back of the room. I squinted in its direction.

It was June.

"Thank you," she said when she reached me. "I have always wondered what happened to my sister. If you see Gloria, you tell her Bug says, 'No more waiting. We got 'em this time.'"

CHAPTER 34

RETURN OF THE DATE KILLERS

il Mil skidded to a perfect hockey-stop in front of me, the show-off, while her bestest friend, Clarisse, spun around like she was in front of an audience. I blinked into the sunlight, thankful for a little warmth as we went into spring.

"If the weather continues like this," Justin said, taking off his jacket. "We won't be able to skate on the lake too much longer."

"Damn," I replied, snapping my fingers. I knew I was making my ice-skating face again.

I looked up in the trees, wondering what else spring had in store for me. New beginnings. New awakenings. Taking sides, whatever that meant.

Parker and Lila laughed behind us, struggling to catch up to their kids. Parker's three-year-old was almost faster than he was now.

I didn't trust Lila one bit. No matter how many times Justin told me the woman wasn't really following me around town, I still got the impression that, yeah, she was. The Donovans were trying to control things, and they wanted me to know about it.

Justin squeezed my hand and I almost slipped on the ice. I

snuggled into him, just listening to the sound of his breathing as he skated, enjoying the warmth of his body.

"Wittle admitted everything," he said. "Not just on camera at the bed and breakfast a couple weeks ago, but he made an official statement yesterday. He was pretty freaked out at the seance."

"Me too," I admitted. "Did they find Freddie Linder and his family?"

He shook his head *no*. "Won't be long, though. Not sure what's going to happen, but everyone's lawyering up. Good job figuring it out."

From what I'd heard, there probably wasn't enough evidence to convict anyone, except Darren Wittle, and only because he'd confessed.

Someone grabbed me from behind and I almost fell on the ice. I turned around, fully expecting to see Mrs. Carmichael again. It was Lynette.

"Getting straight-A's this semester," she said. "They arrested Dan Herndon this morning. And guess who got it all on video. Thanks to my many connections on the police force. Okay, just the one."

She looked over at my boyfriend and I smiled at him.

Justin nodded. "Truck was registered to his son-in-law, bear scratches just like in the report. They think he just wanted to scare you into not being so nosy."

"By almost killing me?" I shook my head. "At least that crazy good-ole-boys network was finally taken down a notch."

"This round, maybe," Justin said.

He waited until Lynette had skated out of earshot to add, "But I have to admit, I was very impressed with the investigation. I can see why ghosts come to you to solve their cases. You and your ex do good work."

Jackson suddenly appeared by our side. "Smarter than the average bear," he said. "I'll give him that."

I shot my ex a look.

He waved his hand, dismissively. "Go on. Go on. Enjoy yourselves like I'm not even here. God forbid I should have some fun." He disappeared, but I knew he was still there. The date killer.

I also knew how hard it must've been for Justin to admit that. Having your girlfriend live with the man she left you for twelve years ago was hard enough, but add in the fact the guy was a ghost and there was nothing you could do about it, and that was probably more than most men would take on.

Passing the same area I'd lost my hat last month, I thought I heard it again. The growling. I searched the trees around us for any signs of the large-beaked birds that growled, remembering the way Clyde had laughed at Gloria, the way the dog had bit through the birds, breaking them in half. A chill shot up my spine along with the feeling that something just wasn't right.

"We should go," I said to Justin.

"You okay?"

"Yeah, let's go back to my place and vedge out."

"Rosalie's recipe strands still holding up?" he asked.

"In all the best places," I said as his radio crackled.

Christine's voice came over it. "Justin, you there?"

He kissed my cheek and put the walkie talkie to his mouth. "Go ahead, Christine."

"Caleb wants you to swing by old George's barber shop. Calm him down."

"I'm supposed to be off tonight."

"I know. I'm sorry. Old George called saying something about a couple bear skins strung up on poles out behind his shop." She hesitated. "Probably won't take long. I'm sure it's someone's idea of a joke, but can you check on that?"

"How many?" he asked.

"What do you mean how many? You asking how many bear skins? I'm sure I don't know that. No wait. I see it here. Three."

"Is the number significant?" I asked, leaning up so I could try to hear better.

"Probably nothing," he replied, skating off. He turned back around, the wind blowing his dark hair along his shoulders. "You okay if I leave you here?" he yelled to me.

"Yeah, I can get a ride home with someone. Parker's here."

He looked at me sideways like he didn't trust Parker as much as I did. But he turned and skated off.

"My. My," Jackson said, suddenly appearing with his arms crossed while we both watched my boyfriend leave. "Parker Blueberg. You would think he'd have objected to that one. I would have."

I bit my lip and ignored my ex-husband's very good point. Justin did seem jealous of Parker.

Justin rushed across the lake toward his truck so fast he slipped a couple of times on the ice and he was an expert skater. My stomach dropped as I suddenly realized why that number might've been significant. Why Justin was in such a hurry.

Shelby's shapeshifting fiancé, Bobby, and his two brothers were still missing. I wondered now if they'd just been found. Another possible sign from the scrapbook.

The End

⁓

READ on to the next chapter for a sneak peek at book four called *Under the Cheater's Table,* coming soon.

From the back cover:

LANDOVER COUNTY IS CHANGING.

KILLER BIRDS ARE COMING. BEAR SHIFTERS HAVE

GONE MISSING. AND NOW, SOME OF THE GHOSTS ARE CHANGING TOO

The fourth installment in the fun, new paranormal series The Ghosts of Landover Mysteries.

There are plenty of signs in Landover County, just none of Shelby's missing fiancé or his brothers. And Carly still doesn't know very much about what's going on, until a ghost follows her home one day with a sob story:

During a snowy weekend in 1923, after a private poker game among lifelong friends, Feldman Winehouse was discovered with his throat slit, under his own poker table at his speakeasy. He wants Carly's help to figure out which one of his best friends murdered him.

There's only one problem. He needs to hurry. His energy is changing into what most people commonly call a demon, and he doesn't have much time.

Carly wants nothing to do with it, or so she tells everyone. **Channeling with a possible demon would be the dumbest thing she's ever done. She's seen The Exorcist.**

But when the entity proves he knows about the signs and why Potter Grove itself is changing, it might be more than the strong medium can resist.

The Ghosts of Landover Mystery series has haunted houses, seances, channelings, curses, shapeshifters, killer birds, and a ton of mysteries. It also has mild profanity and adult humor.

Books in the series so far:

Over My Dead Husband's Body
After the Suffragette's Suicide
Behind the Boater's Cover-Up
Under the Cheater's Table (Coming Soon)
With a Ghost of a Christmas Present (Christmas novelette, coming soon)

UNDER THE CHEATER'S TABLE

CHAPTER ONE: WINEHOUSES

I was the only one who tried to talk Shelby Winehouse out of marrying her awful first husband twelve years ago when she announced her engagement at one of her makeup parties.

Okay, so technically, I just sat on the old floral couch in her parents' living room, quietly scanning the five-page order form, searching for an eyeliner under fifteen bucks (there wasn't one). But I made sure to shift my gaze downward a lot whenever she'd talk about her boyfriend. And that should've been a tipoff.

I would've done more, but at the time, I didn't really know her. Shelby was just the pregnant girlfriend of the route driver who serviced the Thriftway when I worked there in college. I'd just moved out of the dorms, so when the root beer guy came in one day and shoved an invitation into my hands, I jumped on it.

"My girlfriend's having a makeup party," Peter said, practically grunting.

I remember staring at the brightly colored card and then back up at the humungous oaf of a man, wondering just what the hell kind of unibrowed girlfriend he was going to have. But I was torn between two men at the time (one being my dead ex-husband, and the other my now-boyfriend), so I wanted to get away from both and meet some new people.

The route driver wasn't for Shelby. I tried to tell her that with my strategically timed gazes all evening. I tried to tell her about her second husband, Roy, too. That time, I actually said things out loud.

"His name's Roy? C'mon. That's not a real-person's name anymore. That's the name you tell people is your name after you've exhausted every other real-person name. He's obviously been on the run for a while. Either that, or he's a 90-year-old cowboy."

"You're too funny," Shelby said, patting her pregnancy. She was on her third kid at the time, which turned into twins. And I had been right about the fake name. Roy left without a forwarding address, probably goes by John Wayne now.

But, I honestly thought Bobby Franklin had been the one, even though he had always been a ne'er-do-well that I didn't really like. He was good to Shelby.

The grandfather clock in the Winehouse's living room ticked rhythmically in the background, reminding me what an annoying bastard time was. Almost two months had passed since Bobby and his brothers disappeared and there was still no sign of them. But, like the two husbands before him, he was allowed to leave.

I set the cardboard box I was carrying next to the others, in a pile by the faded floral couch, and pulled my curls up into a bun. It did nothing to cool me off. Mrs. Winehouse liked her house more like the Florida Keys in August instead of Wisconsin in March.

The smell of bleach took over my senses because, for some odd reason, most people in Potter Grove treated ordinary spills like crime scenes. And Shelby's kids apparently caused massacres.

Shelby was right behind me. Her hair was pinker today, her makeup extra thick, and she had a new black rose tattoo circling one of her wrists. She told me once a long time ago that she liked to "play with her looks" when she was nervous. Her fiancee was missing and she was moving back in with her parents. It's a wonder that girl looked anything like herself.

Mrs Winehouse moseyed in from the kitchen, a sponge in one hand, Bobby Junior in the other. The baby wouldn't be a year until July, but he took up most of Mrs. Winehouse's hip and seemed to be glaring at the old bulldog laying lazily in the corner like he wished Wisconsin had a Stand Your Ground law he could fudge.

"Take the boxes upstairs before your dad gets back with the boys, okay?" she said to Shelby while scanning the room, probably looking for something else to bleach.

Shelby shuffled over to the stairs, staring off into space like she wasn't really there.

"You okay," I whispered as we took the boxes up to her room.

She didn't say anything.

"Don't worry. He'll come back."

"I don't know about that," she said, pointing me to the room down the hall. It was painted pale pink with black accents. Photos of Shelby in various majorette uniforms from high school sat on her desk. In one, she was twirling a flaming baton in front of a judge's stand. In another, she had red-white-and-blue streamers attached to the ends of her baton. Somehow, I still couldn't picture it.

"I never told anyone this," she said, closing the door behind us. She rummaged through one of the boxes as she talked. "Bobby and I had both been saving for our wedding, stuffing whatever extra money we could into the mattress of our bed. After he left, I checked for that money."

I turned my gaze downward. *Oh God, another Roy.* "At least you didn't marry him this time," I said.

She pulled something tiny and furry out of the box and held it out. It barely took up any space along her palm. "Instead of money, I found this."

It was instantly familiar. One of the signs in the scrapbook I'd found in the basement. Some sort of an animal's foot with white fur, and long yellowed claws protruding out from its three toes.

I realized my lip was curled and I hadn't reached out to take the taxidermied foot from her even though she was still holding it out for me.

"It's a grouse pin," she said. "I looked it up."

Somehow I got myself to take the bony, weird thing with a surprisingly cute silver toe ring on its middle digit, the initials BFF engraved into the metal with a heart.

"Worst Best Friends Forever pin ever," I said, plopping down on her black comforter. She sat down next to me and smoothed out the wrinkles on her 60's-looking capris.

"BFF isn't for best friends forever, or at least I don't think it is. It's Bobby Furgus Franklin. I also read it's a Scottish thing, these grouse pins. They used to wear them when they went hunting. And people also gave them to their significant others when they'd go on a long trip, as a way to remember each other."

"Awww. I knew it had to be romantic," I said, leaning into her, trying to get her to smile. "I need to take this to Justin. Why didn't you show the police this earlier?"

She shrugged. "I guess I didn't want people to know for sure that Shelby Winehouse had been stupid once again. I mean, everybody already knew it. I knew it. But the missing money and this stupid grouse pin with his initials on it, it was like a ha-ha added onto the way things ended for us. And I didn't want people to talk about it and pity me, the stupid woman with five kids and no husband or savings, living out of her parents' house." She put her head in her hands. "I honestly thought he loved me."

I put an arm around her bony shoulder. I knew how this town operated, and she was right. They would've pounced on that part of the story. But, I honestly saw it as a positive sign. "I don't think this was meant as a ha-ha. I think it's an IOU. One of those 'we're not through yet. Here's a tiny, severed foot to prove it' moments."

This made her smile. I had no idea what the severed foot actually meant. All I knew was Bobby and his two brothers were bear shapeshifters that no one had seen for more than a month. Or at least, I hoped not.

Last month, three bear skins had been strung up behind the barber shop. No one knew why or who'd done it. And to make matters weirder, bear skins were in one of the photos on the page in my scrapbook marked "Signs," right next to the foot I now knew was a grouse pin.

Of course, Shelby didn't know her boyfriend was a shapeshifter or that his brothers (and her baby) probably were too. And she always looked at me like I was crazy when I worried about those bear skins.

But we had the "dating a bear shifter" thing in common. I recently discovered Justin was one too. And when you're dating a bear and you see bear skins strung up in your town for no reason, you have to think maybe somebody's trying to tell your bear shifter something.

Thing was, even if Justin knew, he wasn't sharing that with me.

"How much money did Bobby take?" I asked my friend who was still staring off into space.

"Probably around three thousand."

"You had three thousand dollars stashed in your mattress? Are you crazy?"

"You know I don't trust banks. They steal your money."

I resisted the urge to point out the irony here. But at least it explained why Bobby's debit card hadn't been used, something I only knew because Mrs. Carmichael told me, not my police officer boyfriend.

I slipped the foot into the pocket of my skinny jeans and headed downstairs when I stopped midway down. Something was walking with me, close enough for the hairs on my arm to stand on end, but not close enough to touch me. It was like a heavy coldness right by my side, hard to ignore, but I tried.

Ever since I moved back to Potter Grove last summer, strange things had been happening to me. The strangest was my strong mediumship abilities, which I'd never had before. But ghosts were coming out of the woodwork to communicate with me now. So naturally, I'd started taking on their cold cases, helping the dead to solve their murders so they could move on with their after-lives.

The thing that was following me here seemed different, though.

The front door opened and the sound of four rowdy kids arriving home with their grandpa took over my senses, indicating my time to go.

"Staying for dinner," Mr. Winehouse asked when he followed the kids in and saw me coming down the stairs. He was a tall man in his 60s with a ruddy, weathered complexion and reddish gray hair. He took his firefighter jacket off to reveal a t-shirt with the same logo.

I shook my head no. "Can't. I have plans." I was lying. I just had a rule about eating with kids: I tried not to do it. I loved kids, but I didn't grow up with siblings, and I didn't have children yet. So, maybe I was being snobbish about the whole thing, but I liked to eat dinner without someone opening their mouth to show their already-chewed food because someone else farted.

When I went to leave, Mrs. Winehouse pulled me to the side by her husband at the front door and lowered her voice. "I'm real worried about Shelbs. She's usually our trooper. Even when she was a single mom with the four boys, she'd rather have worked three jobs than move back in with us. Isn't that right, Ryan?"

"Yep, but don't get us wrong, we love it," Mr. Winehouse quickly added, looking over at Shelby who was holding the baby while staring aimlessly off at the ceiling while three of her kids ran around her in a circle, the oldest filming it on his phone. "But we're worried."

Mrs. Winehouse continued. "Has Justin mentioned anything? Are there any leads on Bobby yet?"

"Not that I know of," I said. I didn't tell her the part where nobody was really looking. Shelby had given Bobby an ultimatum when his brothers' Christmas visit lasted until almost February, and Bobby was allowed to take the or-else option.

"They haven't given up yet," I said, because, apparently, lies are like potato chips for me.

She nervously cracked her fingers as she talked. "We need to find Bobby, one way or the other. It's this not-knowing thing that's killing Shelby."

Shelby did look like she was dying, but I didn't think it was the not-knowing part that was doing it to her. I maneuvered my way through the circling children and hugged the cadaver goodbye. She barely looked at me.

The cold feeling that had followed me down the stairs suddenly shot over my entire body, making me gasp for air. I searched the room, but didn't see anything. *Was it Bobby? Had he passed? Was he making contact?* I shook the feeling off, refusing to believe it until a painful chill crawled up my spine and across my chest. Someone was riding on me, and unlike every other ghost I'd ever encountered, this one wanted me to know about it.

I concentrated on each step as I trudged over to the front door, my breathing labored.

"You okay?' Mr. Winehouse asked, watching me with a raised eyebrow, his first-responder instincts probably kicking in.

I nodded that I was fine, even though I wasn't sure. I'd never experienced anything like it before.

UNDER THE CHEATER'S TABLE

CHAPTER TWO: TURNING POINTS

I stumbled through my kitchen door. It felt like every cell in my body had been forced to carry a tiny five-pound weight, and it was pretty apparent we were all seriously out of shape. But I somehow managed to make it to my living room where I sunk into the soft crimson fabric of the settee.

The room spun a little when I tried to focus on anything too hard, especially the damask wallpaper. I avoided that, mostly because it made me sick anyway.

The sound of an excited dog's nails clattered along the hardwood, but I was afraid I'd throw up if I turned toward the noise.

My dead ex-husband appeared beside me. He was bright today, full-color almost. I could see every hair on his beard and pockmark in the leather of his jacket's elbow patches. "And just when I was telling the other ghosts how well you were aging," he said, "the old person in you had to come out and prove me wrong."

I closed my eyes but I could still tell the annoying man was hovering right by my face.

"Are you okay?" he asked.

"Fine."

"I would say you're cute when you lie, but I'd be lying," he said. "The upside to that, of course, is that I'm an adorable liar."

I scrunched my already-closed eyes up tighter, which made my head hurt. But I was in no mood for my ex. Rex licked my hand and I smiled, instantly regretting it because it made me realize my mouth-muscles hurt too.

Then, as suddenly as it came on, the chilling, nauseating feeling travelled across my body in a gust that started at my toes and ended through my sinuses like it had taken a flying leap out.

It was gone. I bolted up, relieved. "I feel better now," I said, moving my back and neck around with ease.

"I bet." Jackson pointed to the middle of the living room where a tall, darkened ghost hovered in front of us. I looked the apparition over. It really didn't have much detail or form to it, just a weird dark mist-looking thing that I wasn't even sure had ever been human.

Rex barked uncontrollably at it.

"It's okay, boy," I said, stroking his back to calm him down. He was tense, his fur stiff. "What are you, and what do you want," I asked the thing in the room.

I threw my ex-husband a look. Ghosts were supposed to follow a certain protocol if they wanted my help, which included Jackson vetting and approving them. And part of Jackson's job was making sure they followed it.

"Sorry, Carly," Jackson said, moving between us, glaring at the spirit. "If you've heard of Carly's abilities then you know how this business is run. All clients must meet with my approval first. No exceptions."

The thing hovered closer to my ex. I knew from past experiences that if spirits got too close to one another, they repelled each other like the polar opposites of magnets. It didn't happen this time.

It made a low, almost humming noise, and I wasn't sure what to do or expect, so I backed away, thinking about the bundles of sage I always kept in the top drawer of my credenza. Even burning a little of it seemed to get a ghost to leave, if only momentarily. I turned to get it, but heard something in the humming noise. There was a voice in there.

"I need your help," it said through mostly low-pitched vibrations.

Jackson must have heard it too. He answered. "I'm very sorry. But we have a long list of clients already waiting. You'll have to get in line to be interviewed about your intentions. You must follow the rules."

"I'm about to turn," the voice said, over and over. "Need your help fast."

"What does that mean?" I asked my ex.

"I think it's trying to tell you it wants to skip the line because it doesn't have time to wait. Its energy is transforming from a ghost to something else," Jackson said.

"What the hell else is there?"

"Darker energy. People sometimes mistakenly call them demons or poltergeists."

I turned to the dark form still floating in front of me. "Yeah, I'm not channeling with you, sorry. Hard pass. I've seen the Exorcist, and we are done here. And, not only that, unless you can show yourself in a normal ghostly form, I'm getting the sage."

"Try, try, try," the dark mist said through the humming sound coming off of it as it lightened into some sort of a striped pattern.

"Maybe if we all think happy thoughts and clap our hands," Jackson deadpanned by my side.

The thing balled itself into a swirl of black-and-white stripes, like a dark mist swirling inside a glass ball. But the ball almost took on a pulsating rhythm as it grew larger and smaller again and again.

I watched Jackson's reaction, much the same way I watched flight attendants during turbulence, the only sure way to know when something's normal and when to start screaming that we're all going to die.

Jackson yawned, and shook his head. "Such theatrics," he said. Rex, on the other hand, was still tense, barking every once in a while at the dark thing in the middle of our living room.

After a full minute of pulsating, the thing finally stretched along its ends until it took the shape of a tall, slender human, the stripes fading and turning into the soft pinstripes of an outdated suit.

The ghost in front of us was almost transparent like it was weak, but something told me not to trust that assessment. His eyes were little slits along a long, horse-like face, his hair light, probably blonde. "Feldman Winehouse," he said with a vibrating voice.

"Winehouse. Shelby's relative," I said.

"Quite a showman." Jackson hovered around the apparition, close but not close enough to cause a reaction. "Or should I say a conman?"

"I need your help," the ghost said with almost perfect clarity now, making me wonder if he was conning us before. "And you need my help, too. Neither one of us has much time."

"*We* have all the time in the world," Jackson said. "We're not the ones turning."

I could feel the anger in Feldman's energy now as he glared at my ex-husband. "You think you're clever, huh? You're Henry Bowman's direct descendent, huh? A far cry from your great grandfather. That's for sure."

"So you're saying you knew my great grandfather?"

He nodded. "Did business with him." He looked Jackson up and down. "And you're no Henry Bowman. It's not just the fact that you're smaller and daintier, with a lot of feminine qualities that I'm sure the *ladies* loved back when you were alive…"

"The paid ones liked me fine," Jackson said, making me shake my head. His back was to me, blocking my view of our guest, so I couldn't see much of what was going on.

The ghost went on. "But you don't have Henry's smarts. Henry Bowman knew when to make a deal."

"Get on with your point," Jackson said. "No one here is trying to be Henry Bowman."

"Potter Grove is turning too. You feel it. I know you do. The signs are there."

I thought about the tiny foot I had stuffed in my pocket. The bear skins. The glass figurine. He was right. There were signs. A lot of freakin' signs.

"What are you getting at?" I asked.

"You want answers. I've got answers. But, I want answers too. Maybe we can help each other out. But I need to cut the line."

Jackson whispered to me. "Carly doll, don't believe him. This man is clearly a liar and a charlatan who doesn't want me to check him out. I would've heard if my great grandfather had done business here in Wisconsin, especially with questionable sorts like this. Henry Bowman simply lived off his wealth, a man of leisure."

"Please stop pretending your family wasn't full of question-able sorts," I chimed in.

Jackson's face fell. "You're not seriously going to do a chan-neling with a strong, changing spirit you can't trust. One that hasn't been vetted yet."

He had a point, and I probably should have listened, but instead I said, "I channeled with you, and you are last on my list of trustworthy apparitions. I know you think I'm the dumb version of you, someone who needs your guidance on every-thing. But I don't."

"Sounds like you know everything," Jackson said, disappear-ing. I knew I'd hurt his feelings, but I didn't care.

I turned to Feldman as soon as he left. "Just so we're clear, I'm not saying I'm helping you out. I'm only hearing you out. Go on."

Feldman's smile was wide and confident, a man who thought he had the upper hand on the stupid woman in front of him. His voice was even less shaky now. I could understand him perfectly. "I have to say when I heard there was a strong medium in Potter Grove, I pictured an old bag, not a cute, young bird like yourself."

I didn't respond.

"You should smile when someone compliments you," he said. "Maybe say 'thank you.'"

"And you should stop calling condescending bullshit compliments." I went to the bookshelf in the living room where I'd begun keeping the weird scrapbooks I'd found around Gate House, and pulled out the one labeled *A Crooked Mouse.*

I plopped it on the dining room table and flipped through its pages. "The only reason you're still here and my ex-husband isn't is because there have been signs." As soon as I reached the page about the signs, I pulled the grouse foot out of my pocket.

I tapped on the photo of a glass figurine of a bird. "I saw this one at Delilah Scott's house." Slowly, I moved my finger over to the photo of the bear skins on posts with large empty eye sockets. "Bear skins were recently found staked up on a fence behind the barber shop. Eyeless ones like these. Not bearskin rugs. And now this grouse foot was found at your... relative's house, the Wine-houses. These are hundred-year-old photos that also seem recent. What is going on here?"

"The relatives you're talking about are my brother, Terry's, family. He was probably the one who did me in."

"We'll get to that. What about these signs?"

"Accept my offer and I'll show you. But, I can only tell you what I can tell you. Henry came to me with a business proposal right after those bluenose puritans got their way in '20. He wanted to be a silent partner in what he believed would be a very lucrative business. He was right."

"So you owned a speakeasy or did some bootlegging together."

He looked me up and down, his eyebrows raised. He circled me, a dark smoky kind of force. "I know you." His fading got more color as he circled. I could see the thick waves of his hair now, the deep wrinkles around his eyes. I guessed his age to be around 40. "I can't believe I didn't recognize you before." He shook his head. "You didn't age. You're Henry's nanny."

"I'm not Eliza. I just look like her."

"You're not her, huh? Could've fooled me. Not much of a nanny, though. Never did see you watch any kids." He cocked his head to the side. "Did Henry keep that photograph of you? I mean, her."

My heart raced. *He knew the picture.* The one I'd found in one of the scrapbooks where Eliza was naked and dancing on Henry Bowman's desk, in front of Henry and two other men.

I played dumb and shrugged.

He moved so he was right up next to me. "Maybe you don't know what I'm talking about."

He was trying to intimidate me, and it was working, but I couldn't show it. I kept my breathing normal, my heart rate slow.

He was a chilling dark force of cold vibrations that seemed to be able to stand still in one spot and circle me all at the same time. I took a wide stance with my hands on my hips, focusing only on his face. I couldn't let him know I was afraid.

He went on. "There's only one photograph with that lady in it, as far as I know, a very specific photo indeed," he said in a way that made me fold my arms over my bulky sweater. "A dancing picture taken on the day the bears and birds were supposed to sign a treaty."

I hadn't known anything about a treaty. I was already getting information. Hee-hee. My heart raced.

But something still wasn't right. I had that photo etched in my memory. The faces of those men. Every hair on their chins, every angle of their brows. I'd already identified one of them as James Hind, the father of the suffragette who didn't really commit suicide. He'd mentioned something about a curse when he'd heard a gunshot coming from his daughter's room.

I turned my head to the side. This guy didn't look like the other man, though. The unidentified, younger one in the picture, although the age would've been about right because I'd placed the photo around 1901 to 1906. He was lying.

"I only know about that photo," Feldman continued. "Because I was the one who took it."

"I accept," I said, barely able to get the words out fast enough. A channeling from that day, that moment, was very enticing. I calmed myself down. "I mean, maybe. It does sound like you might be able to tell us a lot. And we need answers... But I also need to check things out to make sure you're telling me the truth."

I knew by Jackson's disappearance I was probably going to be doing my own vetting this time.

"Perfect. Allow me to give you some facts," he said. The man had a crooked smile, and it slowly formed across his horse-long cheeks. He quickly morphed into an almost completely lifelike form now. I could count the pin stripes along his suit if I wanted to, smell the bootleg liquor wafting through his lapels, the remnants of a speakeasy.

He was by far the strongest ghost I'd ever encountered, aside from Mrs. Harpton and Ronald, who might not even be ghosts.

His teeth were a golden shade of yellow and he liked to show them off when he talked, but it was the kind of smile I wasn't entirely sure was intended to be friendly.

"My death," he began. "Took place during a snowed-in weekend at my speakeasy in Landover, Wisconsin in 1923. It was a private poker game, only my best friends were there. One of them slit my throat, that much I know. I want you to figure out which one."

*Thanks for checking out *Under the Cheater's Table,* coming this fall. Follow me on Amazon or sign up for my list if you'd like to know when it comes out.

MORE BOOKS

BY ETTA FAIRE

Must Love Murder: A Sketchy Matchmaker Mystery, book one

P.S. I Poisoned You: A Sketchy Matchmaker Mystery, book two

Rockin' Around the Killing Spree: A Sketchy Matchmaker Mystery, book three

Over My Dead Husband's Body: A Ghosts of Landover Mystery, book one

After the Suffragette's Suicide: A Ghosts of Landover Mystery, book two

Behind the Boater's Cover-Up: A Ghosts of Landover Mystery, book three

Made in the USA
Coppell, TX
31 December 2019